W9-ALK-274

RANDOM
HOUSE
LARGE
PRINT

THE GIRLS

THE GIRLS

A NOVEL

EMMA CLINE

RANDOM HOUSE
LARGE PRINT

The Girls is a work of fiction. Names, characters, places, and incidents are the products of the author's imagination or are used fictitiously. Any resemblance to actual events, locales, or persons, living or dead, is entirely coincidental.

Published in the United States of America by Random House Large Print in association with Random House, an imprint and division of Penguin Random House LLC, New York.

Cover design by Liz Cosgrove

The Library of Congress has established a Cataloging-in-Publication record for this title.

ISBN: 978-0-7352-0818-6

www.randomhouse.com/largeprint

FIRST LARGE PRINT EDITION

Printed in the United States of America

10 9 8 7 6 5 4 3 2 1

This Large Print edition published in accord with the standards of the N.A.V.H.

THE GIRLS

I LOOKED UP because of the laughter, and kept looking because of the girls.

I noticed their hair first, long and uncombed. Then their jewelry catching the sun. The three of them were far enough away that I saw only the periphery of their features, but it didn't matter—I knew they were different from everyone else in the park. Families milling in a vague line, waiting for sausages and burgers from the open grill. Women in checked blouses scooting into their boyfriends' sides, kids tossing eucalyptus buttons at the feral-looking chickens that overran the strip. These long-haired girls seemed to glide above all that was happening around them, tragic and separate. Like royalty in exile.

I studied the girls with a shameless, blatant gape: it didn't seem possible that they might look over and notice me. My hamburger was forgotten in my lap, the breeze blowing in minnow stink from the river. It was an age when I'd immediately scan and rank other girls, keeping up a constant tally of how I fell short, and I saw right away that the black-haired one was the prettiest. I had expected this, even before I'd been able to make out their faces. There was a suggestion of otherworldliness hovering around her, a dirty smock dress barely covering her ass. She was flanked by a skinny redhead and an older girl, dressed with the same shabby afterthought. As if dredged from a lake. All their cheap rings like a second set of knuckles. They were messing with an uneasy threshold, prettiness and ugliness at the same time, and a ripple of awareness followed them through the park. Mothers glancing around for their children, moved by some feeling they couldn't name. Women reaching for their boyfriends' hands. The sun spiked through the trees, like always—the drowsy willows, the hot wind gusting over the picnic blankets—but the familiarity of the day was disturbed by the path the girls cut across the regular world. Sleek and thoughtless as sharks breaching the water.

PART ONE

IT BEGINS WITH THE FORD idling up the narrow drive, the sweet drone of honeysuckle thickening the August air. The girls in the backseat holding hands, the car windows down to let in the seep of night. The radio playing until the driver, suddenly jittery, snaps it off.

They scale the gate, still strung with Christmas lights. Encountering, first, the dumb quiet of the caretaker's cottage; the caretaker taking an evening nap on the couch, his bare feet tucked side by side like loaves. His girlfriend in the bathroom, wiping away the hazy crescents of eye makeup.

Then the main house, where they startle the woman reading in the guest bedroom. The glass of water quivering on the nightstand, the damp cotton of her underpants. Her five-year-old son by her side, murmuring cryptic nonsense to fight sleep.

They herd everyone into the living room. The moment the frightened people understand the sweet dailiness of their lives—the swallow of morning orange juice, the tilting curve taken on a bicycle—is already gone. Their faces change like a shutter opening; the unlocking behind the eyes.

I had imagined that night so often. The dark mountain road, the sunless sea. A woman felled on the night lawn. And though the details had receded over the years, grown their second and third skins, when I heard the lock jamming open near midnight, it was my first thought.

The stranger at the door.

I waited for the sound to reveal its source. A neighbor's kid bumping a trash can onto the sidewalk. A deer thrashing through the brush. That's all it could be, I told myself, this far-off rattle in the other part of the house, and I tried to picture how harmless the space would seem again in daylight, how cool and beyond danger.

But the noise went on, passing starkly into real life. There was now laughter in the other room. Voices. The pressurized **swish** of the refrigerator. I trawled for explanations but kept catching on the worst thought. After everything, this was how it would end. Trapped in someone else's house, among the facts and habits of someone else's life. My bare legs, jotted with varicose veins—how weak I'd appear when they came for me, a middle-aged woman scrabbling for the corners.

I lay in bed, my breath shallow as I stared at the closed door. Waiting for the intruders, the horrors I imagined taking human shape and populating the room—there would be no heroics, I understood. Just the dull terror, the physical pain that would have to be suffered through. I wouldn't try to run.

I only got out of bed after I heard the girl. Her voice was high and innocuous. Though it shouldn't have been comforting—Suzanne and the others had been girls, and that hadn't helped anybody.

I was staying in a borrowed house. The dark maritime cypress packed tight outside the window, the twitch of salt air. I ate in the blunt way I had as a child—a glut of spaghetti, mossed with cheese. The nothing jump of soda in my throat. I watered Dan's plants once a week, ferrying each one to the bathtub, running the pot under the faucet until the soil burbled with wet. More than once I'd showered with a litter of dead leaves in the tub.

The inheritance that had been the leftovers of my grandmother's movies—hours of her smiling her hawkish smile on film, her tidy cap of curls—

I'd spent ten years ago. I tended to the in-between spaces of other people's existences, working as a live-in aide. Cultivating a genteel invisibility in sexless clothes, my face blurred with the pleasant, ambiguous expression of a lawn ornament. The pleasant part was important, the magic trick of invisibility only possible when it seemed to fulfill the correct order of things. As if it were something I wanted, too. My charges were varied. A kid with special needs, frightened of electrical outlets and traffic lights. An elderly woman who watched talk shows while I counted out a saucerful of pills, the pale pink capsules like subtle candy.

When my last job ended and another didn't appear, Dan offered his vacation house—the concerned gesture of an old friend—like I was doing him a favor. The skylight filled the rooms with the hazy murk of an aquarium, the woodwork bloating and swelling in the damp. As if the house were breathing.

The beach wasn't popular. Too cold, no oysters. The single road through town was lined with trailers, built up into sprawling lots—pinwheels snapping in the wind, porches cluttered with bleached buoys and life preservers, the ornaments of humble people. Sometimes I smoked a little of the furry and pungent marijuana from my old landlord, then walked to the store in town. A task I could complete, as defined as washing a dish. It was either dirty or clean, and I welcomed those binaries, the way they shored up a day.

I rarely saw anyone outside. The only teenagers in town seemed to kill themselves in gruesomely rural ways—I heard about their pickups crashing at two in the morning, the sleepover in the garage camper ending with carbon monoxide poisoning, a dead quarterback. I didn't know if this was a problem born of country living, the excess of time and boredom and recreational vehicles, or whether it was a California thing, a grain in the light urging risk and stupid cinematic stunts.

I hadn't been in the ocean at all. A waitress at the café told me this was a breeding ground for great whites.

They looked up from the bright wash of the kitchen lights like raccoons caught in the trash. The girl shrieked. The boy stood to his full, lanky height. There were only two of them. My heart was scudding hard, but they were so young—locals, I figured, breaking into vacation houses. I wasn't going to die.

"What the fuck?" The boy put down his beer bottle, the girl clinging to his side. The boy looked twenty or so, in cargo shorts. High white socks, rosy acne beneath a scrim of beard. But the girl was just a little thing. Fifteen, sixteen, her pale legs tinged with blue.

I tried to gather whatever authority I could, clutching the hem of my T-shirt to my thighs. When I said I'd call the cops, the boy snorted.

"Go ahead." He huddled the girl closer. "Call the cops. You know what?" He pulled out his cellphone. "Fuck it, I'll call them."

The pane of fear I'd been holding in my chest suddenly dissolved.

"Julian?"

I wanted to laugh—I'd last seen him when he was thirteen, skinny and unformed. Dan and Allison's only son. Fussed over, driven to cello competitions all over the western United States. A Mandarin tutor on Thursdays, the brown bread and gummy vitamins, parental hedges against failure. That had all fizzled and he'd ended up at the CSU in Long Beach or Irvine. There'd been some trouble there, I remembered. Expulsion or maybe a milder version of that, a suggestion of a year at junior college. Julian had been a shy, irritable kid, cowering at car radios, unfamiliar foods. Now he had hard edges, the creep of tattoos under his shirt. He didn't remember me, and why should he? I was a woman outside his range of erotic attentions.

"I'm staying here for a few weeks," I said, aware of my exposed legs and embarrassed for the melodrama, the mention of police. "I'm a friend of your dad's."

I could see the effort he made to place me, to assign meaning.

"Evie," I said.

Still nothing.

"I used to live in that apartment in Berkeley? By

your cello teacher's house?" Dan and Julian would come over sometimes after his lessons. Julian lustily drinking milk and scuffing my table legs with robotic kicks.

"Oh, shit," Julian said. "Yeah." I couldn't tell whether he actually remembered me or if I had just invoked enough calming details.

The girl turned toward Julian, her face as blank as a spoon.

"It's fine, babe," he said, kissing her forehead—his gentleness unexpected.

Julian smiled at me and I realized he was drunk, or maybe just stoned. His features were smeary, an unhealthy dampness on his skin, though his upper-class upbringing kicked in like a first language.

"This is Sasha," he said, nudging the girl.

"Hi," she peeped, uncomfortable. I'd forgotten that dopey part of teenage girls: the desire for love flashing in her face so directly that it embarrassed me.

"And Sasha," Julian said, "this is—"

Julian's eyes struggled to focus on me.

"Evie," I reminded him.

"Right," he said, "Evie. Man."

He drank from his beer, the amber bottle catching the blare of the lights. He was staring past me. Glancing around at the furniture, the contents of the bookshelves, like this was my house and he was the outsider. "God, you must've thought we were like, breaking in or something."

"I thought you were locals."

"There was a break-in here once," Julian said. "When I was a kid. We weren't here. They just stole our wet suits and a bunch of abalone from the freezer." He took another drink.

Sasha kept her eyes on Julian. She was in cutoffs, all wrong for the cold coast, and an oversize sweatshirt that must have been his. The cuffs gnawed and wet looking. Her makeup looked terrible, but it was more of a symbol, I suppose. I could see she was nervous with my eyes on her. I understood the worry. When I was that age, I was uncertain of how to move, whether I was walking too fast, whether others could see the discomfort and stiffness in me. As if everyone were constantly gauging my performance and finding it lacking. It occurred to me that Sasha was very young. Too young to be here with Julian. She seemed to know what I was thinking, staring at me with surprising defiance.

"I'm sorry your dad didn't tell you I'd be here," I said. "I can sleep in the other room if you want the bigger bed. Or if you want to be here alone, I'll figure something—"

"Nah," Julian said. "Sasha and I can sleep anywhere, can't we, babe? And we're just passing through. On our way north. A weed run," he said. "I make the drive, L.A. to Humboldt, at least once a month."

It occurred to me that Julian thought I'd be impressed.

"I don't sell it or anything," Julian went on, backpedaling. "Just transport. All you really need is a couple Watershed bags and a police scanner."

Sasha looked worried. Would I get them in trouble?

"How'd you know my dad again?" Julian said. Draining his beer and opening another. They'd brought a few six-packs. The other supplies in sight: the nutty gravel of trail mix. An unopened package of sour worms, the stale crumple of a fast-food bag.

"We met in L.A.," I said. "We lived together for a while."

Dan and I had shared an apartment in Venice Beach in the late seventies, Venice with its third world alleyways, the palm trees that hit the windows in the warm night winds. I was living off my grandmother's movie money while I worked toward my nursing certification. Dan was trying to be an actor. It was never going to happen for him, acting. Instead he'd married a woman with some family money and started a vegetarian frozen-food company. Now he owned a pre-earthquake house in Pacific Heights.

"Oh wait, his friend from Venice?" Julian seemed suddenly more responsive. "What's your name again?"

"Evie Boyd," I said, and the sudden look that came over his face surprised me: recognition, partly, but real interest.

"Wait," he said. He took his arm away from the girl and she looked drained by his absence. "You're that lady?"

Maybe Dan had told him how bad things had

gotten for me. The thought embarrassed me, and I touched my face reflexively. An old, shameful habit from adolescence, how I'd cover up a pimple. A casual hand at my chin, fiddling with my mouth. As if that weren't drawing attention, making it worse.

Julian was excited now. "She was in this cult," he told the girl. "Right?" he said, turning to me.

A socket of dread opened in my stomach. Julian kept looking at me, tart with expectation. His breath hoppy and fractured.

I'd been fourteen that summer. Suzanne had been nineteen. There was an incense the group burned sometimes that made us drowsy and yielding. Suzanne reading aloud from a back issue of **Playboy**. The obscene and luminous Polaroids we secreted away and traded like baseball cards.

I knew how easily it could happen, the past at hand, like the helpless cognitive slip of an optical illusion. The tone of a day linked to some particular item: my mother's chiffon scarf, the humidity of a cut pumpkin. Certain patterns of shade. Even the flash of sunlight on the hood of a white car could cause a momentary ripple in me, allowing a slim space of return. I'd seen old Yardley slickers—the makeup now just a waxy crumble—sell for almost one hundred dollars on the Internet. So grown women could smell it again, that chemical, flowery fug. That's how badly people wanted it—to know that their lives **had** happened, that the person they once had been still existed inside of them.

There were so many things that returned me. The tang of soy, smoke in someone's hair, the grassy hills turning blond in June. An arrangement of oaks and boulders could, seen out of the corner of my eye, crack open something in my chest, palms going suddenly slick with adrenaline.

I anticipated disgust from Julian, maybe even fear. That was the logical response. But I was confused by the way he was looking at me. With something like awe.

His father must have told him. The summer of the crumbling house, the sunburned toddlers. When I'd first tried to tell Dan, on the night of a brownout in Venice that summoned a candlelit, apocalyptic intimacy, he had burst out laughing. Mistaking the hush in my voice for the drop of hilarity. Even after I convinced Dan I was telling the truth, he talked about the ranch with that same parodic goof. Like a horror movie with bad special effects, the boom microphone dipping into the frame and tinting the butchery into comedy. And it was a relief to exaggerate my distance, neatening my involvement into the orderly package of anecdote.

It helped that I wasn't mentioned in most of the books. Not the paperbacks with the title bloody and oozing, the glossed pages of crime scene photographs. Not the less popular but more accurate tome written by the lead prosecutor, gross with specifics, down to the undigested spaghetti they found in the little boy's stomach. The couple of lines that did mention me were buried in an out-of-print book by a former poet, and he'd gotten my name wrong and hadn't made any connection to my grandmother. The same poet also claimed that the CIA was producing porn films starring a drugged Marilyn Monroe, films sold to politicians and foreign heads of state.

"It was a long time ago," I said to Sasha, but her expression was empty.

"Still," Julian said, brightening. "I always thought it was beautiful. Sick yet beautiful," he said. "A fucked-up expression, but an expression, you know. An artistic impulse. You've got to destroy to create, all that Hindu shit."

I could tell he was reading my bewildered shock as approval.

"God, I can't even imagine," Julian said. "Actually being in the middle of something like that."

He waited for me to respond. I was woozy from the ambush of kitchen lights: didn't they notice the room was too bright? I wondered if the girl was even beautiful. Her teeth had a cast of yellow.

Julian nudged her with his elbow. "Sasha doesn't even know what we're talking about."

Most everyone knew at least one of the grisly details. College kids sometimes dressed as Russell for Halloween, hands splashed with ketchup cadged from the dining hall. A black metal band had used the heart on an album cover, the same craggy heart Suzanne had left on Mitch's wall. In the woman's blood. But Sasha seemed so young—why would she have ever heard of it? Why would she care? She was lost in that deep and certain sense that there was nothing beyond her own experience. As if there were only one way things could go, the years leading you down a corridor to the room where your inevitable self waited—embryonic, ready to be revealed. How sad it was to realize that sometimes you never got there. That sometimes you lived a whole life skittering across the surface as the years passed, unblessed.

Julian petted Sasha's hair. "It was like a big fucking deal. Hippies killing these people out in Marin."

The heat in his face was familiar. The same fervor as those people who populated the online forums that never seemed to slow down or die. They jostled for ownership, adopting the same knowing tone, a veneer of scholarship masking the essential ghoulishness of the endeavor. What were they looking for among all the banalities? As though the weather on that day mattered. All of the scraps seemed important, when considered long enough: the station the radio was tuned to in Mitch's kitchen, the number and depth of the stab wounds. How the shadows might have flickered on that particular car driving up that particular road.

"I was only hanging around them for a few months," I said. "It wasn't a big thing."

Julian seemed disappointed. I imagined the woman he saw when he looked at me: her unkempt hair, the commas of worry around her eyes.

"But yeah," I said, "I stayed there a lot."

That answer returned me firmly to his realm of interest.

And so I let the moment pass.

I didn't tell him that I wished I'd never met Suzanne. That I wished I'd stayed safely in my bedroom in the dry hills near Petaluma, the bookshelves packed tight with the gold-foil spines of my childhood favorites. And I did wish that. But some nights, unable to sleep, I peeled an apple slowly at the sink, letting the curl lengthen under the glint of the knife. The house dark around me. Sometimes it didn't feel like regret. It felt like a missing.

Julian shooed Sasha into the other bedroom like a peaceable teenage goatherd. Asking if I needed anything before he said good night. I was taken aback—he reminded me of the boys in school who'd become more polite and high functioning on drugs. Dutifully washing the family dinner dishes while they were tripping, mesmerized by the psychedelic magic of soap.

"Sleep well," Julian said, giving a little geisha bow before closing the door.

The sheets on my bed were mussed, the pang of fear still lingering in the room. How ridiculous I'd been. Being so frightened. But even the surprise of harmless others in the house disturbed me. I didn't want my inner rot on display, even accidentally. Living alone was frightening in that way. No one to police the spill of yourself, the ways you betrayed your primitive desires. Like a cocoon built around you, made of your own naked proclivities and never tidied into the patterns of actual human life.

I was still alert, and it took effort to relax, to regulate my breath. The house was safe, I told myself, I was fine. Suddenly it seemed ridiculous, the bumbling encounter. Through the thin wall, I could hear the sounds of Sasha and Julian settling into the other room. The floor creaking, the closet doors being opened. They were probably putting sheets on the bare mattress. Shaking away years of accumulated dust. I imagined Sasha looking at the family photographs on the shelf, Julian as a toddler holding a giant red telephone. Julian at eleven or twelve, on a whale-watching boat, his face salt lashed and wondrous. She was probably projecting all that innocence and sweetness on the almost-adult man who eased off his shorts and patted the bed for her to join him. The blurry leavings of amateur tattoos rippling along his arms.

I heard the groan of mattress.

I wasn't surprised that they would fuck. But then there was Sasha's voice, whining like a porno. High and curdled. Didn't they know I was right next door? I turned my back to the wall, shutting my eyes.

Julian growling.

"Are you a cunt?" he said. The headboard jacking against the wall.

"Are you?"

I'd think, later, that Julian must have known I could hear everything.

1969

1

It was the end of the sixties, or the summer before the end, and that's what it seemed like, an endless, formless summer. The Haight populated with white-garbed Process members handing out their oat-colored pamphlets, the jasmine along the roads that year blooming particularly heady and full. Everyone was healthy, tan, and heavy with decoration, and if you weren't, that was a thing, too—you could be some moon creature, chiffon over the lamp shades, on a kitchari cleanse that stained all your dishes with turmeric.

But that was all happening somewhere else, not in Petaluma with its low-hipped ranch houses, the covered wagon perpetually parked in front of the Hi-Ho Restaurant. The sun-scorched crosswalks. I was fourteen but looked much younger. People liked to say this to me. Connie swore I could pass for sixteen, but we told each other a lot of lies. We'd been friends all through junior high, Connie waiting for me outside classrooms as patient as a cow, all our energy subsumed into the theatrics of friendship. She was plump but didn't dress like it, in cropped cotton shirts with Mexican embroidery, too-tight skirts that left an angry rim on her upper thighs. I'd always liked her in a way I never had to think about, like the fact of my own hands.

Come September, I'd be sent off to the same boarding school my mother had gone to. They'd built a well-tended campus around an old convent in Monterey, the lawns smooth and sloped. Shreds of fog in the mornings, brief hits of the nearness of salt water. It was an all-girls school, and I'd have to wear a uniform—low-heeled shoes and no makeup, middy blouses threaded with navy ties. It was a holding place, really, enclosed by a stone wall and populated with bland, moon-faced daughters. Camp Fire Girls and Future Teachers shipped off to learn 160 words a minute, shorthand. To make dreamy, overheated promises to be one another's bridesmaids at Royal Hawaiian weddings.

My impending departure forced a newly critical distance on my friendship with Connie. I'd started to notice certain things, almost against my will. How Connie said, "The best way to get over someone is to get under someone else," as if we were shopgirls in

London instead of inexperienced adolescents in the farm belt of Sonoma County. We licked batteries to feel a metallic jolt on the tongue, rumored to be one-eighteenth of an orgasm. It pained me to imagine how our twosome appeared to others, marked as the kind of girls who belonged to each other. Those sexless fixtures of high schools.

Every day after school, we'd click seamlessly into the familiar track of the afternoons. Waste the hours at some industrious task: following Vidal Sassoon's suggestions for raw egg smoothies to strengthen hair or picking at blackheads with the tip of a sterilized sewing needle. The constant project of our girl selves seeming to require odd and precise attentions.

As an adult, I wonder at the pure volume of time I wasted. The feast and famine we were taught to expect from the world, the countdowns in magazines that urged us to prepare thirty days in advance for the first day of school.

Day 28: Apply a face mask of avocado and honey.

Day 14: Test your makeup look in different lights (natural, office, dusk).

Back then, I was so attuned to attention. I dressed to provoke love, tugging my neckline lower, settling a wistful stare on my face whenever I went out in public that implied many deep and promising thoughts, should anyone happen to glance over. As a child, I had once been part of a charity dog show and paraded around a pretty collie on a leash, a silk bandanna around its neck. How thrilled I'd been at the sanctioned performance: the way I went up to strangers and let them admire the dog, my smile as indulgent and constant as a salesgirl's, and how vacant I'd felt when it was over, when no one needed to look at me anymore.

I waited to be told what was good about me. I wondered later if this was why there were so many more women than men at the ranch. All that time I had spent readying myself, the articles that taught me life was really just a waiting room until someone noticed you—the boys had spent that time becoming themselves.

That day in the park was the first time I saw Suzanne and the others. I'd ridden my bike there, aimed at the smoke streaming from the grill. No one spoke to me except the man pressing burgers into the grates with a bored, wet sizzle. The shadows of the oaks moved over my bare arms, my bike tipped in the grass. When an older boy in a cowboy hat ran into me, I purposefully slowed so he would bump into me again. The kind of flirting Connie might do, practiced as an army maneuver.

"What's wrong with you?" he muttered. I opened my mouth to apologize, but the boy was already walking off. Like he'd known he didn't need to hear whatever I was going to say.

The summer gaped before me—the scatter of days, the march of hours, my mother swanning around the house like a stranger. I had spoken to my father a few times on the phone. It had seemed painful for him, too. He'd asked me oddly formal questions, like a distant uncle who knew me only as a series of secondhand facts: Evie is fourteen, Evie is short. The silences between us would've been better if they were colored with sadness or regret, but it was worse—I could hear how happy he was to be gone.

I sat on a bench alone, napkins spread across my knees, and ate my hamburger.

It was the first meat I'd had in a long time. My mother, Jean, had stopped eating meat in the four months since the divorce. She'd stopped doing a lot of things. Gone was the mother who'd made sure I bought new underwear every season, the mother who'd rolled my white bobby socks as sweetly as eggs. Who'd sewn my dolls pajamas that matched mine, down to the exact pearly buttons. She was ready to attend to her own life with the eagerness of a schoolgirl at a difficult math problem. Any spare moment, she stretched. Going up on her toes to work her calves. She lit incense that came wrapped in aluminum foil and made my eyes water. She started drinking a new tea, made from some aromatic bark, and shuffled around the house sipping it, touching her throat absently as if recovering from a long illness.

The ailment was vague, but the cure was specific. Her new friends suggested massage. They suggested the briny waters of sensory deprivation tanks. They suggested E-meters, Gestalt, eating only high-mineral foods that had been planted during a full moon. I couldn't believe my mother took their advice, but she listened to everyone. Eager for an aim, a plan, believing the answer could come from any direction at any time, if only she tried hard enough.

She searched until there was only searching left. The astrologer in Alameda who made her cry, talking about the inauspicious shadow cast by her rising sign. The therapies that involved throwing herself around a padded room filled with strangers and whirling until she hit something. She came home with foggy tinges under the skin, bruises that deepened to a vivid meat. I saw her touch the bruises with something like fondness. When she looked up and saw me watching, she blushed. Her hair was newly bleached, stinking of chemicals and artificial roses.

"Do you like it?" she said, grazing the sheared ends with her fingers.

I nodded, though the color made her skin look washed by jaundice.

She kept changing, day by day. Little things. She bought handcrafted earrings from women in her encounter group, came back swinging primitive bits of wood from her ears, enameled bracelets the color of after-dinner mints jittery on her wrists. She started lining her eyes with an eyeliner pencil she held over a lighter flame. Turning the point until it softened and she could draw slashes at each eye, making her look sleepy and Egyptian.

She paused in my doorway on her way out for the

night, dressed in a tomato-red blouse that exposed her shoulders. She kept pulling the sleeves down. Her shoulders were dusted with glitter.

"You want me to do your eyes too, sweetheart?"

But I had nowhere to be. Who would care if my eyes looked bigger or bluer?

"I might get back late. So sleep well." My mother leaned over to kiss the top of my head. "We're good, aren't we? The two of us?"

She patted me, smiling so her face seemed to crack and reveal the full rush of her need. Part of me did feel all right, or I was confusing familiarity with happiness. Because that was there even when love wasn't—the net of family, the purity of habit and home. It was such an unfathomable amount of time that you spent at home, and maybe that's the best you could get—that sense of endless enclosure, like picking for the lip of tape but never finding it. There were no seams, no interruptions—just the landmarks of your life that had become so absorbed in you that you couldn't even acknowledge them. The chipped willow-print dinner plate I favored for forgotten reasons. The wallpaper in the hallway so known to me as to be entirely incommunicable to another person—every fading copse of pastel palm trees, the particular personalities I ascribed to each blooming hibiscus.

My mother stopped enforcing regular mealtimes, leaving grapes in a colander in the sink or bringing home glass jars of dilled miso soup from her macrobiotic cooking class. Seaweed salads dripping with a nauseating amber oil. "Eat this for breakfast every day," she said, "and you'll never have another zit."

I cringed, pulling my fingers away from the pimple on my forehead.

There had been many late-night planning sessions between my mother and Sal, the older woman she had met in group. Sal was endlessly available to my mother, coming over at odd hours, impatient for drama. Wearing tunics with mandarin collars, her gray hair cut short so her ears showed, making her look like an elderly boy. My mother spoke to Sal about acupuncture, of the movement of energies around meridian points. The charts.

"I just want some space," my mother said, "for me. This world takes it out of you, doesn't it?"

Sal shifted on her wide rear, nodded. Dutiful as a bridled pony.

My mother and Sal were drinking her woody tea from bowls, a new affectation my mother had picked up. "It's European," she'd said defensively, though I had said nothing. When I walked through the kitchen, both women stopped talking, but my mother cocked her head. "Baby," she said, gesturing me closer. She squinted. "Part your bangs from the left. More flattering."

I'd parted my hair that way to cover the pimple, gone scabby from picking. I'd coated it with vitamin E oil but couldn't stop myself from messing with it, flaking on toilet paper to soak up the blood.

Sal agreed. "Round face shape," she said with authority. "Bangs might not be a good idea at all, for her."

I imagined how it would feel to topple Sal over in her chair, how her bulk would bring her down fast. The bark tea spilling on the linoleum.

They quickly lost interest in me. My mother rekindling her familiar story, like the stunned survivor of a car accident. Dropping her shoulders as if to settle even further into the misery.

"And the most hilarious part," my mother went on, "the part that really gets me going?" She smiled at her own hands. "Carl's making money," she said. "That currency stuff." She laughed again. "Finally. It actually worked. But it was my money that paid her salary," she said. "My mother's movie money. Spent on that girl."

My mother was talking about Tamar, the assistant my father had hired for his most recent business. It had something to do with currency exchange. Buying foreign money and trading it back and forth, shifting it enough times so you were left, my father insisted, with pure profit, sleight of hand on a grand scale. That's what the French language tapes in his car had been for: he'd been trying to push along a deal involving francs and lire.

Now he and Tamar were living together in Palo Alto. I'd only met her a few times: she'd picked me up from school once, before the divorce. Waving lazily from her Plymouth Fury. In her twenties, slim and cheerful, Tamar constantly alluded to weekend plans, an apartment she wished were bigger, her life textured in a way I couldn't imagine. Her hair was so blond it was almost gray, and she wore it loose, unlike my mother's smooth curls. At that age I looked at women with brutal and emotionless judgment. Assessing the slope of their breasts, imagining how they would look in various crude positions. Tamar was very pretty. She gathered her hair up in a plastic comb and cracked her neck, smiling over at me as she drove.

"Want some gum?"

I unwrapped two cloudy sticks from their silver jackets. Feeling something adjacent to love, next to Tamar, thighs scudding on the vinyl seat. Girls are the only ones who can really give each other close attention, the kind we equate with being loved. They noticed what we want noticed. And that's what I did for Tamar—I responded to her symbols, to the style of her hair and clothes and the smell of her L'Air du Temps perfume, like this was data that mattered, signs that reflected something of her inner self. I took her beauty personally.

When we arrived home, the gravel crackling under the car wheels, she asked to use the bathroom.

"Of course," I said, vaguely thrilled to have her in my house, like a visiting dignitary. I showed her the nice bathroom, by my parents' room. Tamar peeked at the bed and wrinkled her nose. "Ugly comforter," she said under her breath.

Until then, it had just been my parents' comforter, but abruptly I felt secondhand shame for my mother, for the tacky comforter she had picked out, had even been foolish enough to be pleased by.

I sat at the dining table listening to the muffled sound of Tamar peeing, of the faucet running. She was in there a long time. When Tamar finally emerged, something was different. It took me a moment to realize she was wearing my mother's lipstick, and when she noticed me noticing her, it was as if I'd interrupted a movie she was watching. Her face rapt with the presentiment of some other life.

My favorite fantasy was the sleep cure I had read about in **Valley of the Dolls.** The doctor inducing long-term sleep in a hospital room, the only answer for poor, strident Neely, gone muddy from the Demerol. It sounded perfect—my body kept alive by peaceful, reliable machines, my brain resting in watery space, as untroubled as a goldfish in a glass bowl. I'd wake up weeks later. And even though life would slot back into its disappointing place, there would still be that starched stretch of nothing.

Boarding school was meant to be a corrective, the push I needed. My parents, even in their separate, absorbing worlds, were disappointed in me, distressed by my mediocre grades. I was an average girl, and that was the biggest disappointment of all—there was no shine of greatness on me. I wasn't pretty enough to get the grades I did, the scale not tipping heartily enough in the direction of looks or smarts. Sometimes I would be overtaken with pious impulses to do better, to try harder, but of course nothing changed. Other mysterious forces seemed to be in play. The window near my desk left open so I wasted math class watching the shudder of leaves. My pen leaking so I couldn't take notes. The things I was good at had no real application: addressing envelopes in bubble letters with smiling creatures on the flap. Making sludgy coffee I drank with grave affect. Finding a certain desired song playing on the radio, like a medium scanning for news of the dead.

My mother said I looked like my grandmother, but this seemed suspicious, a wishful lie meant to give false hope. I knew my grandmother's story, repeated like a reflexive prayer. Harriet the date farmer's daughter, plucked from the sunburned obscurity of Indio and brought to Los Angeles. Her soft jaw and damp eyes. Small teeth, straight and slightly pointed, like a strange and beautiful cat. Coddled by the studio system, fed whipped milk and eggs, or broiled liver and five carrots, the same dinner my grandmother ate every night of my childhood. The family holing up in the sprawling ranch in Petaluma after she retired, my grandmother growing show roses from Luther Burbank cuttings and keeping horses.

When my grandmother died, we were like our

own country in those hills, living off her money, though I could bicycle into town. It was more of a psychological distance—as an adult, I would wonder at our isolation. My mother tiptoed around my father, and so did I—his sideways glances at us, his encouragements to eat more protein, to read Dickens or breathe more deeply. He ate raw eggs and salted steaks and kept a plate of beef tartare in the refrigerator, spooning out bites five or six times a day. "Your outer body reflects your inner self," he said, and did his gymnastics on a Japanese mat by the pool, fifty push-ups while I sat on his back. It was a form of magic, being lifted into the air, cross-legged. The oat grass, the smell of the cooling earth.

When a coyote would come down from the hills and fight with the dog—the nasty, quick hiss that thrilled me—my father would shoot the coyote dead. Everything seemed that simple. The horses I copied from a pencil drawing book, shading in their graphite manes. Tracing a picture of a bobcat carrying away a vole in its jaws, the sharp tooth of nature. Later I'd see how the fear had been there all along. The flurry I felt when our mother left me alone with the nanny, Carson, who smelled damp and sat in the wrong chair. How they told me I was having fun all the time, and there was no way to explain that I wasn't. And even moments of happiness were followed by some letdown—my father's laugh, then the scramble to keep up with him as he strode far ahead of me. My mother's hands on my feverish forehead, then the desperate aloneness of my sickroom, my mother disappeared into the rest of the house, talking on the phone to someone in a voice I didn't recognize. A tray of Ritz crackers and chicken noodle soup gone cold, sallow meat breaching the scrim of fat. A starry emptiness that felt, even as a child, something like death.

I didn't wonder how my mother spent her days. How she must have sat in the empty kitchen, the table smelling of the domestic rot of the sponge, and waited for me to clatter in from school, for my father to come home.

My father, who kissed her with a formality that embarrassed us all, who left beer bottles on the steps that trapped wasps and beat his bare chest in the morning to keep his lungs strong. He clung tight to the brute reality of his body, his thick ribbed socks showing above his shoes, flecked from the cedar sachets he kept in his drawers. The way he made a joke of checking his reflection in the hood of the car. I tried to save up things to tell him, combing through my days for something to provoke a glint of interest. It didn't occur to me, until I was an adult, that it was strange to know so much about him when he seemed to know nothing about me. To know that he loved Leonardo da Vinci because he invented solar power and was born poor. That he could identify the make of any car just by the sound of the engine and thought everyone should know the names of trees. He liked when I agreed that business school was a scam or nodded when he said that the teenager in town who'd painted his car with peace signs was a traitor. He'd mentioned once that I should learn classical guitar, though I had never heard him listen to any music except for those theatrical cowboy bands, tapping their emerald cowboy boots and singing about yellow roses. He felt that his height was the only thing that had prevented him from achieving success.

"Robert Mitchum is short too," he'd said to me once. "They make him stand on orange crates."

As soon as I'd caught sight of the girls cutting their way through the park, my attention stayed pinned on them. The black-haired girl with her attendants, their laughter a rebuke to my aloneness. I was waiting for something without knowing what. And then it happened. Quick, but still I saw it: the girl with black hair pulled down the neckline of her dress for a brief second, exposing the red nipple of her bare breast. Right in the middle of a park swarming with people. Before I could fully believe it, the girl yanked her dress back up. They were all laughing, raunchy and careless; none of them even glanced up to see who might be watching.

The girls moved into the alley alongside the restaurant, farther past the grill. Practiced and smooth. I didn't look away. The older one lifted the lid of a dumpster. The redhead bent down and the black-haired girl used her knee as a step, hoisting herself over the edge. She was looking for something inside, but I couldn't imagine what. I stood to throw away my napkins and stopped at the garbage can, watching. The black-haired girl was handing things from the dumpster to the others: a bag of bread, still in its packaging, an anemic-looking cabbage that they sniffed, then tossed back in. A seemingly well-established procedure—would they actually eat the food? When the black-haired girl emerged for the last time, climbing over the rim and slinging her weight onto the ground, she was holding something in her hands. It was a strange shape, the color of my own skin, and I edged closer.

When I realized it was an uncooked chicken, sheened in plastic, I must have stared harder, since the black-haired girl turned and caught my glance. She smiled and my stomach dropped. Something seemed to pass between us, a subtle rearranging of air. The frank, unapologetic way she held my gaze. But she jarred back to attention when the screen door of the restaurant banged open. Out came a hefty man, already shouting. Shooing them like dogs. The girls grabbed the bag of bread and the chicken and took off running. The man stopped and watched them for a minute. Wiping his large hands on his apron, his chest moving with effort.

By then the girls were a block away, their hair streaming behind them like flags, and a black school bus heaved past and slowed, and the three of them disappeared inside.

The sight of them; the gruesomely fetal quality of the chicken, the cherry of the girl's single nipple. All of it was so garish, and maybe that's why I kept thinking of them. I couldn't put it together. Why these girls needed food from the dumpster. Who had been driving the bus, what kind of people would paint it that color. I'd seen that they were dear to one another, the girls, that they'd passed into a familial contract—they were sure of what they were together. The long night that stretched ahead, my mother out with Sal, suddenly seemed unbearable.

That was the first time I ever saw Suzanne—her black hair marking her, even at a distance, as different, her smile at me direct and assessing. I couldn't explain it to myself, the wrench I got from looking at her. She seemed as strange and raw as those flowers that bloom in lurid explosion once every five years, the gaudy, prickling tease that was almost the same thing as beauty. And what had the girl seen when she looked at me?

I used the bathroom inside the restaurant. **Keep truckin'**, scrawled with a marker. **Tess Pyle eats dick!** The accompanying illustrations had been crossed out. All the silly, cryptic marks of humans who were resigned to being held in a place, shunted through the perfunctory order of things. Who wanted to make some small protest. The saddest: **Fuck,** written in pencil.

While I washed my hands, drying them with a stiff towel, I studied myself in the mirror over the sink. For a moment, I tried to see myself through the eyes of the girl with the black hair, or even the boy in the cowboy hat, studying my features for a vibration under the skin. The effort was visible in my face, and I felt ashamed. No wonder the boy had seemed disgusted: he must have seen the longing in me. Seen how my face was blatant with need, like an orphan's empty dish. And that was the difference between me and the black-haired girl—her face answered all its own questions.

I didn't want to know these things about myself. I splashed water on my face, cold water, like Connie had once told me to do. "Cold water makes your pores close up," and maybe it was true: I felt my skin tighten, water dripping down my face and neck. How desperately Connie and I thought that if we performed these rituals—washed our faces with cold water, brushed our hair into a static frenzy with a boar-bristle brush before bed—some proof would solve itself and a new life would spread out before us.

2

Cha ching, the slot machine in Connie's garage went, like a cartoon, Peter's features soaked in its rosy glow. He was eighteen, Connie's older brother, and his forearms were the color of toast. His friend Henry hovered at his side. Connie decided she had a crush on Henry, so our Friday night would be devoted to perching on the weight-lifting bench, Henry's orange motorcycle parked beside us like a prize pony. We'd watch the boys play the slot machine, drinking the off-brand beer Connie's father kept in the garage fridge. Later they'd shoot the empty bottles with a BB gun, crowing at each glassy burst.

I knew I'd see Peter that night, so I'd worn an embroidered shirt, my hair foul with hairspray. I'd dotted a pimple on my jaw with a beige putty of Merle

Norman, but it collected along the rim and made it glow. As long as my hair stayed in place, I looked nice, or at least I thought so, and I tucked in my shirt to show the tops of my small breasts, the artificial press of cleavage from my bra. The feeling of exposure gave me an anxious pleasure that made me stand straighter, holding my head on my neck like an egg in a cup. Trying to be more like the black-haired girl in the park, that easy cast of her face. Connie narrowed her eyes when she saw me, a muscle by her mouth twitching, but she didn't say anything.

Peter had really only spoken to me for the first time two weeks before. I'd been waiting for Connie downstairs. Her bedroom was much smaller than mine, her house meaner, but we spent most of our time there. The house done up in a maritime theme, her father's misguided attempt to approximate female decoration. I felt bad for Connie's father: his night job at a dairy plant, the arthritic hands he clenched and unclenched nervously. Connie's mother lived somewhere in New Mexico, near a hot spring, had twin boys and another life no one ever spoke of. For Christmas, she had once sent Connie a compact of cracked blush and a Fair Isle sweater that was so small neither of us could squeeze our head through the hole.

"The colors are nice," I said hopefully.

Connie just shrugged. "She's a bitch."

Peter crashed through the front door, dumping a book on the kitchen table. He nodded at me in his mild way and started making a sandwich—pulling out slices of white bread, an acid-bright jar of mustard.

"Where's the princess?" he said. His mouth was chapped a violent pink. Slightly coated, I imagined, with pot resin.

"Getting a jacket."

"Ah." He slapped the bread together and took a bite. He watched me while he chewed.

"Looking good these days, Boyd," he said, then swallowed hard. His assessment knocked me so off balance that I felt I had almost imagined it. Was I even supposed to say anything back? I'd already memorized the sentence.

He turned then at a noise from the front door, a girl in a denim jacket, her shape muffled by the screen. Pamela, his girlfriend. They were a constant couple, porous with each other; wearing similar clothes, silently passing the newspaper back and forth on the couch or watching **The Man from U.N.C.L.E.** Picking lint off each other as if from their own selves. I had seen Pamela at the high school, those times I'd ridden my bike past the dun-colored building. The rectangles of half-dry grass, the low, wide steps where older girls were always sitting in poor-boy shirts, pinkies linked, palming packs of Kents. The whiff of death among them, the boyfriends in humid jungles.

They were like adults, even in the way they flicked the ashes of their cigarettes with weary snaps of the wrist.

"Hey, Evie," Pamela said.

It was easy for some girls to be nice. To remember your name. Pamela was beautiful, it was true, and I felt that submerged attraction to her that everyone felt for the beautiful. The sleeves of her jean jacket were bulked at her elbows, her eyes doped looking from liner. Her legs were tan and bare. My own legs were dotted with the pricks of mosquito bites I worried into open wounds, my calves hatched with pale hairs.

"Babe," Peter said with his mouth full, and loped over to give her a hug, burying his face in her neck. Pamela squealed and pushed him away. When she laughed, her snaggletooth flashed.

"Beyond foul," Connie whispered, entering the room. But I was quiet, trying to imagine how that would feel: to be so known to someone that you had become almost the same person.

We were upstairs, later, smoking weed Connie had stolen from Peter. Stuffing the space below the door with the fat twist of a towel. She kept having to pinch the rolling paper shut again with her fingers, the two of us smoking in our solemn, hothouse silence. I could see Peter's car out the window, parked awry like he'd had to abandon it under great duress. I'd always been aware of Peter, in the way I liked any older boy at that age, their mere existence demanding attention. But my feelings were suddenly amplified and pressing, as exaggerated and inevitable as events seem in dreams. I stuffed myself on banalities of him, the T-shirts he wore in rotation, the tender skin where the back of his neck disappeared into his collar. The looping horns of Paul Revere and the Raiders sounding from his bedroom, how he'd sometimes stumble around with a proud, overt secrecy, so I would know he had taken acid. Filling and refilling a glass of water in the kitchen with extravagant care.

I'd gone into Peter's bedroom while Connie was showering. It reeked of what I'd later identify as masturbation, a damp rupture in the air. All his possessions suffused with a mysterious import: his low futon, a plastic bag full of ashy-looking nugs by his pillow. Manuals to become a trainee mechanic. The glass on the floor, greased with fingerprints, was half-full of stale-looking water, and there was a line of smooth river stones on the top of his dresser. A cheap copper bracelet I had seen him wear sometimes. I took in everything as if I could decode the private meaning of each object, puzzle together the interior architecture of his life.

So much of desire, at that age, was a willful act. Trying so hard to slur the rough, disappointing edges of boys into the shape of someone we could love. We spoke of our desperate need for them with rote and familiar words, like we were reading lines from a play.

Later I would see this: how impersonal and grasping our love was, pinging around the universe, hoping for a host to give form to our wishes.

When I was young, I'd seen magazines in a drawer of the bathroom, my father's magazines, the pages bloated with humidity. The insides crowded with women. The tautness of mesh pulled across crotches, the gauzy light that made their skin illuminate and pale. My favorite girl had a gingham ribbon tied around her throat in a bow. It was so odd and stirring that someone could be naked but also wear a ribbon around her neck. It made her nakedness formal.

I visited the magazine with the regularity of a penitent, replacing it carefully each time. Locking the bathroom door with breathless, ill pleasure that quickly morphed into rubbing my crotch along the seams of carpets, the seam of my mattress. The back of a couch. How did it work, even? That by holding the hovering image of the girl in my mind, I could build the sensation, a sheet of pleasure that grew until it was compulsive, the desire to feel that way again and again. It seemed strange that it was a girl I was imagining, not a boy. And that the feeling could be reignited by other oddities: a color-plate illustration in my fairy-tale book of a girl trapped in a spider's web. The faceted eyes of evil creatures, watching her. The memory of my father cupping a neighbor's ass through her wet swimsuit.

I'd done things before—not quite sex, but close. The dry fumbles in the hallways of school dances. The overheated suffocation of a parent's couch, the backs of my knees sweaty. Alex Posner worming his hand down my shorts in his exploratory, detached fashion, jerking away roughly when we heard footsteps. None of it—the kissing, the clawing hand in my underwear, the raw jumpiness of a penis in my fist—seemed in any way kin to what I did alone, the spread of pressure, like stairs going up. I imagined Peter almost as a corrective to my own desires, whose compulsion sometimes frightened me.

I lay back on the thin tapestry covering Connie's bed. She had a bad sunburn; I watched her rub cloudy skin loose from her shoulder and roll it into tiny gray balls. My faint revulsion was tempered by the thought of Peter, who lived in the same house as Connie, who breathed the same air. Who ate from the same utensils. They were conflated in an essential way, like two different species raised in the same laboratory.

From downstairs, I heard Pamela's tripping laugh.

"When I get a boyfriend, I'm going to make him take me out to dinner," Connie said with authority. "She doesn't even mind Peter just brings her here to screw."

Peter never wore underwear, Connie had complained, and the fact grew in my mind, making me nauseous in a not unpleasant way. The sleepy crease of his eyes from his permanent high. Connie paled in comparison: I didn't really believe that friendship could be an end in itself, not just the background fuzz to the dramatics of boys loving you or not loving you.

Connie stood at the mirror and tried to harmonize with one of the sweet, sorrowful forty-fives we listened to with fanatic repetition. Songs that overheated my own righteous sadness, my imagined alignment with the tragic nature of the world. How I loved to wring myself out that way, stoking my feelings until they were unbearable. I wanted all of life to feel that frantic and pressurized with portent, so even colors and weather and tastes would be more saturated. That's what the songs promised, what they trawled out of me.

One song seemed to vibrate with a private echo, as if marked. The simple lines about a woman, about the shape of her back when she turns it on the man for the last time. The ashes she leaves in bed from her cigarettes. The song played once through, and Connie hopped up to flip the record.

"Play it again," I said. I tried to imagine myself in the same way the singer saw the woman: the dangle of her silver bracelet, tinged with green, the fall of her hair. But I only felt foolish, opening my eyes to the sight of Connie at the mirror, separating her eyelashes with a safety pin, her shorts wedged into her ass. It wasn't the same to notice things about yourself. Only certain girls ever called forth that kind of attention. Like the girl I'd seen in the park. Or Pamela and the girls on the high school steps, waiting for the lazy agitation of their boyfriends' idling cars, the signal to leap to their feet. To brush off their seat and trip out into the full sun, waving goodbye to the ones left behind.

Soon after that day, I'd gone to Peter's room while Connie was sleeping. His comment to me in the kitchen felt like a time-stamped invitation I had to redeem before it slipped away. Connie and I had drunk beer before bed, lounging against the wicker legs of her furniture and scooping cottage cheese from a tub with our fingers. I drank much more than she had. I wanted some other momentum to take over, forcing action. I didn't want to be like Connie, never changing, waiting around for something to happen, eating an entire sleeve of sesame crackers, then doing ten jumping jacks in her room. I stayed awake after Connie passed into her deep, twitchy sleep. Listening for Peter's footsteps on the stairs.

He crashed to his room, finally, and I waited for what seemed like a long time before I followed. Creeping along the hallway like a specter in shortie pajamas, their polyester slickness stuck in the broody stretch between princess costumes and lingerie. The silence of the house was a living thing, oppressive and present but also coloring everything with a foreign freedom, filling the rooms like a denser air.

Peter's form under the blankets was still, his knobby man's feet exposed. I heard his breathing, brambled from the aftereffects of whatever drugs he'd taken. His room seemed to cradle him. This might have been enough—to watch him sleep as a parent would, indulging the privilege of imagining happy dreams. His breaths like the beads of a rosary, each in and out a comfort. But I didn't want it to be enough.

When I got closer, his face clarified, his features completing as I adjusted to the dark. I let myself watch him without shame. Peter opened his eyes, suddenly, and somehow didn't seem startled by my presence at his bedside. Giving me a look as mild as a glass of milk.

"Boyd," he said, his voice still drifty from sleep, but he blinked and there was a resignation in the way he said my name that made me feel he'd been waiting for me. That he'd known I would come.

I was embarrassed to be standing like I was.

"You can sit," he said. I crouched by the futon, hovering foolishly. My legs already starting to burn with effort. Peter reached a hand to pull me fully onto the mattress and I smiled, though I wasn't sure he could even see my face. He was quiet and so was I. His room looked strange, as seen from the floor; the bulk of the dresser, the slivered doorway. I couldn't imagine Connie in the rooms beyond. Connie mumbling in her sleep, as she often did, sometimes announcing a number like an addled bingo player.

"You can get under the blankets if you're cold," he said, caping open the covers so I saw his bare chest, his nakedness. I got in beside him with ritual silence. It was as easy as this—I'd entered a possibility that had always been there.

He didn't speak, after that, and neither did I. He hitched me close so my back was pressed against his chest and I could feel his dick rear against my thighs. I didn't want to breathe, feeling that it would be an imposition on him, even the fact of my ribs rising and falling too much of a bother. I was taking tiny breaths through my nose, a light-headedness overtaking me. The strident rank of him in the dark, his blankets, his sheets—it was what Pamela got all the time, this easy occupation of his presence. His arm was around me, a weight I kept identifying as the weight of a boy's arm. Peter acted like he was going to sleep, the casual sigh and shuffle, but that kept the whole thing together. You had to act as if nothing strange were happening. When he brushed my nipple with his finger, I kept very still. I could feel his steady breath on my neck. His hand taking an impersonal measurement. Twisting the nipple so I inhaled audibly, and he hesitated for a moment but kept going. His dick smearing at my bare thighs. I would be shunted along whatever would happen, I understood. However he piloted the night. And there wasn't fear, just a feeling adjacent to excitement, a viewing from the wings. What would happen to Evie?

When the floorboards creaked from the hall, the spell cracked. Peter withdrew his hand, rolling abruptly onto his back. Staring at the ceiling so I could see his eyes.

"I've gotta get some sleep," he said in a voice carefully drained. A voice like an eraser, its insistent dullness meant to make me wonder if anything had happened. And I was slow to get to my feet, a little stunned, but also in a happy swoon, like even that little bit had fed me.

The boys played the slot machine for what seemed like hours. Connie and I sat on the bench, vibrating with forced inattention. I kept waiting for some acknowledgment from Peter of what had happened. A catch in the eye, a glance serrated with our history. But he didn't look at me. The humid garage smelled of chilly concrete and the funk of camping tents, folded while still wet. The gas station calendar on the wall: a woman in a hot tub with the stilled eyes and bared teeth of taxidermy. I was grateful for Pamela's absence that night. There'd been some fight between her and Peter, Connie had told me. I wanted to ask for more details, but there was a warning in her face—I couldn't be too interested.

"Don't you kids have somewhere better to be?" Henry asked. "Some ice-cream social somewhere?"

Connie tossed her hair, then walked over to get more beer. Henry watched her approach with amusement.

"Give those to me," she whined when Henry held two bottles out of reach. I remember noticing for the first time how loud she was, her voice hard with silly aggressiveness. Connie with her whines and feints, the grating laugh that sounded, and was, practiced. A space opened up between us as soon as I started to notice these things, to catalog her shortcomings the way a boy would. I regret how ungenerous I was. As if by putting distance between us, I could cure myself of the same disease.

"What are you gonna give me for them?" Henry said. "Nothing's free in this world, Connie."

She shrugged, then lunged for the beers. Henry pressed the solid mass of his body against her, grinning as she struggled. Peter rolled his eyes. He didn't like this kind of thing either, the bleating vaudeville. He had older friends who'd disappeared in sluggish jungles, rivers thick with sediment. Who'd returned home babbling and addicted to tiny black cigarettes, their hometown girlfriends cowering behind them like nervous little shadows. I tried to sit up straighter, to compose my face with adult boredom. Willing Peter to look over. I wanted the parts of him I was sure Pamela couldn't see, the pricks of sorrow I sometimes caught in his gaze or the secret kindness he showed to Connie, taking us to Arrowhead Lake the year their mother had forgotten Connie's birthday entirely. Pamela didn't know those things, and I held on to that certainty, whatever leverage might belong to me alone.

Henry pinched the soft skin above the waist of Connie's shorts. "Hungry lately, huh?"

"Don't touch me, perv," she said, hitting his hand away. She giggled a little. "Fuck you."

"Fine," he said, grabbing Connie's hands by the wrist. "Fuck me." She tried halfheartedly to pull away, whining until Henry finally let her go. She rubbed her wrists.

"Asshole," she muttered, but she wasn't really mad. That was part of being a girl—you were resigned to whatever feedback you'd get. If you got mad, you were crazy, and if you didn't react, you were a bitch. The only thing you could do was smile from the corner they'd backed you into. Implicate yourself in the joke even if the joke was always on you.

I didn't like the taste of beer, the granular bitterness nothing like the pleasing hygienic chill of my father's martinis, but I drank one and then another. The boys fed the slot machine from a shopping bag full of nickels until they were almost out of coins.

"We need the machine keys," Peter said, lighting a thin joint he pulled from his pocket. "So we can open it up."

"I'll get them," Connie said. "Don't miss me too

much," she crooned to Henry, fluttering a little wave before she left. To me, she just raised her eyebrows. I understood this was part of some plan she had hatched to get Henry's attention. To leave, then return. She had probably read about it in a magazine.

That was our mistake, I think. One of many mistakes. To believe that boys were acting with a logic that we could someday understand. To believe that their actions had any meaning beyond thoughtless impulse. We were like conspiracy theorists, seeing portent and intention in every detail, wishing desperately that we mattered enough to be the object of planning and speculation. But they were just boys. Silly and young and straightforward; they weren't hiding anything.

Peter let the lever ratchet to a starting position and stepped back to give Henry a turn, the two of them passing the joint back and forth. They both wore white T-shirts that were thin from washings. Peter smiled at the carnival racket when the slot machine clattered out a pile of coins, but he seemed distracted, finishing another beer, smoking the joint until it was crushed and oily. They were speaking low. I heard bits and pieces.

They were talking about Willie Poteracke: we all knew him, the first boy in Petaluma to enlist. His father had driven him to register. I'd seen him later at the Hamburger Hamlet with a petite brunette whose nostrils streamed snot. She called him stubbornly by his full name, Will-**iam**, like the extra syllable was the secret password that would transform him into a grown, responsible man. She clung to him like a burr.

"He's always out in the driveway," Peter said. "Washing his car like nothing's different. He can't even drive anymore, I don't think."

This was news from the other world. I felt ashamed, seeing Peter's face, for how I only playacted at real feelings, reaching for the world through songs. Peter could actually be sent away, he could actually die. He didn't have to force himself to feel that way, the emotional exercises Connie and I occupied ourselves with: What would you do if your father died? What would you do if you got pregnant? What would you do if a teacher wanted to fuck you, like Mr. Garrison and Patricia Bell?

"It was all puckered, his stump," Peter said. "Pink."

"Disgusting," Henry said from the machine. He didn't turn away from the looping images of cherries that scrolled in front of him. "You wanna kill people, you better be okay with those people blowing your legs off."

"He's proud of it, too," Peter said, his voice rising as he flicked the end of the joint onto the garage floor. He watched it snuff out. "Wanting people to see it. That's what's crazy."

The dramatics of their conversation made me feel dramatic, too. I was stirred by the alcohol, the burn in my chest I exaggerated until I became moved by an authority not my own. I stood up. The boys didn't notice. They were talking about a movie they had seen in San Francisco. I recognized the title—they hadn't shown it in town because it was supposed to be perverted, though I couldn't remember why.

When I finally watched the movie, as an adult, the palpable innocence of the sex scenes surprised me. The humble pudge of fat above the actress's pubic hair. How she laughed when she pulled the yacht captain's face to her saggy, lovely breasts. There was a good-natured quality to the raunch, like fun was still an erotic idea. Unlike the movies that came later, girls wincing while their legs dangled like a dead thing's.

Henry was fluttering his eyelids, tongue in an obscene rictus. Aping some scene from the movie.

Peter laughed. "Sick."

They wondered aloud whether the actress had actually been getting fucked. They didn't seem to care that I was standing right there.

"You can tell she liked it," Henry said. "Ooh," he crowed in a high feminine voice. "Ooh, yeah, mmm." He banged the slot machine with his hips.

"I saw it, too." I spoke before thinking. I wanted an entry point in the conversation, even if it was a lie. They both looked at me.

"Well," Henry said, "the ghost finally speaks."

I flushed.

"You saw it?" Peter seemed doubtful. I told myself he was being protective.

"Yeah," I said. "Pretty wild."

They exchanged a glance. Did I really think they'd believe I had somehow gotten a ride to the city? That I'd gone to see what was, essentially, a porno?

"So." Henry's eyes glinted. "What was your favorite part?"

"That part you were talking about," I said. "With the girl."

"But what part of that did you like best?" Henry said.

"Leave her alone," Peter said mildly. Already bored.

"Did you like the Christmas scene?" Henry continued. His smile lulled me into thinking we were having a real conversation, that I was making progress. "The big tree? All the snow?"

I nodded. Almost believing my own lie.

Henry laughed. "The movie was in Fiji. The whole thing's on an island." Henry was snorting, helpless with laughter, and cut a look at Peter, who seemed embarrassed for me, like you would be embarrassed for a stranger who tripped on the street, like nothing had ever happened between us at all.

I pushed Henry's motorcycle. I hadn't expected it to tip over, not really: maybe just wobble, just enough to interrupt Henry so he'd be scared for a second, so he'd make some jokey exclamations of dismay and forget my lie. But I had pushed with real force. The motorcycle fell over and crunched hard on the cement floor.

Henry stared at me. "You little bitch." He hurried

to the downed motorcycle like it was a shot pet. Practically cradling it in his arms.

"It's not broken," I said inanely.

"You're a fucking nutcase," he muttered. He ran his hands along the body of the bike and held a shard of orange metal up to Peter. "You believe this shit?"

When Peter looked at me, his face solidified with pity, which was somehow worse than anger. I was like a child, warranting only abbreviated emotions.

Connie appeared in the doorway.

"Knock knock," she called, the keys hanging from a crooked finger. She took in the scene: Henry squatting by the motorcycle; Peter's arms crossed.

Henry let out a harsh laugh. "Your friend's a real bitch," he said, shooting me a look.

"Evie knocked it over," Peter said.

"You fucking kids," Henry said. "Get a babysitter next time, don't hang around with us. Fuck."

"I'm sorry," I said, my voice small, but nobody was listening.

Even after Peter helped Henry right the motorcycle, peering closely at the break—"It's just cosmetic," he announced, "we can fix it pretty easy"—I understood that other things had broken. Connie studied me with cold wonder, like I'd betrayed her, and maybe I had. I'd done what we were not supposed to do. Illuminated a slice of private weakness, exposed the twitchy rabbit heart.

3

The owner of the Flying A was a fat man, the counter cutting into his belly, and he leaned on his elbows to track my movements around the aisles, my purse banging against my thighs. There was a newspaper open in front of him, though he never seemed to turn the page. He had a weary air of responsibility about him, both bureaucratic and mythological, like someone doomed to guard a cave for all eternity.

I was alone that afternoon. Connie probably fuming in her small bedroom, playing "Positively 4th Street" with wounded, righteous indulgence. The thought of Peter was gutting—I wanted to skim over that night, calcifying my shame into something blurry and manageable, like a rumor about a stranger. I'd tried to apologize to Connie, the boys still worrying over the motorcycle like field medics. I even offered to pay for repairs, giving Henry everything I had in my purse. Eight dollars, which he'd accepted with a stiff jaw. After a while, Connie said it was best if I just went home.

I'd gone back a few days later—Connie's father answered the door almost instantly, like he'd been waiting for me. He usually worked at the dairy plant past midnight, so it was odd to see him at home.

"Connie's upstairs," he said. On the counter behind him, I saw a glass of whiskey, watery and catching the sunlight. I was so focused on my own plans that I didn't pick up the air of crisis in the house, the unusual information of his presence.

Connie was lying on her bed, her skirt hitched so I could see the crotch of her white underwear, the entirety of her stippled thighs. She sat up when I entered, blinking.

"Nice makeup," she said. "Did you do that just for me?" She threw herself back on the pillow. "You'll like this news. Peter's gone. Like, gone gone. With Pamela, **quelle** surprise." She rolled her eyes but articulated Pamela's name with a perverse happiness. Cutting me a look.

"What do you mean, left?" Panic was already dislocating my voice.

"He's so **selfish**," she said. "Dad told us we might have to move to San Diego. The next day, Peter takes off. He took a bunch of his clothes and stuff. I think they went to her sister's house in Portland. I mean, I'm pretty sure they went there." She blew at her bangs. "He's a coward. And Pamela is the kind of girl who's gonna get fat after she has a baby."

"Pamela's pregnant?"

She gave me a look. "Surprise—you don't even care I might have to move to San Diego?"

I knew I was supposed to start enumerating the ways I loved her, how sad I would be if she left, but I was hypnotized by an image of Pamela next to Peter in his car, falling asleep against his shoulder. Avis maps at their feet gone translucent with hamburger grease, the backseat filled with clothes and his mechanic manuals. How Peter would look down and see the white line of Pamela's scalp through her part. He might kiss her, moved by a domestic tenderness, even though she was sleeping and would never know.

"Maybe he's just messing around," I said. "I mean, couldn't he still show up?"

"Screw you," Connie said. She seemed surprised by these words, too.

"What'd I even do to you?" I said.

Of course we both knew.

"I think I'd rather be alone right now," Connie announced primly, and stared hard out the window.

Peter, fleeing north with the girlfriend who might even have his baby—there was no imagining the biology away, the fact of the multiplying proteins in Pamela's stomach. But here was Connie, her chubby shape on the bed so familiar that I could map her freckles, point out the blip on her shoulder from chicken pox. There was always Connie, suddenly beloved.

"Let's go to a movie or something," I said.

She sniffed and studied the pale rim of her nails. "Peter's not even around anymore," she said. "So you really have no reason to be here. You're gonna be at boarding school, anyway."

The hum of my desperation was obvious. "Maybe we can go to the Flying A?"

She bit her lip. "May says you're not very nice to me."

May was the dentist's daughter. She wore plaid pants with matching vests, like a junior accountant.

"You said May was boring."

Connie was quiet. We used to feel sorry for May, who was rich but ridiculous, but I understood that now Connie was feeling sorry for me, watching me pant after Peter, who'd probably been planning to go to Portland for weeks. Months.

"May's nice," Connie said. "Real nice."

"We could all see a movie together." I was pedaling now, for any kind of traction, a bulwark against the empty summer. May wasn't so bad, I told myself, even though she wasn't allowed to eat candy or popcorn because of her braces, and yes, I could imagine it, the three of us.

"She thinks you're trashy," Connie said. She turned back to the window. I stared at the lace curtains I had helped Connie hem with glue when we were twelve. I had waited too long, my presence in the room an obvious error, and it was clear that there was nothing to do but leave, to say a tight-throated goodbye to Connie's father downstairs—he gave me a distracted nod—and clatter my bike out into the street.

Had I ever felt alone like this before, the whole day to spend and no one to care? I could almost imagine the ache in my gut as pleasure. It was about keeping busy, I told myself, a frictionless burning of hours. I made a martini the way my father had taught me, sloshing the vermouth over my hand and ignoring the spill on the bar table. I'd always hated martini glasses—the stem and the funny shape seemed embarrassing, like the adults were trying too hard to be adults. I poured it in a juice cup instead, rimmed with gold, and forced myself to drink. Then I made another and drank that, too. It was fun to feel loose and amused with my own house, realizing, in a spill of hilarity, that the furniture had always been ugly, chairs as heavy and mannered as gargoyles. To notice the air was candied with silence, that the curtains were always drawn. I opened them and struggled to lift a window. It was hot outside—I imagined my father, snapping that I was letting the warm air in—but I left the window open anyway.

My mother would be gone all day, the liquor aiding the shorthand of my loneliness. It was strange that I could feel differently so easily, that there was a sure way to soften the crud of my own sadness. I could drink until my problems seemed compact and pretty, something I could admire. I forced myself to like the taste, to breathe slowly when I felt nauseous. I burbled acrid vomit onto my blankets, then cleaned so there was just a tart, curdled spice in the air that I almost liked. I knocked over a lamp and put on dark eye makeup with inexpert but avid attention. Sat in front of my mother's lighted mirror with its different settings: Office. Daylight. Dusk. Washes of colored light, my features spooking and bleaching as I clicked through the artificial day.

I tried reading parts of books I'd liked when I was young. A spoiled girl gets banished underground, to a city ruled by goblins. The girl's bared knees in her childish dress, the woodcuts of the dark forests. The illustrations of the bound girl stirred me so I had to parcel how long I could look at them. I wished I could draw something like that, like the terrifying inside of someone's own mind. Or draw the face of the black-haired girl I'd seen in town—studying her long enough so I could see how the features worked together. The hours I lost to masturbation, face pressed into my pillow, passing some point of caring. I'd get a headache after a while, muscles jumpy, my legs quivering and tender. My underpants wet, the tops of my thighs.

Another book: a silversmith accidentally spills molten silver on his hand. His arm and hand probably looked skinned after the burn had scabbed over and peeled. The skin tight and pink and fresh, without hair or freckles. I thought of Willie and his stump, the warm hose water he sloshed over his car. How the puddles would slowly evaporate from the asphalt. I practiced peeling an orange as if my arm were burned to the elbow and I had no fingernails.

Death seemed to me like a lobby in a hotel. Some civilized, well-lit room you could easily enter or leave. A boy in town had shot himself in his finished basement after getting caught selling counterfeit raffle tickets: I didn't think of the gore, the wet insides, but only the ease of the moment before he pulled the trigger, how clean and winnowed the world must have seemed. All the disappointments, all of regular life with its punishments and indignities, made surplus in one orderly motion.

The aisles of the store seemed new to me, my thoughts formless from drinking. The constant flickering of the lights, stale lemon drops in a bin, the makeup arranged in pleasing, fetishistic groupings. I uncapped a lipstick, to test it on my wrist like I'd read I should. The door rang its chime of commerce. I looked up. It was the black-haired girl from the park, in denim sneakers, a dress whose sleeves had been cut at the shoulder. Excitement moved through me. Already I was trying to imagine what I would say to her. Her sudden appearance made the day seem tightly wound with synchronicity, the angle of sunlight newly weighted.

The girl wasn't beautiful, I realized, seeing her again. It was something else. Like pictures I had seen of the actor John Huston's daughter. Her face could have been an error, but some other process was at work. It was better than beauty.

The man behind the counter scowled.

"I told you," he said. "I won't let any of you in here, not anymore. Get on."

The girl gave him a lazy smile, holding up her hands. I saw a prick of hair in her armpits. "Hey," she said, "I'm just trying to buy toilet paper."

"You stole from me," the man said, shading red. "You and your friends. Not wearing shoes, running around with your filthy feet. Trying to confuse me."

I would have been terrified in the focus of his anger, but the girl was calm. Even jokey. "I don't think that's true." She cocked her head. "Maybe it was someone else."

He crossed his arms. "I remember you."

The girl's face shifted, something hardening in her eyes, but she remained smiling. "Fine," she said. "Whatever your thing is." She looked over at me, her glance cool and distant. Like she hardly saw me. Desire moved through me: I surprised myself with how much I didn't want her to disappear.

"Get on outside," the man said. "Go."

Before she left, she stuck out her tongue at the man. Just a peep, like a droll little cat.

...

I'd only hesitated for a moment before following the girl outside, but she was already cutting across the parking lot, keeping up a brisk pace. I hurried behind.

"Hey," I called. She kept walking.

I said it again, louder, and she stopped. Letting me catch up to her.

"What a jerk," I said. I must have looked shiny as an apple. Cheeks flushed with half-drunk effort.

She glared in the direction of the store. "Fat fuck," she muttered. "I can't even buy toilet paper."

She finally seemed to acknowledge me, studying my face for a long moment. I could tell she saw me as young. That my bib shirt, a gift from my mother, was considered fancy. I wanted to do something bigger than those facts. I made the offer before I'd really thought about it.

"I'll lift it," I said, my voice unnaturally bright. "The toilet paper. Easy. I steal stuff from there all the time."

I wondered if she believed me. It must have been obvious how lightly I was wearing the lie. But maybe she respected that. The desperation of my desire. Or maybe she wanted to see how it would play out. The rich girl, trying out kid-glove criminality.

"You sure?" she said.

I shrugged, my heart hammering. If she felt sorry for me, I didn't see that part.

...

My unexplained return agitated the man behind the counter.

"Back again?"

Even if I'd really planned to try to steal something, it would have been impossible. I dawdled down the aisles, making an effort to wipe my face of any delinquent glimmer, but the man didn't look away. He glared until I grabbed the toilet paper and brought it to the register, shamed at how easily I snapped into the habit. Of course I wasn't going to steal anything. That was never going to happen.

He got on a tear as he rang up the toilet paper. "A nice girl like you shouldn't hang out with girls like that," he said. "So filthy, that group. Some guy with a black dog." He looked pained. "Not in my store."

Through the pocked glass, I could see the girl ambling in the parking lot outside. Hand shading her eyes. This sudden and unexpected fortune: she was waiting for me.

After I paid, the man looked at me for a long moment. "You're just a kid," he said. "Why don't you go on home?"

I had felt bad for him until then. "I don't need a bag," I said, and stuffed the toilet paper in my purse. I was silent while the man gave me change, licking his lips as if to chase away a bad taste.

...

The girl perked up as I came over.

"You get it?"

I nodded, and she huddled me around the corner, her arm hurrying me along. I could almost believe I had actually stolen something, adrenaline brightening my veins as I held out my bag.

"Ha," she said, peeking inside. "Serves him right, the asshole. Was it easy?"

"Pretty easy," I said. "He's so out of it, anyway." I was thrilling at our collusion, the way we'd become a team. A triangle of stomach showed where the girl's dress wasn't fully buttoned. How easily she invoked a kind of sloppy sexual feeling, like her clothes had been hurried on a body still cooling from sweat.

"I'm Suzanne," she said. "By the way."

"Evie." I stuck out my hand. Suzanne laughed in a way that made me understand shaking hands was the wrong thing to do, a hollow symbol from the straight world. I flushed. It was hard to know how to act without all the usual polite gestures and forms. I wasn't sure what took their place. There was a silence: I scrambled to fill it.

"I think I saw you the other day," I said. "By the Hi-Ho?"

She didn't respond, giving me nothing to grab on to.

"You were with some girls?" I said. "And a bus came?"

"Oh," she said, her face reanimating. "Yeah, that idiot was real mad." She relaxed into the memory.

"I have to keep the other girls in line, you know, or they'd just fall all over themselves. Get us caught." I was watching Suzanne with an interest that must have been obvious: she let me look at her without any self-consciousness.

"I remembered your hair," I said.

Suzanne seemed pleased. Touching the ends, absently. "I never cut it."

I would find out, later, that this was something Russell told them not to do.

Suzanne nestled the toilet paper to her chest, suddenly proud. "You want me to give you some money for this?"

She had no pockets, no purse.

"Nah," I said. "It's not like it cost me anything."

"Well, thanks," she said, with obvious relief. "You live around here?"

"Pretty close," I said. "With my mom."

Suzanne nodded. "What street?"

"Morning Star Lane."

She made a hum of surprise. "Fancy."

I could see it meant something to her, me living in the nice part of town, but I couldn't imagine what, beyond the vague dislike for the rich that all young people had. Mashing up the wealthy and the media and the government into an indistinct vessel of evil, perpetrators of the grand hoax. I was only just starting to learn how to rig certain information with apology. How to mock myself before other people could.

"What about you?"

She made a fluttery motion with her fingers. "Oh," she said, "you know. We've got some things going on. But a lot of people in one place"—she held up the bag—"means a lot of asses that need wiping. We're low on money, at this exact moment, but that'll turn, soon, I'm sure."

We. The girl was part of a **we**, and I envied her ease, her surety of where she was aimed after the parking lot. Those two other girls I'd seen with her in the park, whoever else she lived with. People who'd notice her absence and exclaim at her return.

"You're quiet," Suzanne said after a moment.

"Sorry." I willed myself not to scratch my mosquito bites, though my skin was twisting with itchiness. I reeled for conversation, but all the possibilities that appeared were the things I couldn't say. I should not tell her how often and idly I had thought of her since that day. I should not tell her I had no friends, that I was being shunted to boarding school, that perpetual municipality of unwanted children. That I was not even a blip to Peter.

"It's cool." She waved her hand. "People are the way they are, you know? I could tell when I saw you," she continued. "You're a thoughtful person. On your own trip, all caught up in your mind."

I was not used to this kind of unmediated attention. Especially from a girl. Usually it was only a way of apologizing for being zeroed in on whatever boy was around. I let myself imagine I was a girl people saw as thoughtful. Suzanne shifted: I could tell this was a prelude to departure, but I couldn't think of how to extend our exchange.

"Well," she said. "That's me over there." She nodded to a car parked in the shade. It was a Rolls-Royce, shrouded in dirt. When she saw my confusion, she smiled.

"We're borrowing it," she said. As if that explained everything.

I watched her walk away without trying to stop her. I didn't want to be greedy: I should be happy I had gotten anything at all.

4

My mother was dating again. First, a man who introduced himself as Vismaya and kept massaging my mother's scalp with his clawed fingers. Who told me that my birthday, on the cusp of Aquarius and Pisces, meant my two phrases were "I believe" and "I know."

"Which is it?" Vismaya asked me. "Do you believe you know, or do you know you believe?"

Next, a man who flew small silver planes and told me that my nipples were showing through my shirt. He said it plainly, as if this were helpful information. He made pastel portraits of Native Americans and wanted my mother to help open a museum of his work in Arizona. Next, a real estate developer from Tiburon who took us out for Chinese food. He kept encouraging me to meet his daughter. Repeating again and again how sure he was that we'd get along like a house on fire. His daughter was eleven, I came to realize. Connie would have laughed, dissecting the way the man's teeth gummed up with rice, but I hadn't spoken to her since the day at her house.

"I'm fourteen," I said. The man looked to my mother, who nodded.

"Of course," he said, a tang of soy sauce on his breath. "I see now you're practically a grown-up."

"I'm sorry," my mother mouthed across the table, but when the man turned to feed her a slimy-looking snow pea from his fork, she opened her mouth obediently, like a bird.

The pity I felt for my mother in these situations was new and uncomfortable, but also I sensed that I deserved to carry it around—a grim and private responsibility, like a medical condition.

There had been a cocktail party my parents had thrown, the year before the divorce. It was my father's idea—until he left, my mother wasn't social, and I could sense a deep agitation in her during parties or events, a heave of discomfort she willed into a stiff smile. It had been a party to celebrate the investor my father had found. It was the first time, I think, that he'd gotten money from someone other than my mother, and he got even bigger in the heat of that, drinking before the guests arrived. His hair saturated with the dense fatherly scent of Vitalis, his breath notched with liquor.

My mother had made Chinese ribs with ketchup and they had a glandular sheen, like a lacquer. Olives from a can, buttered nuts. Cheese straws. Some sludgy dessert made from mandarin oranges, a recipe she'd seen in **McCall's**. She asked me before the guests arrived if she looked all right. Smoothing her damask skirt. I remember being taken aback by the question.

"Very nice," I said, feeling strangely unsettled. I'd been allowed some sherry in a cut pink glass: I liked the rotted pucker and snuck another glass.

The guests were my father's friends, mostly, and I was surprised at the breadth of his other life, a life I saw only from the perimeter. Because here were people who seemed to know him, to hold a vision of him informed by lunches and visits to Golden Gate Fields and discussions of Sandy Koufax. My mother hovered nervously around the buffet: she'd put out chopsticks, but no one was using them, and I could tell this disappointed her. She tried to urge them on a heavyset man and his wife, and they shook their heads, the man making some joke I couldn't hear. I saw something desperate pass over my mother's face. She was drinking, too. It was the kind of party where everyone was drunk early, a communal haze slurring over conversation. Earlier, one of my father's friends had lit a joint, and I saw my mother's expression downshift from disapproval to patient indulgence. Certain lines were getting dim. Wives staring up at the pass of an airplane, arcing toward SFO. Someone dropped a glass in the pool. I saw it drift slowly to the bottom. Maybe it was an ashtray.

I floated around the party, feeling like a much younger child, that desire for invisibility coupled with a wish to participate in an adjacent way. I was happy enough to point out the bathroom when asked, to parcel into a napkin buttered nuts that I ate by the pool, one by one, their salty grit fleecing my fingers. The freedom of being so young that no one expected anything from me.

I hadn't seen Tamar since the day she'd dropped me off after school, and I remember feeling disappointed when she arrived—I'd have to act like a grown-up now that she was there as witness. She had a man with her, slightly older. She introduced him around, kissing someone on the cheek, shaking hands. Everyone seemed to know her. I was jealous of how Tamar's boyfriend rested his hand on her back while she spoke, on the sliver of skin between her skirt and top. I wanted her to see that I was drinking: I made my way to the bar table when she did, pouring myself another glass of sherry.

"I like your outfit," I said, pushed to speak by the burn in my chest. She had her back to me and didn't hear. I repeated myself and she startled.

"Evie," she said, pleasantly enough. "You scared me."

"Sorry." I felt foolish, blunt in my shift dress. Her outfit was bright and new looking, wavy diamonds in violet and green and red.

"Fun party," she said, her eyes scanning the crowd.

Before I could think of a rejoinder, some crack to show that I knew the tiki torches were stupid, my mother joined us. I quickly put my glass back on the table. Hating the way I felt: all my comfort before Tamar's arrival had transformed into painful awareness of every object in my house, every detail of my parents, as if I were responsible for all of it. I was embarrassed for my mother's full skirt, which seemed outdated next to Tamar's clothes, for the eager way my mother greeted her. Her neck getting blotchy with nerves. I slunk away while they were distracted with their polite chatter.

Queasy and sunbaked with discomfort, I wanted to sit in one place without having to talk to anyone, without having to track Tamar's gaze or see my mother using her chopsticks, announcing gaily that it wasn't so hard, even as a mandarin orange slithered back onto her plate. I wished Connie were there—we were still friends then. My spot by the pool had been occupied by a gossipy scrum of wives: from across the yard, I heard my father's booming laugh, the group surrounding him laughing as well. I pulled my dress down, awkwardly, missing the weight of a glass in my hands. Tamar's boyfriend was standing nearby, eating ribs.

"You're Carl's daughter," he said, "right?"

I remember thinking it was strange that he and Tamar had floated apart, that he was just standing by himself, powering through his plate. It was strange that he would even want to talk to me. I nodded.

"Nice house," he said, his mouth full. Lips bright and wet from the ribs. He was handsome, I saw, but there was something cartoonish about him, the upturn of his nose. The extra ruff of skin under his chin. "So much land," he added.

"It was my grandparents' house."

His eyes shifted. "I heard about her," he said. "Your grandmother. I used to watch her when I was little." I didn't realize how drunk he was until that moment. His tongue lingering in the corner of his mouth. "That episode where she finds the alligator in the fountain. Classic."

I was used to people speaking of my grandmother fondly. How they liked to perform their admiration, tell me that they'd grown up with her on their television screens, beamed into their living rooms like another, better, family member.

"Makes sense," the boyfriend said, looking around. "That this was her place. 'Cause your old man couldn't afford it, no way."

I understood that he was insulting my father.

"It's just strange," he said, wiping his lips with his hand. "What your mother puts up with."

My face must have been blank: he waggled his fingers in the direction of Tamar, still at the bar. My father had joined her. My mother was nowhere in sight. Tamar's bracelets were making noise as she waved her glass. She and my father were just talking. Nothing was happening. I didn't get why her boyfriend was smiling so rabidly, waiting for me to say something.

"Your father fucks anything he can," he said.

"Can I take your plate?" I asked, too stunned to flinch. That was something I'd learned from my mother: revert to politeness. Cut pain with a gesture of civility. Like Jackie Kennedy. It was a virtue to that generation, an ability to divert discomfort, tamp it down with ceremony. But it was out of fashion now, and I saw something like disdain in his eyes when he handed me his plate. Though maybe that is something I imagined.

The party ended after dark. A few of the tiki torches stayed lit, sending their bleary flames streaking into the navy night. The vivid oversize cars lumbering down the driveway, my father calling out goodbyes while my mother stacked napkins and brushed olive pits, washed in other people's saliva, into her open palm. My father restarted the record; I looked out my bedroom window and saw him trying to get my mother to dance. "I'll be looking at the moon," he sang, the moon's far-off face the focus of so much longing back then.

I knew I should hate my father. But I only felt foolish. Embarrassed—not for him, but for my mother.

Smoothing her full skirt, asking me how she looked. The way she sometimes had flecks of food in her teeth and blushed when I told her so. The times she stood at the window when my father was late coming home, trying to decode new meaning out of the empty driveway.

She must know what was going on—she had to have known—but she wanted him anyway. Like Connie, jumping for the beer knowing she would look stupid. Even Tamar's boyfriend, eating with his frantic, bottomless need. Chewing faster than he could swallow. He knew how your hunger could expose you.

The drunk was wearing off. I was sleepy and hollow, cast uncomfortably back to myself. I had scorn for everything: my room with my childhood leftovers, the trim of lace around my desk. The plastic record player with a chunky Bakelite handle, a wet-looking beanbag chair that stuck to the backs of my legs. The party with its eager hors d'oeuvres, the men wearing aloha shirts in a sartorial clamor for festivity. It all seemed to add up to an explanation for why my father would want something else. I imagined Tamar with her throat circled by a ribbon, lying on some carpet in some too-small Palo Alto apartment. My father there—watching her? sitting in a chair? The perverse voltage of Tamar's pink lipstick. I tried to hate her but couldn't. I couldn't even hate my father. The only person left was my mother, who'd let it happen, who'd been as soft and malleable as dough. Handing money over, cooking dinner every night, and no wonder my father had wanted something else—Tamar's outsize opinions, her life like a TV show about summer.

It was a time when I imagined getting married in a simple, wishful way. The time when someone promised to take care of you, promised they would notice if you were sad, or tired, or hated food that tasted like the chill of the refrigerator. Who promised their lives would run parallel to yours. My mother must have known and stayed anyway, and what did that mean about love? It was never going to be safe—all the mournful refrains of songs that despaired **you didn't love me the way I loved you.**

The most frightening thing: It was impossible to detect the source, the instant when things changed. The sight of a woman's back in her low dress mingled with the knowledge of the wife in another room.

When the music stopped, I knew my mother would come say good night. It was a moment I'd been dreading—having to notice how her curls had wilted, the haze of lipstick around her mouth. When she knocked, I thought about pretending to be asleep. But my light was on: the door edged open.

She grimaced a little. "You're still all dressed."

I would've ignored her or made some joke, but I didn't want to cause her any pain. Not then. I sat up.

"That was nice, wasn't it?" she said. She leaned

against the door frame. "The ribs came out good, I thought."

Maybe I genuinely thought my mother would want to know. Or maybe I wanted to be soothed by her, for her to offer a calming adult summary.

I cleared my throat. "Something happened."

I felt her tense in the doorway.

"Oh?"

Later I cringed, thinking of it. She must have already known what was coming. Must have willed me to be quiet.

"Dad was talking." I turned back to my shoes, working intently at the buckle. "With Tamar."

She let out a breath. "And?" She was smiling a little. An untroubled smile.

I was confused: she must know what I meant. "That's all," I said.

My mother looked at the wall. "That dessert was the one thing," she said. "Next time I would do macaroons instead, coconut macaroons. Those mandarins were too hard to eat."

I was silent, shock making me wary. I slipped off my shoes and put them under my bed, side by side. I murmured good night, tilted my head to receive her kiss.

"You want me to turn off the light?" my mother asked, pausing in the doorway.

I shook my head. She shut the door gently. How conscientious she was, turning the handle so it clicked shut. I stared at my red feet, marked by the outline of my shoes. Thought about how strangled and strange they looked, all out of proportion, and who would ever love someone whose feet could look like this?

My mother spoke of the men she dated, after my father, with the desperate optimism of the born-again. And I saw the devout labor it took: she did exercises on a bath towel in the living room, her leotard striped with sweat. Licked her palm and sniffed to test her own breath. She went out with men whose necks raised boils where they cut themselves shaving, men who fumbled for the check but looked grateful when my mother removed her Air Travel Card. She found men like this and seemed happy about it.

I'd imagine Peter, during our dinners with these men. Asleep with Pamela in a basement apartment in an unfamiliar Oregon town. Jealousy mingled strangely with a protectiveness for the two of them, for the child growing inside Pamela. There were only so many girls, I understood, that could be marked for love. Like that girl Suzanne, who commanded that response just by existing.

The man my mother liked best was a gold miner. Or that's how Frank introduced himself, laughing, a scud of spit in the corner of his mouth.

"Pleased to meet you, darlin'," he said the first

night, his big arm reining me toward him in a clumsy hug. My mother was giddy and a little drunk, as if life were a world where nuggets of gold were hidden in streambeds or clustered at cliff bases, picked off as easily as peaches.

I had heard my mother tell Sal that Frank was still married but wouldn't be for long. I didn't know if that was true. Frank didn't seem the type to leave his family. He wore a shirt with creamy buttons, peonies embroidered in raised red thread on the shoulders. My mother was acting nervous, touching her hair, slipping her fingernail between her front teeth. She looked from me to Frank. "Evie's a very smart girl," she said. She was talking too loud. Still, it was nice to hear her say it. "She'll really blossom at Catalina." This was the boarding school I'd attend, though September seemed years away.

"Big brains," Frank boomed. "Can't go wrong there, can you?"

I didn't know if he was joking or not, and my mother didn't seem to know either.

We ate a casserole in silence in the dining room, and I picked out the blats of tofu and built a pile on my plate. I watched my mother decide not to say anything.

Frank was good-looking, even if his shirt was strange, too fussy and feminine, and he made my mother laugh. He was not as handsome as my father, but still. She kept reaching out to touch his arm with her fingertips.

"Fourteen years old, huh?" Frank said. "Bet you have a ton of boyfriends."

Adults always teased me about having boyfriends, but there was an age where it was no longer a joke, the idea that boys might actually want you.

"Oh, heaps," I said, and my mother perked to attention, hearing the coldness in my voice. Frank didn't seem to notice, smiling widely at my mother, patting her hand. She was smiling, too, in a mask-like way, her eyes bouncing from me to him across the table.

Frank had gold mines in Mexico. "No regulations down there," he said. "Cheap labor. It's pretty much a sure thing."

"How much gold have you found?" I asked. "So far, I mean."

"Well, once all the equipment is in place, I'll be finding a ton." He drank from a wineglass, his fingers leaving ghosts of grease. My mother went soft, in his glance; her shoulders relaxing, her lips parting. She was young looking that night. I had a queer twinge of motherly feeling for her, and the discomfort of it made me wince.

"Maybe I'll take you down there," Frank said. "Both of you. Little trip to Mexico. Flowers in your hair." He burped under his breath, swallowing it, and my mother blushed, wine moving in her glass.

My mother liked this man. Did her stupid exercises so she would look beautiful to him without any clothes on. She was groomed and oiled, her face eager for love. It was a painful thought, my mother needing anything, and I looked over at her, wanting to smile, to show her how we were fine, the two of us. But she wasn't watching me. She was alert to Frank instead, waiting to receive whatever he wanted to give her. I balled my hands tight under the table.

"What about your wife?" I asked.

"Evie," my mother hissed.

"That's all right," Frank said, holding up his hands. "That's a fair question." He rubbed his eyes hard, then put down his fork. "It's complicated stuff."

"It's not that complicated," I said.

"You're a rude girl," my mother said. Frank put his hand on her shoulder, but she'd already stood up to clear the plates, a grim busyness fixed on her face, and Frank handed over his plate with a concerned smile. Wiping his dry hands on his jeans. I didn't look at her or him. I was picking at the skin around my fingernail, tugging until there was a satisfying tear.

When my mother left the room, Frank cleared his throat.

"You shouldn't make your mom so mad," he said. "She's a nice lady."

"None of your business." My cuticle was bleeding a little: I pressed to feel the sting.

"Hey," he said, his voice easy, like he was trying to be my friend. "I get it. You wanna be out of the house. Tired of living with ol' mom, huh?"

"Pathetic," I mouthed.

He didn't understand what I had said, only that I

hadn't responded how he wanted. "Biting your nails is an ugly habit," he said hotly. "An ugly, dirty habit for dirty people. Are you an ugly person?"

My mother reappeared in the doorway. I was sure she had overheard, and now she knew that Frank wasn't a nice man. She would be disappointed, but I resolved to be kinder, to help more around the house.

But my mother just wrinkled her face. "What's happening?"

"I was just telling Evie she shouldn't bite her nails."

"I tell her that, too," my mother said. Her voice rattled, her lips twitching. "She could get sick, ingesting germs."

I cycled through the possibilities. My mother was simply stalling. She was taking a moment to figure out how best to drive Frank from our lives, to tell him I was no one else's business. But when she sat down and allowed Frank to rub her arm, even leaning toward him, I understood how it would go.

When Frank went to the bathroom, I figured there would be some kind of an apology from her.

"That shirt is too tight," she whispered harshly. "It's inappropriate, at your age."

I opened my mouth to speak.

"We'll talk tomorrow," she said. "You better believe we'll talk." When she heard Frank's footsteps returning, she gave me one last look, then rose to meet him. They left me alone at the table. The overhead light on my arms and hands was severe and unlovely.

They went on the porch to sit, my mother keeping her cigarette butts in a mermaid tin. From my bedroom I heard their staggered talk late into the night, my mother's laugh, simple and thoughtless. The smoke from their cigarettes drifting through the screen. The night boiled inside me. My mother thought life was as easy as picking gold from the ground, as if things could be that way for her. There was no Connie to temper my upset, just the suffocating constancy of my own self, that numb and desperate company.

There are ways I made sense of my mother later. How fifteen years with my father had left great blanks in her life that she was learning to fill, like those stroke victims relearning the words for car and table and pencil. The shy way she looked at herself in the oracle of the mirror, as critical and hopeful as an adolescent. Sucking in her stomach to zip her new jeans.

In the morning, I came into the kitchen and found my mother at the table, her bowl of tea already drained, sediment flecking the bottom. Her lips were tight, her eyes wounded. I walked past her without speaking, opening a bag of ground coffee, purple and heady, my mother's replacement for the Sanka that my father liked.

"What was that about?" She was trying to be calm, I could tell, but the words were rushed.

I shook the grounds into the maker, turned on the burner. Keeping a Buddhist calm on my face as I went about my tasks, untroubled. This was my best weapon, and I could feel her getting agitated.

"Well, now you're quiet," she said. "You were very rude to Frank last night."

I didn't respond.

"You want me to be unhappy?" She got to her feet. "I'm talking to you," she said, reaching to snap the stove off.

"Hey," I said, but her face made me shut up.

"Why can't you let me have anything?" she said. "Just one little thing."

"He's not going to leave her." The intensity of my feeling startled me. "He's never going to be with you."

"You don't know anything about his life," she said. "Not anything. You think you know so much."

"Oh yeah," I said. "Gold. Right. Big success there. Just like Dad. I bet he asked you for money."

My mother flinched.

"I try with you," she said. "I've always tried, but you aren't trying at all. Look at yourself. Doing nothing." She shook her head, tightening her robe. "You'll see. Life will come up on you so fast, and guess what, you'll be stuck with the person you are. No ambition, no drive. You have a real chance at Catalina, but you have to try. You know what my mother was doing at your age?"

"You never did anything!" Something tipped over inside me. "All you did was take care of Dad. And he left." My face was burning. "I'm sorry I disappoint you. I'm sorry I'm so awful. I should pay people to tell me I'm great, like you do. Why did Dad leave if you're so fucking great?"

She reached forward and slapped me, not hard, but hard enough so there was an audible sound. I smiled, like a crazed person, showing too many teeth.

"Get out." Her neck was mottled with hives, her wrists thin. "Get out," she hissed again, weakly, and I darted away.

I took the bicycle down the dirt road. My heart thudding, the tightness of pressure behind my eyes. I liked feeling the sting of my mother's slap, the aura of goodness she had so carefully cultivated for the last month—the tea, the bare feet—curdled in an instant. Good. Let her be ashamed. All her classes and cleanses and readings had done nothing. She was the same weak person as always. I pedaled faster, a flurry in my throat. I could go to the Flying A and buy a bag of chocolate stars. I could see what was playing at the movie theater or walk along the brothy soup of the river. My hair lifted a little in the dry heat. I felt hatred hardening in me, and it was almost nice, how big it was, how pure and intense.

My furious pedaling went abruptly slack: the chain slipped its bearings. The bike was slowing. I lurched to a stop in the dirt by the fire road. My armpits were sweating, the backs of my knees. The sun hot through the cutwork lattice of a live oak. I was trying not to cry. I crouched on the ground to realign the chain, tears skimming off my eyes in the sting of the breeze, my fingers slippery with grease. It was too hard to grip, the chain falling away.

"Fuck," I said, then said it louder. I wanted to kick the bicycle, silence something, but that would be too pitiful, the theater of upset performed for no one. I tried one more time to hook the chain onto the spoke, but it wouldn't catch, snapping loose. I let the bike drop into the dirt and sank down beside it. The front wheel spun a little, then slowed to a stop. I stared at the bike, splayed and useless: the frame was "Campus Green," a color that had conjured, in the store, a hale college boy walking you home from an evening class. A prissy fantasy, a stupid bike, and I let the string of disappointments grow until they looped into a dirge of mediocrity. Connie was probably with May Lopes. Peter and Pamela buying houseplants for an Oregon apartment and soaking lentils for supper. What did I have? The tears dripped off my chin into the dirt, pleasing proof of my suffering. This absence in me that I could curl around like an animal.

I heard it before I saw it: the black bus lumbering heavily up the road, dust rising behind the wheels. The windows were pocked and gray, the blurred shapes of people within. Painted on the hood was a crude heart, crowned with drippy lashes, like an eye.

...

A girl wearing a man's shirt and knitted vest stepped down from the bus, shaking back her flat orange hair. I could hear other voices, a flurry at the windows. A moony face appeared: watching me.

The girl's voice was singsongy. "What's wrong?" she said.

"The bike," I said, "the chain's messed up." The girl toed the wheel with her sandaled foot. Before I could ask who she was, Suzanne came down the steps, and my heart surged. I got to my feet, trying to brush the dirt from my knees. Suzanne smiled but seemed distracted. I realized I had to remind her of my name.

"From the store on East Washington," I said. "The other day?"

"Oh yeah."

I expected her to say something about the bizarre luck of encountering each other again, but she looked a little bored. I kept glancing at her. I wanted to remind her of our conversation, how she'd said I was thoughtful. But she wouldn't exactly meet my eye.

"We saw you sitting there and thought, Oh shit, poor thing," the redhead said. This was Donna, I was to learn. She had a touched look, her eyebrows invisible so her face took on an alien blankness. She squatted to study my bike. "Suzanne said she knew you."

...

The three of us worked together to get the chain back on. The smell of their sweat as we propped the bike on its stand. I'd bent the gears somehow when the bike fell, and the teeth wouldn't line up with the spokes.

"Fuck." Suzanne sighed. "This is all messed up."

"You need pliers or something," Donna said. "You aren't gonna fix it now. Stick it in the bus, come hang with us for a while."

"Let's just give her a ride into town," Suzanne said.

She spoke briskly, like I was a mess that needed to be cleaned up. Even so, I was glad. I was used to thinking about people who never thought about me.

"We're having a solstice party," Donna said.

I didn't want to go back to my mother, to the forlorn guardianship of my own self. I had the sense that if I let Suzanne go, I would not see her again.

"Evie wants to come," Donna said. "I can tell she's up for it. You like to have fun, don't you?"

"Come on," Suzanne said. "She's a kid."

I surged with shame. "I'm sixteen," I lied.

"She's **sixteen,**" Donna repeated. "Don't you think Russell would want us to be hospitable? I think he'd be upset if I told him we weren't being hospitable."

I didn't read any threat in Donna's voice, only teasing.

Suzanne's mouth was tight; she finally smiled.

"Okay," she said. "Put the bike in the back."

...

I saw that the bus had been emptied and rebuilt, the interior cruddy and overworked in the way things were back then—the floor gridded with Oriental carpets, grayed with dust, the drained tufts of thrift store cushions. The stink of a joss stick in the air, prisms ticking against the windows. Cardboard scrawled with dopey phrases.

There were three other girls in the bus, and they turned to me with eagerness, a feral attention I read as flattering. Cigarettes going in their hands while they looked me up and down, an air of festivity and timelessness. A sack of green potatoes, pasty hot dog buns. A crate of wet, overripe tomatoes. "We were on a food run," Donna said, though I didn't really understand what that meant. My mind was preoccupied with this sudden shift of luck, with monitoring the slow trickle of sweat under my arms. I kept waiting to be spotted, to be identified as an intruder who didn't belong. My hair too clean. Little nods toward presentation and decorum that seemed to concern no one else. My hair cut crazily across my vision from the open windows, intensifying the dislocation, the abruptness of being in this strange bus. A feather hanging from the rearview with a cluster of beads. Some dried lavender on the dashboard, colorless from the sun.

"She's coming to the solstice," Donna chimed, "the summer solstice."

It was early June and I knew the solstice was at the end of the month: I didn't say anything. The first of many silences.

"She's gonna be our offering," Donna told the others. Giggling. "We're gonna sacrifice her."

I looked to Suzanne—even our brief history seemed to ratify my presence among them—but she was sitting off to the side, absorbed by the box of tomatoes. Applying pressure to the skins, sifting out the rot. Waving away the bees. It would occur to me later that Suzanne was the only one who didn't seem overjoyed to come upon me, there on the road. Something formal and distant in her affect. I can only think it was protective. That Suzanne saw the weakness in me, lit up and obvious: she knew what happened to weak girls.

Donna introduced me around, and I tried to remember their names. Helen, a girl who seemed close to my age, though maybe it was just her pigtails. She was pretty in the youthful way of hometown beauties, snub-nosed, her features accessible, though with an obvious expiration date. Roos. "Short for Roosevelt," she told me. "As in, Franklin D." She was older than the other girls, with a face as round and rosy as a storybook character.

I couldn't remember the name of the tall girl who was driving: I never saw her again after that day.

Donna made a space, patting the nub of an embroidered cushion.

"Come here," she said, and I sat down on the itchy pile. Donna seemed odd, slightly oafish, but I liked her. All of her greed and pettiness was right on the surface.

The bus lurched forward: my gut went jostled and tight, but I took the jug of cheap red wine when they passed it, splashing out over my hands. They looked happy, smiling, their voices sometimes breaking into snippets of song like campers around a fire. I was picking up the particularities—how they held hands without any self-consciousness and dropped words like "harmony" and "love" and "eternity." How Helen acted like a baby, pulling on her pigtails and talking in her baby voice, abruptly sinking into Roos's lap like she could trick Roos into taking care of her. Roos didn't complain: she seemed stolid, nice. Those pink cheeks, her lank blond hair falling in her eyes. Though later I'd think maybe it was less niceness than a muted void where niceness should be. Donna asked me about myself, and so did the others, a constant stream of questions. I couldn't help my pleasure at being the focus of their attention. Inexplicably, they seemed to like me, and the thought was foreign and cheering, a mysterious gift I didn't want to probe too much. I could even cast Suzanne's silence in a welcoming light, imagining she was shy, like me.

"Nice," Donna said, touching my shirt. Helen pinched a sleeve, too.

"You're just like a little doll," Donna said. "Russell's gonna love you."

She tossed out his name just like that, as if it were

unimaginable that I might not know who Russell was. Helen giggled at the sound of his name, rolling her shoulders with pleasure, like she was sucking on a sweet. Donna saw my blink of uncertainty and laughed.

"You'll love him," she said. "He's not like anyone else. No bullshit. It's like a natural high, being around him. Like the sun or something. That big and right."

She looked over to be sure I was listening, seemed pleased that I was.

She said that the place we were headed was about a way of living. Russell was teaching them how to discover a path to truth, how to free their real selves from where it was coiled inside them. She talked about someone named Guy, who'd once trained falcons but had joined their group and now wanted to be a poet.

"When we met him, he was on some weird trip, just eating meat. He thought he was the devil or something. But Russell helped him. Taught him how to love," Donna said. "Everyone can love, can transcend the bullshit, but so many things get us all stopped up."

I didn't know how to imagine Russell. I had only the limited reference point of men like my father or boys I'd had crushes on. The way these girls spoke of Russell was different, their worship more practical, with none of the playful, girlish longing I knew. Their certainty was unwavering, invoking Russell's power and magic as though it were as widely acknowledged as the moon's tidal pull or the earth's orbit.

Donna said Russell was unlike any other human. That he could receive messages from animals. That he could heal a man with his hands, pull the rot out of you as cleanly as a tumor.

"He sees every part of you," Roos added. As if that were a good thing.

The possibility of judgment being passed on me supplanted any worries or questions I might have about Russell. At that age, I was, first and foremost, a thing to be judged, and that shifted the power in every interaction onto the other person.

The hint of sex that crossed their faces when they spoke of Russell, a prom-night giddiness. I understood, without anyone exactly saying so, that they all slept with him. The arrangement made me blush, inwardly shocked. No one seemed jealous of anyone else. "The heart doesn't own anything," Donna chimed. "That's not what love is about," she said, squeezing Helen's hand, a look passing between them. Even though Suzanne was mostly silent, sitting apart from us, I saw her face change at the mention of Russell. A wifely tenderness in her eyes that I wanted to feel, too.

I may have smiled to myself as I watched the familiar pattern of the town pass, the bus cruising through shade to sunshine. I'd grown up in this place, had the knowledge of it so deep in me that I didn't even know most street names, navigating instead by landmarks, visual or memorial. The corner where my mother had twisted her ankle in a mauve pantsuit. The copse of trees that had always looked vaguely attended by evil. The drugstore with its torn awning. Through the window of that unfamiliar bus, the burr of old carpet under my legs, my hometown seemed scrubbed clean of my presence. It was easy to leave it behind.

They discussed plans for the solstice party. Helen up on her knees, tightening her pigtails with happy, brisk habit. Thrilling while they described the dresses they'd change into, some goofy solstice song Russell had made up. Someone named Mitch had given them enough money to buy alcohol: Donna said his name with a confusing emphasis.

"You know," she repeated. "Mitch. Like Mitch Lewis?"

I hadn't recognized Mitch's name, but I'd heard of his band—I'd seen them on TV, playing in the hot lights of a studio set, sweat needling their foreheads. The background was a shag of tinsel, the stage revolving so the band members turned like jewelry-box ballerinas.

I affected nonchalance, but here it was: the world I had always suspected existed, the world where you called famous musicians by their first names.

"Mitch did a recording session with Russell," Donna told me. "Russell blew his mind."

There it was again, their wonder at Russell, their certainty. I was jealous of that trust, that someone else could stitch the empty parts of your life together so you felt there was a net under you, linking each day to the next.

"Russell's gonna be famous, like **that**," Helen added. "He has a record deal, already." It was like she was recounting a fairy tale, but this was even better, because she knew it would happen.

"You know what Mitch calls Russell?" Donna spooked her hands dreamily. "The Wizard. Isn't that a trip?"

After I'd been at the ranch a while, I saw how everyone spoke of Mitch. Of Russell's imminent record deal. Mitch was their patron saint, sending Clover Dairy shipments to the ranch so the kids could get calcium, supporting the place financially. I wouldn't hear the whole story until much later. Mitch had met Russell at Baker Beach, at a love-in of sorts. Russell attending in his buckskins, a Mexican guitar strapped to his back. Flanked by his women, begging for change with their air of biblical poverty. The cold, dark sand, a bonfire, Mitch on a break between records. Someone in a porkpie hat tending a pot of steamed clams.

Mitch, I'd learn, had been having a crisis—money disputes with a manager who'd been a childhood friend, a marijuana arrest that had been expunged, but still—and Russell must have seemed like a citizen of a realer world, stoking Mitch's guilt over the gold records, the parties where he covered the pool in Perspex. Russell offered up a mystic salvation, buttressed by the young girls who cast their eyes down in adoration when Russell spoke. Mitch invited the whole group back to his house in Tiburon, letting them gorge on the contents of his refrigerator, crash in his guest room. They drained bottles of apple juice and pink champagne and tracked mud onto the bed, thoughtless as an occupying army. In the morning, Mitch gave them a lift back to the ranch: by then Russell had seduced Mitch, speaking softly of truth and love, those invocations especially potent to wealthy searchers.

I believed everything the girls told me that day, their buzzy, swarming pride as they spoke of Russell's brilliance. How pretty soon he wouldn't be able to walk down the street without getting mobbed. How he'd be able to tell the whole world how to be free. And it was true that Mitch had set up a recording session for Russell. Thinking maybe Mitch's label would find Russell's vibe interesting and of the moment. I didn't know it until much later, but the session had gone badly, the failure legendary. This was before everything else happened.

. . .

There are those survivors of disasters whose accounts never begin with the tornado warning or the captain announcing engine failure, but always much earlier in the timeline: an insistence that they noticed a strange quality to the sunlight that morning or excessive static in their sheets. A meaningless fight with a boyfriend. As if the presentiment of catastrophe wove itself into everything that came before.

Did I miss some sign? Some internal twinge? The bees glittering and crawling in the crate of tomatoes? An unusual lack of cars on the road? The question I remember Donna asking me in the bus—casually, almost as an afterthought.

"You ever hear anything about Russell?"

The question didn't make sense to me. I didn't understand that she was trying to gauge how many of the rumors I'd heard: about orgies, about frenzied acid trips and teen runaways forced to service older men. Dogs sacrificed on moonlit beaches, goat heads rotting in the sand. If I'd had friends besides Connie, I might've heard chatter of Russell at parties, some hushed gossip in the kitchen. Might've known to be wary.

But I just shook my head. I hadn't heard anything.

5

Even later, even knowing the things I knew, it was impossible, that first night, to see beyond the immediate. Russell's buckskin shirt, smelling of flesh and rot and as soft as velvet. Suzanne's smile blooming in me like a firework, losing its colored smoke, its pretty, drifting cinders.

"Home on the range," Donna said as we climbed down from the bus that afternoon.

It took me a moment to see where I was. The bus had gone far from the highway, bumping down a dirt road that ended deep in the blond summer hills, cupped with oaks. An old wooden house: the knobby rosettes and plaster columns giving it the air of a minor castle. It was part of a grid of ad hoc existence that included, as far as I could see, a barn and a swampy-looking pool. Six fleecy llamas drowsing in a pen. Far-off figures were hacking at brush along the fence. They raised their hands in greeting, then bent again to their work.

"The creek is low, but you can still swim," Donna said.

It seemed magical to me that they actually lived there together. The Day-Glo symbols crawling up the side of the barn, clothes on a line ghosting in a breeze. An orphanage for raunchy children.

They had once filmed a car commercial at the ranch, Helen said in her baby voice. "A while ago, but still."

Donna nudged me. "Pretty wild out here, huh?"

I said, "How'd you even find this place?"

"This old guy used to live here, but he had to move out 'cause the roof was bad." Donna shrugged. "We fixed it, kind of. His grandson rents it to us."

To make money, she explained, they took care of the llamas and worked for the farmer next door, harvesting lettuce with their pocketknives and selling his haul at the farmer's market. Sunflowers and jars of marmalade gluey with pectin.

"Three bucks an hour. Not bad," Donna said. "But money gets tight."

I nodded, like I understood such concerns. I watched a young boy, four or five, hurtle himself at Roos, crash-landing into her leg. He was badly sunburned, his hair bleached white, and he seemed too old to still be wearing a diaper. I assumed the boy was Roos's child. Was Russell the father? The quick thought of sex raised a queasy rush in my chest. The boy lifted his head, like a dog roused from sleep, and looked at me with a bored, suspicious squint.

Donna leaned into me. "Come meet Russell," she said. "You'll love him, I swear."

"She'll meet him at the party," Suzanne said, cutting into our conversation. I hadn't noticed her approach: her closeness startled me. She handed a sack of potatoes to me and took up a cardboard box in her arms. "We're gonna dump this stuff in the kitchen, first. For the feast."

Donna pouted, but I followed Suzanne.

"Bye, dolly," she called, frittering her thin fingers and laughing, not unkindly.

I followed Suzanne's dark hair through a jumble of strangers. The ground was uneven, a disorienting slope. It was the smell, too, a heavy smokiness. I was flattered Suzanne had enlisted my help, like it confirmed I was one of them. There were young people milling around in bare feet or boots, their hair drifty and sun lightened. I overheard feverish invocations of the solstice party. I didn't know it yet, but it was rare for the ranch, all this efficient work. Girls wore their best thrift store rags and carried instruments in their arms as gently as babies, the sun catching the steel of a guitar and fractaling into hot diamonds of light. The tambourines rattling tuneless in their arms.

"Those fuckers bite me all night," Suzanne said, swatting at one of the vicious horseflies that droned around us. "I wake up all bloody from scratching."

Beyond the house, the land was scarred with boulders and the filtery oaks, a few hollow cars in a state of disrepair. I liked Suzanne but couldn't shake the feeling that I was struggling to keep pace with her: it was an age when I often conflated liking people with feeling nervous around them. A boy with no shirt and a chunky silver belt buckle catcalled when we passed. "What you got there? A solstice present?"

"Shut up," Suzanne said.

The boy smiled, raffish, and I tried to smile back. He was young, his hair long and dark, a medieval droop to his face I took as romantic. Handsome with the feminine duskiness of a cinematic villain, though I'd find out he was just from Kansas.

This was Guy. A farm boy who'd defected from Travis AFB when he'd discovered it was the same bullshit scene as his father's house. He'd worked in Big Sur for a while, then drifted north. Gotten caught up in a group fermenting around the borders of the Haight, the hobby Satanists who wore more jewelry than a teenage girl. Scarab lockets and platinum daggers, red candles and organ music. Then Guy had come across Russell playing guitar in the park one day. Russell in the frontier buckskins that maybe reminded Guy of the adventure books of his youth, serials starring men who scraped caribou hides and forded frigid Alaskan rivers. Guy had been with Russell ever since.

Guy was the one who would drive the girls later that summer. Tighten his own belt around the caretaker's wrists, that big silver buckle notching into the tender skin and leaving behind an oddly shaped stamp, like a brand.

But that first day he was just a boy, giving off a dirty fritz like a warlock, and I glanced back at him with a thrilled shiver.

Suzanne stopped a girl walking by: "Tell Roos to get Nico back to the nursery. He shouldn't be out here."

The girl nodded.

Suzanne glanced at me as we kept going, reading my confusion. "Russell doesn't want us to get too attached to the kids. Especially if they're ours." She let out a grim laugh. "They aren't our property, you know? We don't get to fuck them up just because we want something to cuddle."

It took me a moment to process this idea that parents didn't have the right. It suddenly seemed blaringly true. My mother didn't own me just because she had given birth to me. Sending me to boarding school because the spirit moved her. Maybe this was a better way, even though it seemed alien. To be part of this amorphous group, believing love could come from any direction. So you wouldn't be disappointed if not enough came from the direction you'd hoped.

The kitchen was much darker than outside, and I blinked in the sudden wash. All the rooms smelled pungent and earthy, some mix of high-volume cooking and bodies. The walls were mostly bare, except for streaks of a daisy-patterned wallpaper and another funny heart painted there, too, like on the bus. The window sashes were crumbling, T-shirts tacked up instead of curtains. Somewhere nearby, a radio was on.

There were ten or so girls in the kitchen, focused on their cooking tasks, and everyone was healthy looking, their arms slim and tan, their hair thick. Bare feet gripping the rough boards of the floor. They cackled and snipped at one another, pinching exposed flesh and swatting with spoons. Everything seemed sticky and a little rotten. As soon as I put the bag of potatoes on the counter, a girl started picking through them.

"Green potatoes are poisonous," she said. Sucking her teeth, sifting through the sack.

"Not if you cook them," Suzanne shot back. "So cook them."

Suzanne slept in a small outbuilding with a dirt floor, a bare twin mattress against each of the four walls.

"Mostly girls crash here," she said, "it depends. And Nico, sometimes, even though I don't want him to. I want him to grow up free. But he likes me."

A square of stained silk was tacked above a mattress, a Mickey Mouse pillowcase on the bed. Suzanne passed me a rolled cigarette, the end wet with her saliva. Ash fell on her bare thigh, but she didn't seem to notice. It was weed, but it was stronger than what Connie and I smoked, the dry refuse from Peter's sock drawer. This was oily and dank, and the cloying smoke it produced didn't dissipate quickly. I waited to start feeling differently. Connie would hate all this. Think this place was dirty and strange, that Guy was frightening—this knowledge made me proud. My thoughts were softening, the weed starting to surface.

"Are you really sixteen?" Suzanne asked.

I wanted to keep up the lie, but her gaze was too bright.

"I'm fourteen," I said.

Suzanne didn't seem surprised. "I'll give you a ride home, if you want. You don't have to stay."

I licked my lips—did she think I couldn't handle this? Or maybe she thought I would embarrass her. "I don't have to be anywhere," I said.

Suzanne opened her mouth to say something, then hesitated.

"Really," I said, starting to feel desperate. "It's fine."

There was a moment, when Suzanne looked at me, when I was sure she'd send me home. Pack me back to my mother's house like a truant. But then the look drained into something else, and she got to her feet.

"You can borrow a dress," she said.

There was a rack of clothes hanging and more spilling out of a garbage bag—torn denim. Paisley shirts, long skirts. The hems stuttering with loose stitching. The clothes weren't nice, but the quantity and unfamiliarity stirred me. I'd always been jealous of girls who wore their sister's hand-me-downs, like the uniform of a well-loved team.

"This stuff is all yours?"

"I share with the girls." Suzanne seemed resigned to my presence: Maybe she'd seen that my desperation was bigger than any desire or ability she had to shoo me off. Or maybe the admiration was flattering, my wide eyes, greedy for the details of her. "Only Helen makes a fuss. We have to go get things back; she hides them under her pillow."

"Don't you want some for yourself?"

"Why?" She took a draw from the joint and held her breath. When she spoke, her voice was crackled. "I'm not on that kind of trip right now. Me me me. I love the other girls, you know. I like that we share. And they love me."

She watched me through the smoke. I felt shamed. For doubting Suzanne or thinking it was strange to share. For the limits of my carpeted bedroom at home. I shoved my hands in my shorts. This wasn't bullshit dabbling, like my mother's afternoon workshops.

"I get it," I said. And I did, and tried to isolate the flutter of solidarity in myself.

The dress Suzanne chose for me stank like mouse shit, my nose twitching as I pulled it over my head, but I was happy wearing it—the dress belonged to someone else, and that endorsement released me from the pressure of my own judgments.

"Good," Suzanne said, surveying me. I ascribed more meaning to her pronouncement than I ever had to Connie's. There was something grudging about Suzanne's attention, and that made it doubly valued. "Let me braid your hair," she said. "Come here. It'll tangle if you dance with it loose."

I sat on the floor in front of Suzanne, her legs on either side of me, and tried to feel comfortable with the closeness, the sudden, guileless intimacy. My parents were not affectionate, and it surprised me that someone could just touch me at any moment, the gift of their hand given as thoughtlessly as a piece of gum. It was an unexplained blessing. Her tangy breath on my neck as she swept my hair to one side. Walking her fingers along my scalp, drawing a straight part. Even the pimples I'd seen on her jaw seemed obliquely beautiful, the rosy flame an inner excess made visible.

...

Both of us were silent as she braided my hair. I picked up one of the reddish rocks from the floor, lined up beneath the mirror like the eggs of a foreign species.

"We lived in the desert for a while," Suzanne said. "That's where I got that."

She told me about the Victorian they had rented in San Francisco. How they'd had to leave after Donna had accidentally started a fire in the bedroom. The time spent in Death Valley where they were all so sunburned they couldn't sleep for days. The remains of a gutted, roofless salt factory in the Yucatán where they'd stayed for six months, the cloudy lagoon where Nico had learned to swim. It was painful to imagine what I had been doing at the same time: drinking the tepid, metallic water from my school's drinking fountain. Biking to Connie's house. Reclining in the dentist's chair, hands politely in my lap, while Dr. Lopes worked in my mouth, his gloves slick with my idiot drool.

The night was warm and the celebration started early. There were maybe forty of us, swarming and massing in the stretch of dirt, hot air gusting over the run of tables, the wavy light from a kerosene lamp. The party seemed much bigger than it actually was. There was an antic quality that distorted my memory, the house looming behind us so everything gained a cinematic flicker. The music was loud, the sweet thrum occupying me in an exciting way, and people were dancing and grabbing for one another, hand over wrist: they skipped in circles, threading in and out. A drunken, yelping chain that broke when Roos sat down hard in the dirt, laughing. Some little kids skulked around the table like dogs, full and lonesome for the adult excitement, their lips scabby from picking.

"Where's Russell?" I asked Suzanne. She was stoned, like me, her black hair loose. Someone had given her a shrub rose, half-wilted, and she was trying to knot it in her hair.

"He'll be here," she said. "It doesn't really start till he's here."

She brushed some ash off my dress and the gesture stirred me.

"There's our little doll," Donna cooed when she saw me. She had a tinfoil crown on her head that kept falling off. She'd drawn an Egyptian pattern on her hands and freckled arms with kohl before clearly losing interest—it was all over her fingers, smeared on her dress, along her jaw. Guy swerved, avoiding her hands.

"She's our sacrifice," Donna told him, her words already careening around. "Our solstice offering."

Guy smiled at me, his teeth stained from wine.

They burned a car that night in celebration, and the flames were hot and jumpy and I laughed out loud, for no reason—the hills were so dark against the sky and no one from my real life knew where I was and it was the solstice, and who cared if it wasn't actually the solstice? I had distant thoughts of my mother, houndish nips of worry, but she'd assume I was at Connie's. Where else would I be? She couldn't conceive of this kind of place even existing, and even if she could, even if by some miracle she showed up, she wouldn't be able to recognize me. Suzanne's dress was too big, and it often slipped off my shoulders, but pretty soon I wasn't as quick to pull the sleeves back up. I liked the exposure, the way I could pretend I didn't care, and how I actually started not to care, even when I accidentally flashed most of a breast as I hitched up the sleeves. Some stunned, blissed-out boy—a painted crescent moon on his face—grinned at me like I'd always been there among them.

The feast was not a feast at all. Bloated cream puffs sweating in a bowl until someone fed them to the dogs. A plastic container of Cool Whip, green beans boiled to structureless gray, augmented by the winnings of some dumpster. Twelve forks clattered in a giant pot—everyone took turns scooping out a watery vegetal pabulum, the mash of potatoes and ketchup and onion soup packets. There was a single watermelon, rind patterned like a snake, but no one could find a knife. Finally Guy cracked it open violently on the corner of a table. The kids descended on the pulpy mess like rats.

It was nothing like the feast I'd been imagining.

The distance made me feel a little sad. But it was only sad in the old world, I reminded myself, where people stayed cowed by the bitter medicine of their lives. Where money kept everyone slaves, where they buttoned their shirts up to the neck, strangling any love they had inside themselves.

How often I replayed this moment again and again, until it gained a meaningful pitch: when Suzanne nudged me so I knew the man walking toward the fire was Russell. My first thought was shock—he'd looked young as he approached, but then I saw he was at least a decade older than Suzanne. Maybe even as old as my mother. Dressed in dirty Wranglers and a buckskin shirt, though his feet were bare—how strange that was, how they all walked barefoot through the weeds and the dog shit as if nothing were there. A girl got to her knees beside him, touching his leg. It took me a moment to remember the girl's name—my brain was sludgy from the drugs—but then I had it, Helen, the girl from the bus with her pigtails, her baby voice. Helen smiled up at him, enacting some ritual I didn't understand.

I knew Helen had sex with this man. Suzanne did, too. I experimented with that thought, imagining the man hunched over Suzanne's milky body. Closing his hand on her breast. I knew only how to dream about boys like Peter, the unformed muscles under their skin, the patchy hair they tended along their jaws. Maybe I would sleep with Russell. I tried on the thought. Sex was still colored by the girls in my father's magazines, everything glossy and dry. About beholding. The people at the ranch seemed beyond that, loving one another indiscriminately, with the purity and optimism of children.

The man held up his hands and boomed out a greeting: the group surged and twitched like a Greek chorus. At moments like that, I could believe Russell was already famous. He seemed to swim through a denser atmosphere than the rest of us. He walked among the group, giving benedictions: a hand on a shoulder, a word whispered in an ear. The party was still going, but everyone was now aimed at him, their faces turned expectantly, as if following the arc of the sun. When Russell reached Suzanne and me, he stopped and looked in my eyes.

"You're here," he said. Like he'd been waiting for me. Like I was late.

I'd never heard another voice like his—full and slow, never hesitating. His fingers pressed into my back in a not unpleasant way. He wasn't much taller than me, but he was strong and compact, pressurized. The hair haloed around his head was coarsened by oil and dirt into a boggy mass. His eyes didn't seem to water, or waver, or flick away. The way the girls had spoken of him finally made sense. How he took me in, like he wanted to see all the way through.

"Eve," Russell said when Suzanne introduced me. "The first woman."

I was nervous I'd say the wrong thing, expose the error of my presence. "It's Evelyn, really."

"Names are important, aren't they?" Russell said. "And I don't see any snake in you."

Even this mild approval relieved me.

"What do you think of our solstice celebration, Evie?" he said. "Our spot?"

All the while his hand was pulsing a message on my back I couldn't decode. I slivered a glance at Suzanne, aware that the sky had darkened without me noticing, the night gliding deeper. I felt drowsy from the fire and the dope. I hadn't eaten and there was an empty throb in my stomach. Was he saying my name a lot? I couldn't tell. Suzanne's whole body was directed at Russell, her hand moving uneasy in her hair.

I told Russell I liked it here. Other meaningless, nervous remarks, but even so, he was getting other information from me. And I never did lose that feeling. Even after. That Russell could read my thoughts as easily as taking a book from a shelf.

When I smiled, he tilted my chin up with his hand. "You're an actress," he said. His eyes were like hot oil, and I let myself feel like Suzanne, the kind of girl a man would startle at, would want to touch. "Yeah, that's it. I see it. You gotta be standing on a cliff and looking out to sea."

I told him I wasn't an actress, but my grandmother was.

"Right on," he said. As soon as I said her name, he was even more attentive. "I picked that up right off. You look like her."

Later I'd read about how Russell sought the famous and semifamous and hangers-on, people he could court and wring for resources, whose cars he could borrow and houses he could live in. How pleased he must have been at my arrival, not even needing to be coaxed. Russell reached out to draw Suzanne closer. When I caught her eye, she seemed to retreat. I hadn't thought, until that moment, that she might be nervous about me and Russell. A new feeling of power flexed within me, a quick tightening of ribbon so unfamiliar I didn't recognize it.

"And you'll be in charge of our Evie," Russell said to Suzanne. "Won't you?"

Neither looked at me. The air between them crisscrossed with symbols. Russell held my hand for a moment, his eyes avalanching over me.

"Later, Evie," he said.

Then a few whispered words to Suzanne. She rejoined me with a new air of briskness.

"Russell says you can stick around, if you want," she said.

I felt how energized she was by seeing Russell. Alert with renewed authority, studying me as she spoke. I didn't know if the jump I felt was fear or interest.

My grandmother had told me about getting movie roles—how quickly she was plucked from a group. "That's the difference," she'd told me. "All the other girls thought the director was making the choice. But it was really me telling the director, in my secret way, that the part was mine."

I wanted that—a sourceless, toneless wave carried from me to Russell. To Suzanne, to all of them. I wanted this world without end.

The night began to show ragged edges. Roos was naked from the waist up, her heavy breasts flushed from the heat. Falling into long silences. A black dog trotted into the darkness. Suzanne had disappeared to find more grass. I kept searching for her, but I'd get distracted by the flash and shuffle, the strangers who danced by and smiled at me with blunt kindness.

Little things should have upset me. Some girl burned herself, raising a ripple of skin along her arm, and stared down at the scorch with idle curiosity. The outhouse with its shit stench and cryptic drawings, walls papered in pages torn from porno mags. Guy describing the warm entrails of the pigs he'd gutted on his parents' farm in Kansas.

"They knew what was coming," he said to a rapt audience. "They'd smile when I brought food and flip out when I had the knife."

He adjusted his big belt buckle, cackling something I couldn't hear. But it was the solstice, I explained to myself, pagan mutterings, and whatever disturbance I felt was just a failure to understand the place. And there was so much else to notice and favor—the silly music from the jukebox. The silver guitar that caught the light, the melted Cool Whip dripping from someone's finger. The numinous and fanatic faces of the others.

Time was confusing on the ranch: there were no clocks, no watches, and hours or minutes seemed arbitrary, whole days pouring into nothing. I don't know how much time passed. How long I was waiting for Suzanne to return before I heard his voice. Right next to my ear, whispering my name.

"Evie."

I turned, and there he was. I twisted with happiness: Russell had remembered me, he'd found me in the crowd. Had maybe even been looking for me. He took my hand in his, working the palm, my fingers. I was beaming, indeterminate; I wanted to love everything.

The trailer he brought me to was larger than any of the other rooms, the bed covered with a shaggy blanket that I'd realize later was actually a fur coat. It was the only nice thing in the room—the floor matted with clothes, empty cans of soda and beer glinting among the detritus. A peculiar smell in the air, a cut of fermentation. I was being willfully naïve, I suppose, pretending like I didn't know what was happening. But part of me really didn't. Or didn't fully dwell on the facts: it was suddenly difficult to remember how I'd gotten there. That lurching bus ride, the cheap sugar of the wine. Where had I left my bike?

Russell was watching me intently. Tilting his head when I looked away, forcing me to catch his eyes. He brushed my hair behind my ear, letting his fingers fall to my neck. His fingernails uncut so I felt the ridge of them.

I laughed, but it was uneasy. "Is Suzanne gonna be here soon?" I said.

He'd told me, back at the fire, that Suzanne was coming, too, though maybe that was only something I wished.

"Suzanne's just fine," Russell said. "I wanna talk about you right now, Evie."

My thoughts slowed to the pace of drifting snow. Russell spoke slowly and with seriousness, but he made me feel as though he had been waiting all night for the chance to hear what I had to say. How different this was from Connie's bedroom, listening to records from some other world we'd never be a part of, songs that just reinforced our own static misery. Peter seemed drained to me, too. Peter, who was just a boy, who ate oleo on white bread for dinner. This was real, Russell's gaze, and the flattered sickness in me was so pleasurable, I could barely keep hold of it.

"Shy Evie," he said. Smiling. "You're a smart girl. You see a lot with those eyes, don't you?"

He thought I was smart. I grabbed on to it like proof. I wasn't lost. I could hear the party outside. A fly buzzed in the corner, hitting the walls of the trailer.

"I'm like you," Russell went on. "I was so smart when I was young, so smart that of course they told me I was dumb." He let out a fractured laugh. "They taught me the word **dumb.** They taught me those words, then they told me that's what I was." When Russell smiled, his face soaked with a joy that seemed foreign to me. I knew I'd never felt that good. Even as a child I'd been unhappy—I saw, suddenly, how obvious that was.

As he talked, I hugged myself with my arms. It all started making sense to me, what Russell was saying, in the drippy way things could make sense. How drugs patchworked simple, banal thoughts into phrases that seemed filled with importance. My glitchy adolescent brain was desperate for causalities, for conspiracies that drenched every word, every gesture, with meaning. I wanted Russell to be a genius.

"There's something in you," he said. "Some part that's real sad. And you know what? That really makes me sad. They've tried to ruin this beautiful, special girl. They've made her sad. Just because they are."

I felt the press of tears.

"But they didn't ruin you, Evie. 'Cause here you are. Our special Evie. And you can let all that old shit float away."

He sat back on the mattress with the dirty soles of his bare feet on the fur coat, a strange calm in his face. He would wait as long as it took.

I don't remember what I said at that point, just that I chattered nervously. School, Connie, the hollow nonsense of a young girl. My gaze slid around the trailer, fingers nipping at the fabric of Suzanne's dress. Eyes coursing the fleur-de-lis pattern of the filthy bedspread. I remember that Russell smiled, patiently, waiting for me to lose energy. And I did. The trailer silent except for my own breathing and Russell shifting on the mattress.

"I can help you," he said. "But you have to want it."

His eyes fixed on mine.

"Do you want it, Evie?"

The words slit with scientific desire.

"You'll like this," Russell murmured. Opening his arms to me. "Come here."

I edged toward him, sitting on the mattress. Struggling to complete the full circuit of comprehension. I knew it was coming, but it still surprised me. How he took down his pants, exposing his short, hairy legs, his penis in his fist. The hesitant catch in my gaze—he watched me watching him.

"Look at me," he said. His voice was smooth, even while his hand worked furiously. "Evie," he said, "Evie."

The undercooked look of his dick, clutched in his hand: I wondered where Suzanne was. My throat tightened. It confused me at first, that it was all Russell wanted. To stroke himself. I sat there, trying to impose sense on the situation. I transmuted Russell's behavior into proof of his good intentions. Russell was just trying to be close, to break down my hang-ups from the old world.

"We can make each other feel good," he said. "You don't have to be sad."

I flinched when he pushed my head toward his lap. A singe of clumsy fear filled me. He was good at not seeming angry when I reared away. The indulgent look he gave me, like I was a skittish horse.

"I'm not trying to hurt you, Evie." Holding out his hand again. The strobe of my heart going fast. "I just want to be close to you. And don't you want me to feel good? I want you to feel good."

When he came, he gasped, wetly. The salt damp of semen in my mouth, the alarming swell. He held me there, bucking. How had I gotten here, in the trailer, found myself in the dark woods without any crumbs to follow home, but then Russell's hands were in my hair, and his arms were around me, pulling me up, and he said my name with intention and surety so it sounded strange to me, but smooth, too, valuable, like some other, better, Evie. Was I supposed to cry? I didn't know. I was crowded with idiot trivia. A red sweater I had lent Connie and never gotten back. Whether Suzanne was looking for me or not. A curious thrill behind my eyes.

Russell handed me a bottle of Coke. The soda was tepid and flat, but I drank the whole thing. As intoxicating as champagne.

I experienced the whole night as fated, me as the center of a singular drama. But Russell had put me through a series of ritual tests. Perfected over the years that he had worked for a religious organization near Ukiah, a center that gave away food, found shelter and jobs. Attracting the thin, harried girls with partial college degrees and neglectful parents, girls with hellish bosses and dreams of nose jobs. His bread and butter. The time he spent at the center's outpost in San Francisco in the old fire station. Collecting his followers. Already he'd become an expert in female sadness—a particular slump in the shoulders, a nervous rash. A subservient lilt at the end of sentences, eyelashes gone soggy from crying. Russell did the same thing to me that he did to those girls. Little tests, first. A touch on my back, a pulse of my hand. Little ways of breaking down boundaries. And how quickly he'd ramped it up, easing his pants to his knees. An act, I thought, calibrated to comfort young girls who were glad, at least, that it wasn't sex. Who could stay fully dressed the whole time, as if nothing out of the ordinary were happening.

But maybe the strangest part—I liked it, too.

...

I floated through the party in a stunned hush. The air on my skin insistent, my armpits sliding with sweat. It had happened—I had to keep telling myself so. I assumed everyone would see it on me. An obvious aura of sex. I wasn't anxious anymore, wasn't roaming the party squeezed by nervous need, the certainty that there was a hidden room I wasn't allowed access to—that worry had been satisfied, and I took dreamy steps, looked back into passing faces with a smile that asked nothing.

When I saw Guy, tapping a pack of cigarettes, I stopped without hesitation.

"Can I have one?"

He grinned at me. "The girl wants a cigarette, she shall have her cigarette." He held it to my mouth and I hoped people were watching.

I finally found Suzanne in a group near the fire. When she caught my eye, she gave me an odd, airless smile. I'm sure she recognized the inward shift you sometimes see in young girls, newly sexed. It's that pride, I think, a solemnity. I wanted her to know. Suzanne was giddy from something, I could tell. Not alcohol. Something else, her pupils seeming to eat the iris, a flush lacing up her neck like a trippy Victorian collar.

Maybe Suzanne felt some hidden disappointment when the game fulfilled itself, when she saw that I'd gone with Russell, after all. But maybe she'd expected it. The car was still smoldering, the noise of the party cutting up the darkness. I felt the night churn in me like a wheel.

"When's the car gonna stop burning?" I said.

I couldn't see her face, but I could feel her, the air soft between us.

"Jesus, I don't know," she said. "Morning?"

In the flicker, my arms and hands in front of me looked scaly and reptilian, and I welcomed the distorted vision of my body. I heard the brood of a motorcycle ignition, someone's wicked hoot—they'd thrown a box spring in the fire, and the flames soared and deepened.

"You can crash in my room if you want," Suzanne said. Her voice gave away nothing. "I don't care. But you have to actually be here, if you're going to be here. Get it?"

Suzanne was asking me something else. Like those fairy tales where goblins can enter a house only if invited by its inhabitants. The moment of crossing the threshold, the careful way Suzanne constructed her statements—she wanted me to say it. And I nodded, and said I understood. Though I couldn't understand, not really. I was wearing a dress that didn't belong to me in a place I had never been, and I couldn't see much farther than that. The possibility that my life was hovering on the brink of a new and permanent happiness. I thought of Connie with a beatific indulgence—she was a sweet girl, wasn't she—and even my father and mother fell under my generous purview, sufferers of a tragic foreign malady. The beam of motorcycle headlights blanched the tree branches and illuminated the exposed foundation of the house, the black dog crouching over an unseen prize. Someone kept playing the same song over and over. **Hey, baby,** the first lines went. The song repeated enough times that I started to get the phrase in my head, **Hey, baby.** I worked the words around with unspecific effort, like the idle rattle of a lemon drop against the teeth.

PART TWO

I WOKE TO A WASH OF FOG pressed against the windows, the bedroom filled with snowy light. It took a moment to reoccupy the disappointing and familiar facts—I was staying in Dan's house. It was his bureau in the corner, his glass-topped nightstand. His blanket, bordered in sateen ribbon, that I pulled over my own body. I remembered Julian and Sasha, the thin wall between us. I didn't want to think of the previous night. Sasha's mewlings. The slurred, obsessive muttering, "Fuck me fuck mefuckmefuckme," repeated so many times it failed to mean anything.

I stared at the monotony of ceiling. They'd been thoughtless, as all teenagers are, and the night didn't mean anything beyond that. Still. The polite thing to do was to wait in my room until they had left for

Humboldt. Let them clear off without having to perform any dutiful morning niceties.

As soon as I heard the car back out of the garage, I got out of bed. The house was mine again, and though I expected relief, there was some sadness, too. Sasha and Julian were aimed at another adventure. Clicking back into the momentum of the larger world. I'd recede in their minds—the middle-aged woman in a forgotten house—just a mental footnote getting smaller and smaller as their real life took over. I hadn't realized until then how lonely I was. Or something less urgent than loneliness: an absence of eyes on me, maybe. Who would care if I ceased to exist? Those silly phrases I remembered Russell saying—cease to exist, he urged us, disappear the self. And all of us nodding like golden retrievers, the reality of our existence making us cavalier, eager to dismantle what seemed permanent.

I started the kettle. Opened the window to let a slash of cold air circulate. I gathered what seemed to be a lot of empty beer bottles—had they drunk more while I slept?

After taking out the trash, the tight heave of plastic and my own garbage, I caught myself staring at the poky blankets of ice plants along the driveway. The beach beyond. The fog had started to burn off, and I could see the crawl of waves, the cliffs above looking rusted and dry. A few people were out walking, obvious in performance wear. Most of them had dogs—this was the only beach around where you could take dogs off-leash. I'd seen the same rottweiler a few times, his coat a color deeper than black, his heavy churning run. A pit bull had recently killed a woman in San Francisco. Was it strange that people loved these creatures that could harm them? Or was it understandable—that they maybe even loved animals more for their restraint, for the way they blessed humans with temporary safety.

I hustled back inside. I couldn't stay in Dan's house forever. Another aide job would turn up soon. But how familiar that was—lifting someone into the warm, persistent waters of a therapy tub. Sitting in the waiting rooms of doctor's offices, reading articles on the effects of soy on tumors. The importance of filling your plate with a rainbow. The usual wishful lies, tragic in their insufficiency. Did anyone really believe in them? As if the bright flash of your efforts could distract death from coming for you, keep the bull snorting harmlessly after the scarlet flag.

The kettle was whistling, so at first I didn't hear Sasha come into the kitchen. Her abrupt presence startled me.

"Morning," she said. A streak of spit had dried along her cheek. She was wearing high-cut shorts made of sweatpant material, her socks dotted with tiny hot-pink symbols I realized were skulls. She swallowed, her mouth furry with sleep. "Where's Julian?" she asked.

I tried to hide my surprise. "I heard the car leave awhile ago."

She squinted. "What?" she asked.

"Didn't he tell you he was going?"

Sasha saw my pity. Her face tightened.

"Of course he told me," she said after a moment. "Yeah, of course. He'll be back tomorrow."

So he had left her. My first thought was irritation. I wasn't a babysitter. Then relief. Sasha was a kid—she shouldn't go with him to Humboldt. Ride an ATV through barbed-wire checkpoints to some shit-hole tarp ranch in Garberville just to pick up a duffel bag of weed. I was even a little glad for her company.

"I don't like the drive, anyway," Sasha said, gamely adapting to the situation. "I get sick on those small roads. He drives so crazy, too. Super fast." She leaned up against the counter, yawning.

"Tired?" I said.

She told me that she had been trying polyphasic sleep but had to quit. "It was too weird," she said. Her nipples were apparent through her shirt.

"Polyphasic sleep?" I said, pulling my own robe tight in a prudish surge.

"Thomas Jefferson did it. You sleep in hour bursts, like, six times a day."

"And you're awake the rest of the time?"

Sasha nodded. "It's kind of great, the first couple

of days. But I crashed hard. It seemed like I'd never sleep normal again."

I couldn't link the girl I'd overheard the night before to the girl in front of me, talking about sleep experiments.

"There's enough hot water in the kettle if you want some," I said, but Sasha shook her head.

"I don't eat in the mornings, like a ballerina." She glanced at the window, the sea a pewter sheet. "Do you ever swim?"

"It's really cold." I had only seen the occasional surfer venture into the waves, their bodies sheathed in neoprene, hoods over their heads.

"So you've gone in?" she asked.

"No."

Sasha's face moved with sympathy. Like I was missing out on some obvious pleasure. But no one swam, I thought, feeling protective of my life in this borrowed house, the local orbits of my days. "There are sharks out there, too," I added.

"They don't really attack humans," Sasha said, shrugging. She was pretty, like a consumptive, eaten by an internal heat. I tried to spot some pornographic residue of the night before, but there was nothing. Her face as pale and blameless as a lesser moon.

Sasha's proximity, even for the day, forced some normalcy. The built-in preventative of another person meant I couldn't indulge the animal feelings, couldn't leave orange peels in the kitchen sink. I dressed right after breakfast instead of haunting my robe all day. Swiped on mascara from a mostly dried-up tube. These were the cogent human labors, the daily tasks that staved larger panics, but living alone had gotten me out of the habit—I didn't feel substantial enough to warrant this kind of effort.

I'd last lived with someone years ago, a man who taught ESL classes at one of the sham colleges that advertised on bus-stop benches. The students were mostly wealthy foreigners who wanted to design videogames. It was surprising to think of him, of David, to remember a time when I imagined a life with another person. Not love, but the pleasant inertia that could substitute. The agreeable quiet that passed over us both in car rides. The way I'd once seen him look at me as we crossed a parking lot.

But then it started—a woman who knocked on the apartment door at strange hours. An ivory hairbrush that had belonged to my grandmother went missing from the bathroom. I'd never told David certain things, so that whatever closeness we had was automatically corrupted, the grub twisting in the apple. My secret was sunk deep, but it was there. Maybe that was the reason it had happened, the other women. I had left open a space for such secrets. And how much could you ever know another person, anyway?

...

I'd imagined that Sasha and I would spend the day in courteous silence. That Sasha would be as hidden as a mouse. She was polite enough, but soon her presence was obvious. I found the refrigerator door left open, filling the kitchen with an alien buzz. Her sweatshirt thrown on the table, a book about the Enneagram splayed on a chair. Music came loud from her room through tinny laptop speakers. It surprised me—she was listening to the singer whose plaintive voice had been the perpetual aural backdrop for a certain kind of girl I remembered from college. Girls already swampy with nostalgia, girls who lit candles and stayed up late kneading bread dough in Danskin leotards and bare feet.

I was used to encountering remnants—the afterburn of the sixties was everywhere in that part of California. Ragged blips of prayer flags in the oak trees, vans eternally parked in fields, missing their tires. Older men in decorative shirts with common-law wives. But those were the expected sixties ghosts. Why would Sasha have any interest?

I was glad when Sasha changed the music. A woman singing over gothy electronic piano, nothing I recognized at all.

That afternoon, I tried to take a nap. But I couldn't sleep. I lay there, staring at the framed photo that hung over the bureau: a sand dune, rippling with mint grass. The ghoulish whorls of cobwebs in the corners. I shifted in the sheets, impatient. I was too aware of Sasha in the room next door. The music from her laptop hadn't stopped all afternoon, and sometimes I could make out scraps of digital noise over the songs, beeps and chimes. What was she doing—playing games on her phone? Texting with Julian? I had a sudden ache for the obliging ways she must be tending to her loneliness.

I knocked on her door, but the music was too loud. I tried again. Nothing. I was embarrassed by the exposure of effort, about to scurry back to my room, but Sasha appeared in the doorway. Her face still muted with sleep, her hair scraggled by the pillow—maybe she'd been trying to nap, too.

"Do you want some tea?" I asked.

It took her a moment to nod, like she'd forgotten who I was.

Sasha was quiet at the table. Studying her fingernails, sighing with cosmic boredom. I remembered this pose from my own adolescence—thrusting my jaw forward, staring out the car window like a wrongfully accused prisoner, all along desperately wishing that my mother would say something. Sasha was waiting for me to breach her reserve, to ask her questions, and I could feel her eyes on me while I poured the tea. It was nice to be watched, even suspiciously. I used the good cups and the buckwheat crackers I fanned along the saucers were only a little stale. I wanted to please her, I realized, setting the plate gently in front of her.

The tea was too hot; there was a lull while we huddled over the cups, my face dampening in the thin vegetal steam. When I asked Sasha where she was from, she grimaced.

"Concord," she said. "It sucks."

"And you go to college with Julian?"

"Julian's not in college."

I wasn't sure if this was information Dan knew. I tried to remember what I'd last heard. When Dan did mention his son, it was with performative resignation, playing the clueless dad. Any trouble reported with sitcom sighs: boys will be boys. Julian had been diagnosed with some behavioral disorder in high school, though Dan made it sound mild.

"Have you guys been together long?" I asked.

Sasha sipped at the tea. "A few months," she said. Her face grew animate, like just talking about Julian was a source of sustenance. She must have already forgiven him for leaving her behind. Girls were good at coloring in those disappointing blank spots. I thought of the night before, her exaggerated moans. Poor Sasha.

She probably believed that any sadness, any flicker of worry over Julian, was just a problem of logistics. Sadness at that age had the pleasing texture of imprisonment: you reared and sulked against the bonds of parents and school and age, the things that kept you from the certain happiness that awaited. When I was a sophomore in college, I had a boyfriend who spoke breathlessly of running away to Mexico—it didn't occur to me that we could no longer run away from home. Nor did I imagine what we would be running to, beyond the vagueness of warm air and more frequent sex. And now I was older, and the wishful props of future selves had lost their comforts. I might always feel some form of this, a depression that did not lift but grew compact and familiar, a space occupied like the sad limbo of hotel rooms.

"Listen," I said, slotting into a parental role that was laughably unearned. "I hope Julian is being nice to you."

"Why wouldn't he be nice?" she said. "He's my boyfriend. We live together."

I could imagine so easily what would pass for living. A month-to-month apartment that smelled of freezer meals and Clorox, Julian's childhood comforter on the mattress. The girlish effort of a scented candle by the bed. Not that I was doing much better.

"We might get a place with a washing machine," Sasha said, a new defiance in her tone as she invoked their meager domesticity. "Probably in a few months."

"And your parents are okay with you living with Julian?"

"I can do what I want." She shuffled her hands into the sleeves of Julian's sweatshirt. "I'm eighteen."

That couldn't be true.

"Besides," she said, "weren't you my age when you were in that cult?"

Her tone was blank, but I imagined a slant of accusation.

Before I could say anything, Sasha got up from the table, listing toward the refrigerator. I watched her affected swagger, the easy way she removed one of the beers they'd brought. The cutout silvered mountains gleaming from the label. She met my gaze.

"Want one?" she asked.

This was a test, I understood. Either I could be the kind of adult to be ignored or pitied or I could be someone she could maybe talk to. I nodded and Sasha relaxed.

"Think fast," she said, tossing the bottle to me.

Night came on quick, as it did on the coast, with no mediation of buildings to temper the change. The sun was so low that we could look directly at it, watching it drift from sight. We each had had a few beers. The kitchen grew dark, but neither of us got up to turn on the lights. Everything had a blue shadow, soft and royal, the furniture simplifying into shapes. Sasha asked if we could make a fire in the fireplace.

"It's gas," I said. "And it's broken."

A lot of things in the house were broken or forgotten: the kitchen clock stopped, a closet doorknob coming off in my hand. The sparkly mess of flies I'd swept from the corners. It took sustained, constant living to ward off decay. Even my presence for the last few weeks hadn't made much of a dent.

"But we can try making one out in the yard," I said.

The sandy lot behind the garage was sheltered from the wind, wet leaves matted on the seats of plastic chairs. There had once been a fire pit of sorts, the stones scattered among the senseless archaeological relics of family life: add-ons to forgotten toys, a chewed-looking shard of Frisbee. We were both distracted by the hustle of preparation, tasks that allowed for companionable silence. I found a stack of three-year-old newspapers in the garage and a bundle of wood from the general store in town. Sasha toed the stones back into a circle.

"I was always bad at this," I said. "There's something you're supposed to do, right? Some special shape with the logs?"

"Like a house," Sasha said. "You're supposed to make it look like a cabin." She used her foot to neaten the ring. "We used to camp a lot in Yosemite when I was little."

Sasha was the one who actually got the fire going: squatting in the sand, keeping up a steady stream of breath. Gentling the flames until there was a satisfying burn.

We sat down in the plastic chairs, their surfaces stippled from sand and wind. I pulled mine close to the fire—I wanted to feel hot, to sweat. Sasha was quiet, looking at the jump of flames, but I could sense the whir of her mind, the faraway place she had disappeared to. Maybe she was imagining what Julian was doing up in Garberville. The musky futon he'd sleep on, using a towel for a blanket. All part of the adventure. How nice it must be to be a twenty-year-old boy.

"That stuff Julian was talking about," Sasha said, clearing her throat like she was embarrassed, though her interest was obvious. "Were you, like, in love with that guy or something?"

"Russell?" I said, poking at the fire with a stick. "I didn't think about him like that."

It was true: the other girls had circled around Russell, tracking his movements and moods like weather patterns, but he stayed mostly distant in my mind. Like a beloved teacher whose home life his students never imagined.

"Why'd you hang out with them, then?" she asked.

My first impulse was to avoid the subject. I'd have to pin down all the edges. Act out the whole morality play: the regret, the warnings. I tried to sound businesslike.

"People were falling into that kind of thing all the time, back then," I said. "Scientology, the Process people. Empty-chair work. Is that still a thing?" I glanced at her—she was waiting for me to go on. "It was partly bad luck, I guess. That it was the group I found."

"But you stayed."

I could feel the full force of Sasha's curiosity for the first time.

"There was a girl. It was more her than Russell." I hesitated. "Suzanne." It was odd to say her name, to let it live in the world. "She was older," I said. "Not by much, really, but it felt like a lot."

"Suzanne Parker?"

I stared across the fire at Sasha.

"I looked some things up today," she said. "Online."

I'd once lost hours to that kind of stuff. The fan sites or whatever you called them. The stranger corners. The website devoted to Suzanne's artwork from prison. Watercolors of mountain ranges, puff-ball clouds, the captions filled with misspellings. I'd felt a pang, imagining Suzanne working with great concentration, but closed the website when I saw the photo: Suzanne, in blue jeans and a white T-shirt—her jeans stuffed with middle-aged fat, her face a vacant scrim.

The thought of Sasha gorging on that macabre glut made me uneasy. Packing herself with particulars: the autopsy reports, the testimony the girls gave of that night, like the transcript of a bad dream.

"It's nothing to be proud of," I said. Recounting

the usual things—it was awful. Not glamorous, not enviable.

"There wasn't anything about you," Sasha said. "Not that I could find."

I felt a lurch. I wanted to tell her something valuable, my existence traced with enough care that I would become visible.

"It's better that way," I said. "So the lunatics don't search me out."

"But you were there?"

"I lived there. Basically. For a while. I didn't kill anyone or anything." My laugh came out flat. "Obviously."

She was huddling into her sweatshirt. "You just left your parents?" Her voice was admiring.

"It was a different time," I said. "Everyone ran around. My parents were divorced."

"So are mine," Sasha said, forgetting to be shy. "And you were my age?"

"A little younger."

"I bet you were really pretty. I mean, duh, you're pretty now, too," she said.

I could see her puff up with her own generosity.

"How'd you even meet them?" Sasha asked.

It took me a moment to gather myself, to remember the sequence of things. "Revisit" is the word they always used in anniversary articles about the murder. "Revisiting the horror of Edgewater Road," as if the event existed singularly, a box you could close a lid on. As if I hadn't been stopped by hundreds of ghosted Suzannes on the streets or in the background of movies.

I fielded Sasha's questions about what they had been like in real life, those people who had become totems of themselves. Guy had been less interesting to the media, just a man doing what men had always done, but the girls were made mythic. Donna was the unattractive one, slow and rough, often cast as a pity case. The hungry harshness in her face. Helen, the former Camp Fire Girl, tan and pigtailed and pretty—she was the fetish object, the pinup murderess. But Suzanne got the worst of it. Depraved. Evil. Her sneaky beauty didn't photograph well. She looked feral and meager, like she might have existed only to kill.

Talking about Suzanne raised a rev in my chest that I was sure Sasha could see. It seemed shameful. To feel that helpless excitement, considering what had happened. The caretaker on the couch, the coiled casing of his guts exposed to the air. The mother's hair soaked with gore. The boy so disfigured the police weren't sure of his gender. Surely Sasha had read about those things, too.

"Did you ever think you could have done what they did?" she asked.

"Of course not," I said reflexively.

In all the times I had ever told anyone about the ranch, few had ever asked me that question. Whether I could have done it, too. Whether I almost had.

Most assumed a base level of morality separated me, as if the girls had been a different species.

Sasha was quiet. Her silence seemed like a kind of love.

"I guess I do wonder, sometimes," I said. "It seems like an accident that I didn't."

"An accident?"

The fire was getting weak and jumpy. "There wasn't that much difference. Between me and the other girls."

It was strange to say this aloud. To edge, even vaguely, around the worry I had worked over all this time. Sasha didn't seem disapproving or even wary. She simply looked at me, her watchful face on mine, as if she could take in my words and make a home for them.

We went to the one bar in town that had food. This seemed like a good idea, a goal we could aim toward. Sustenance. Movement. We'd talked until the fire had burned itself into a glowy mottle of newspaper. Sasha kicked sand over the mess, her scout's diligence making me laugh. I was happy to be with someone, despite the provisional reprieve—Julian would come back, Sasha would be gone, and I'd be alone again. Even so, it was nice to be the subject of someone's admiration. Because that's what it was, mostly: Sasha seemed to respect the fourteen-year-old girl I had been, to think I was interesting, had been somehow brave. I tried to correct her, but an expansive comfort had spread in my chest, a reoccupation of my body, like I'd woken from the twilight of pharmaceutical sleep.

We walked side by side on the shoulder of the road, along the aqueduct. The pointed trees were dense and dark, but I didn't feel afraid. The night had taken on a strange, festive air, and Sasha had started calling me Vee for some reason.

"Mama Vee," she said.

She seemed like a kitten, affable and mild, her warm shoulder bumping against mine. When I looked over, I saw that she was gnawing at her bottom lip, her face turned to the sky. But there was nothing to see—the stars were hidden by fog.

There were a few stools in the bar and not much else. The usual patchwork of rusted signs, a pair of humming neon eyes over the door. Someone in the kitchen was smoking cigarettes—the sandwich bread was humid with smoke. We stayed awhile after we'd finished eating. Sasha looked fifteen, but they didn't care. The bartender, a woman in her fifties, seemed grateful for any business. She looked worked over, her hair crispy from drugstore dye. We were almost the same age, but I wouldn't glance into the mirror to confirm the similarities, not with Sasha beside me. Sasha, whose features had the clean, purified cast of a saint on a religious medal.

Sasha swiveled around on her stool like a young child.

"Look at us." She laughed. "Partying hard." She took a drink of beer, then a drink of water, a conscientious habit I'd noticed, though it didn't prevent a visible slump from taking over. "I'm kind of glad Julian's not here," she said.

The words seemed to thrill her. I knew by then not to spook her, but instead to give her space to dawdle toward her actual point. Sasha kicked the bar rail absently, her breath beery and close.

"He didn't tell me he was leaving," she said. "For Humboldt." I pretended surprise. She laughed flatly. "I couldn't find him this morning and I just thought he was like, outside. That's kind of weird, right? That he just took off?"

"Yeah, weird." Too cautious, maybe, but I was wary of inciting a righteous defense of Julian.

"He texted me all sorry. He thought we'd talked about it, I guess."

She sipped her beer. Drawing a smiley face in the wood of the bar with a wet finger. "You know why he got kicked out of Irvine?" She was half-giddy, half-wary. "Wait," she said, "you're not gonna tell his dad, are you?"

I shook my head, an adult willing to keep a teenager's secrets.

"Okay." Sasha took a breath. "He had some comp teacher he hated. He was kind of a jerk, I guess. The teacher. He didn't let Julian turn in this paper late, even though he knew Julian would fail without a grade for it.

"So Julian went to the guy's house and did something to his dog. Fed him something that made him sick. Like bleach or rat poison, I don't really know what." Sasha caught my eye. "The dog died. This old dog."

I struggled to keep my face even. The plainness of her retelling, devoid of any inflection, made the story worse.

"The school knew he did it, but they couldn't prove it," Sasha said. "So they suspended him for other stuff, but he couldn't go back or anything. It's messed up." She looked at me. "I mean, don't you think?"

I didn't know what to say.

"He said he didn't mean to kill it or anything, just make it sick." Sasha's tone was tentative, testing out the thought. "That's not so bad, right?"

"I don't know," I said. "It sounds bad to me."

"But I live with him, you know," Sasha said. "Like he pays all the rent and stuff."

"There are always places to go," I said.

Poor Sasha. Poor girls. The world fattens them on the promise of love. How badly they need it, and how little most of them will ever get. The treacled pop songs, the dresses described in the catalogs with words like "sunset" and "Paris." Then the dreams are taken away with such violent force; the hand wrenching the buttons of the jeans, nobody looking at the man shouting at his girlfriend on the bus. Sorrow for Sasha locked up my throat.

She must have sensed my hesitation.

"Whatever," she said. "It was a while ago."

This is what it might be like to be a mother, I thought, watching Sasha drain her beer, wipe her mouth like a boy. To feel this unexpected, boundless tenderness for someone, seemingly out of nowhere. When a pool player sauntered over, I was prepared to scare him away. But Sasha smiled big, showing her pointed teeth.

"Hi," she said, and then he was buying us each another beer.

Sasha drank steadily. Alternating between distracted boredom and manic interest, feigned or not, in what the man was saying.

"You two from out of town?" he asked. His hair graying and long, a turquoise ring on his thumb—another sixties ghost. Maybe we'd even crossed paths back then, haunting the same well-worn trail. He hitched up his pants. "Sisters?"

His voice barely tried to include me in the purview of his effort, and I almost laughed. Still, even sitting next to Sasha, I was aware of some of the attention washing onto me. It was shocking to remember the voltage, even secondhand. How it felt to be a desired thing. Maybe Sasha was so used to it that she didn't even notice. Caught up in the rush of her own life, in her certainty of the meliorative trajectory.

"She's my mother," Sasha said. Her eyes were taut, wanting me to keep the joke going.

And I did. I huddled my arm around her. "We're

on a mother-daughter trip," I said. "Driving the 1. All the way up to Eureka."

"Adventurers!" the man exclaimed, pounding the table. His name was Victor, we learned, and the background wallpaper on Victor's cellphone was an Aztec image, he told us, so imbued with powers that just the contemplation of said image made you smarter. He was convinced that world events were orchestrated by complicated and persistent conspiracies. He took out a dollar bill to show us how the Illuminati communicated with one another.

"Why would a secret society lay out their plans on common currency?" I asked.

He nodded like he'd anticipated the question. "To display the reach of their power."

I envied Victor's certainty, the idiot syntax of the righteous. This belief—that the world had a visible order, and all we had to do was look for the symbols—as if evil were a code that could be cracked. He kept talking. His teeth wet from drink, the gray blush of a dead molar. He had plenty of conspiracies to explain to us in detail, plenty of inside information he could clue us into. He spoke of "getting on the level." Of "hidden frequencies" and "shadow governments."

"Wow," Sasha said, deadpan. "Did you know that, Mom?"

She kept calling me Mom, her voice exaggerated and comical, though it took me a while to see how drunk she was. To realize how drunk I was, too. The night had sailed into foreign waters. The fritzing of the neon signs, the bartender smoking in the doorway. I watched the bartender stamp the butt out, her flip-flops sliding around her feet. Victor said it was nice to see how well Sasha and I got along.

"You don't always see that, these days." He nodded, thoughtful. "Mothers and daughters who'd take a trip together. Who are sweet with each other like you two."

"Oh, she's great," Sasha said. "I love my mom."

She cut me a tricky smile before she leaned her face close to mine. The dry press of her lips, the stingy brine of pickles on her mouth. The most chaste of kisses. Still. Victor was shocked. As she'd hoped he would be.

"Goddamn," Victor said, both disgusted and titillated. Straightening his bulky shoulders, retucking his blousy shirt. He suddenly seemed wary of us, glancing around for support, for confirmation, and I wanted to explain that Sasha wasn't my daughter, but I was past the point of caring, the night stoking a foolish, confused sense that I had somehow returned to the world after a period of absence, had taken up residence again in the realm of the living.

1969

6

My father had always been in charge of pool maintenance—skimming the surface with a net, heaping wet leaves into a pile. The colored vials he used to test chlorine levels. He'd never been that assiduous with upkeep, but the pool had gotten bad since he'd left. Salamanders idling around the filter. When I propelled myself along the rim, there was some sloggy resistance, crud dispersing in my wake. My mother was at group. She'd forgotten a promise to buy me a new swimsuit, so I was wearing my old orange one: pale as cantaloupe, the stitching puckered and gaping around the leg holes. The top was too small, but the adult mass of cleavage pleased me.

It had only been a week since the solstice party, and already I'd been back to the ranch, and already

I was stealing money for Suzanne, bill by bill. I like to imagine that it took more time than that. That I had to be convinced over a period of months, slowly broken down. Wooed as carefully as a valentine. But I was an eager mark, anxious to offer myself.

I kept bobbing in the water, algae speckling the hair on my legs like filings to a magnet. A forgotten paperback ruffled on the seat of the lawn chair. The leaves in the trees were silvery and spangled, like scales, everything full with June's lazy heat. Had the trees around my house always looked like that, so strange and aquatic? Or were things already shifting for me, the dumb litter of the normal world transforming into the lush stage sets of a different life?

Suzanne had driven me home the morning after the solstice, my bike shoved in the backseat. My mouth was leached and unfamiliar from smoking so much, and my clothes were stale from my body and smelled of ash. I kept picking bits of straw from my hair—proof of the night before that thrilled me, like a stamped passport. It had happened, after all, and I kept up a vivid catalog of happy data: the fact that I was sitting beside Suzanne, our friendly silence. My perverse pride that I'd been with Russell. I took pleasure in replaying the facts of the act, even the messy and boring parts. The odd lulls while Russell made himself hard. There was some power in the bluntness of human functions. Like Russell had explained to me: your body could hurtle you past your hang-ups, if you let it.

Suzanne smoked steadily as she drove, occasionally offering her cigarette to me with serene ritual. The quiet between us wasn't slack or uncomfortable. Outside the car, olive trees flashed by, the scorched summer earth. Far-off waterways, sloughing to the sea. Suzanne kept changing the radio station until she abruptly snapped it off.

"We need gas," she announced.

We, I echoed silently, **we** need gas.

Suzanne pulled into the Texaco, empty except for a teal-and-white pickup towing a boat trailer.

"Hand me a card," Suzanne said. Nodding at the glove box.

I scrambled to open it, loosing a jumble of credit cards. All with different names.

"The blue one," she said. She seemed impatient. When I handed her the card, she saw my confusion.

"People give them to us," she said. "Or we take them." She fingered the blue card. "Like this one is Donna's. She lifted it from her mom."

"Her mom's gas card?"

"Saved our ass—we would've starved," Suzanne said. She gave me a look. "Like you hustling that toilet paper, right?"

I flushed at the mention. Maybe she'd known I had lied, but I couldn't tell from her shuttered face—maybe not.

"Besides," she continued, "it's better than what

they'd do with it—more crap, more stuff, more me, me, me. Russell's trying to help people. He's not judgmental, that's not his trip. He doesn't care if you're rich or poor."

It made a kind of sense, what Suzanne was saying. They were just trying to equalize the forces in the world.

"It's ego," she went on, leaning against the car but keeping a sharp eye on the gas gauge: none of them ever filled up a tank more than a quarter full. "Money is ego, and people won't give it up. Just want to protect themselves, hold on to it like a blanket. They don't realize it keeps them slaves. It's sick."

She laughed.

"What's funny is that as soon as you give everything away, as soon as you say, Here, take it—that's when you really have everything."

One of the group had been detained for dumpster diving on a garbage run, and Suzanne was incensed, recounting the story as she pulled the car back onto the road.

"More and more stores get wise to it. Bullshit," she said. "They throw something away and they still want it. That's America."

"That is bullshit." The tone of the word was strange in my mouth.

"We'll figure something out. Soon." She glanced in the rearview. "Money's tight. But you just can't escape it. You probably don't know what that's like."

She wasn't sneering, not really—she spoke like

she was just stating the truth. Acknowledging reality with an affable shrug. That's when the idea came to me, fully formed, as if I had thought of it myself. And that's how it seemed, like the exact solution, a baubled ornament shining within reach.

"I can get some money," I said, later cringing at my eagerness. "My mom leaves her purse out all the time."

It was true. I was always coming across money: in drawers, on tables, forgotten by the bathroom sink. I had an allowance, but my mother often gave me more, by accident, or just gestured vaguely in the direction of her purse. "Take what you need," she'd always said. And I'd never taken more than I should have and was always conscious of returning the change.

"Oh no," Suzanne said, flicking the last of her cigarette out the window. "You don't have to do that. You're a sweet kid, though," she said. "Nice of you to offer."

"I want to."

She pursed her lips, affecting uncertainty, igniting a tilt in my gut.

"I don't want you to do something you don't want to." She laughed a little. "That's not what I'm about."

"But I do want to," I said. "I want to help."

Suzanne didn't speak for a minute, then smiled without looking over. "Okay," she said. I didn't miss the test in her voice. "You want to help. You can help."

...

My task made me a spy in my mother's house, my mother the clueless quarry. I could even apologize for our fight when I ran into her that night across the stillness of the hallway. My mother gave a little shrug but accepted my apology, smiling in a brave way. It would bother me, normally, that wavery brave smile, but the new me bowed my head in abject regret. I was imitating a daughter, acting like a daughter would. Part of me thrilled at the knowledge I held out of her reach, how every time I looked at her or spoke to her, I was lying. The night with Russell, the ranch, the secret space I tended to the side. She could have the husk of my old life, all the dried-up leftovers.

"You're home so early," she said. "I thought you might sleep at Connie's again."

"I didn't feel like it."

It was strange to be reminded of Connie, to jar back to the regular world. I'd been surprised, even, that I could feel the ordinary desire for food. I wanted the world to reorder itself visibly around the change, like a mend marking a tear.

My mother softened. "I'm just glad because I wanted to spend some time with you. Just us. It's been a while, huh? Maybe I'll make Stroganoff," she said. "Or meatballs. What do you think?"

I was suspicious of her offer: she didn't buy food for the house unless I wrote notes for her to find when she got back from group. And we hadn't eaten meat in forever. Sal told my mother that to eat meat was to eat fear and that ingesting fear would make you gain weight.

"Meatballs would be good," I allowed. I didn't want to notice how happy it made her.

My mother turned on the radio in the kitchen, playing the kind of slight, balmy songs that I'd loved as a child. Diamond rings, cool streams, apple trees. If Suzanne or even Connie caught me listening to that sort of music, I'd be embarrassed—it was bland and cheerful and old-fashioned—but I had a grudging, private love of those songs, my mother singing along to the parts she knew. Rosy with theatrical enthusiasm, so it was easy to get caught up in her giddiness. Her posture was shaped by years of horse shows in adolescence, smiling from the backs of sleek Arabians, arena lights catching the crust of rhinestones on her collar. She had been so mysterious to me when I was younger. The shyness I had felt watching her move around the house, shuffling in her night slippers. The drawer of jewelry whose provenance I made her describe, piece by piece, like a poem.

The house was clean, the windows segmenting the dark night, the carpets plush beneath my bare feet. This was the opposite of the ranch, and I sensed I should be guilty—that it was wrong to be comfortable like this, to want to eat this food with my mother in the primness of our tidy kitchen. What were Suzanne and the others doing at that same moment? It was suddenly hard to imagine.

"How's Connie these days?" she asked, flicking through her handwritten recipe cards.

"Fine." She probably was. Watching May Lopes's braces scum up.

"You know," she said, "she can always come over here. You guys have been spending an awful lot of time at her house lately."

"Her dad doesn't care."

"I miss her," she said, though my mother had always seemed mystified by Connie, like a barely tolerated maiden aunt. "We should go on a trip to Palm Springs or something." It was clear she'd been waiting to offer this. "You could invite Connie, if you wanted."

"I don't know." It could be nice. Connie and I shoving each other in the sun-stifled backseat, drinking shakes from the date farm outside Indio.

"Mm," she murmured. "We could go in the next few weeks. But you know, sweetheart"—a pause. "Frank might come, too."

"I'm not going on a trip with you and your boyfriend."

She tried to smile, but I saw that she wasn't saying everything. The radio was too loud. "Sweetheart," she started. "How are we ever going to live together—"

"What?" I hated how automatically my voice tilted bratty, cutting any authority.

"Not right away, definitely not." Her mouth puckered. "But if Frank moves in—"

"I live here, too," I said. "You were just gonna let him move in one day, without even telling me?"

"You're fourteen."

"This is bullshit."

"Hey! Watch it," she said, tucking her hands into her armpits. "I don't know why you're being so rude, but you need to quit it, and fast." The nearness of my mother's pleading face, her naked upset—it stoked a biological disgust for her, like when I smelled the bellow of iron in the bathroom and knew she had her period. "This is a nice thing I'm trying to do," she said, "inviting your friend along. Can I get a break here?"

I laughed, but it was dripping with the sickness of betrayal. That's why she'd wanted to make dinner. It was worse now, because I'd been so easily pleased. "Frank's an asshole."

Her face flared, but she pushed herself to get calm. "Watch your attitude. This is my life, understand? I'm trying to get just a little bit happy," she said, "and you need to give me that. Can you give me that?"

She deserved her anemic life, its meager, girlish uncertainties. "Fine," I said. "Fine. Good luck with Frank."

Her eyes narrowed. "What does that mean?"

"Forget it." I could smell the raw meat coming to room temperature, a biting tinge of cold metal. My stomach tightened. "I'm not hungry anymore," I said, and left her standing in the kitchen. The radio still playing songs about first loves, about dancing by the river, the meat thawed enough so my mother would be forced to cook it, though no one would eat it.

It was easy after that to tell myself that I deserved the money. Russell said that most people were selfish, unable to love, and that seemed true of my mother, and my father, too, tucked away with Tamar in the Portofino Apartments in Palo Alto. So it was a tidy trade, when I thought about it like that. Like the money I was filching, bill by bill, added up to something that could replace what had gone missing. It was too depressing to think it had maybe never been there in the first place. That none of it had—Connie's friendship. Peter ever feeling anything for me besides annoyance at the obviousness of my kiddish worship.

My mother left her purse lying around, like always, and that made the money inside seem less valuable, something she didn't care enough about to take seriously. Still, it was uncomfortable, poking around in her purse, like the rattly inside of my mother's brain. The litter was too personal—the wrapper from a butterscotch candy, a mantra card, a pocket mirror. A tube of cream, the color of a Band-Aid, that she patted under her eyes. I pinched a ten, folding it into my shorts. Even if she saw me, I'd just say I was getting groceries—why would she suspect me? Her daughter, who had always been good, even if that was more disappointing than being great.

I'm surprised that I felt so little guilt. On the contrary—there was something righteous in the way I hoarded my mother's money. I was picking up some of the ranch bravado, the certainty that I could take what I wanted. The knowledge of the hidden bills allowed me to smile at my mother the next morning, to act like we hadn't said the things we'd said the night before. To stand patiently when she brushed at my bangs without warning.

"Don't hide your eyes," my mother said, her breath close and hot, her fingers raking at my hair.

I wanted to shake her off, to step back, but I didn't.

"There," she said, pleased. "There's my sweet daughter."

I was thinking of the money while I kicked in the pool, my shoulders above the waterline. There was a purity to the task, amassing the bills in my little zip purse. When I was alone, I liked to count the money, each new five or ten a particular boon. I folded the crisper bills on top, so the bundle looked nicer. Imagining Suzanne's and Russell's pleasure when I brought the money to them, lulled into the sweet wayward fog of daydreams.

My eyes were closed as I floated, and I only opened them when I heard thrashing beyond the tree line. A deer, maybe. I tensed, stirring uneasily in the water. I didn't think that it could be a person: we didn't worry about those kinds of things. Not until later. And it was a dalmatian anyway, the creature that came trotting out of the trees and right up to the pool's edge. He regarded me soberly, then started to bark.

The dog was strange looking, speckled and spotted, and it barked with high, human alarm. I knew it belonged to the neighbors on our left, the Dutton family. The father had written some movie theme song, and at parties I had heard the mother hum it, mockingly, to a gathered group. Their son was younger than me—he often shot his BB gun in the yard, the dog yelping in agitated chorus. I couldn't remember the dog's name.

"Get," I said, splashing halfheartedly. I didn't want to have to haul myself out of the water. "Go on."

The dog kept barking.

"Go," I tried again, but the dog just barked louder.

My cutoffs were damp from my swimsuit by the time I made it to the Dutton house. I'd put on my cork sandals, grimed with the ghost of my feet, and taken the dog by the collar, the ends of my hair dripping. Teddy Dutton answered the door. He was eleven or twelve, his legs studded with scabs and scrapes. He'd broken his arm last year falling from a tree, and my mother had been the one to drive him to the hospital: she'd muttered darkly that his parents left him alone too much. I had never spent much time with Teddy, beyond the familiarity of being young at neighborhood parties, anyone under age eighteen herded together in a forced march to friendship. Sometimes I'd see him riding his bike along the fire road with a boy in glasses: he'd once let me pet a barn kitten they'd found, holding the tiny thing under his shirt. The kitten's eyes were leaky with pus, but Teddy had been gentle with it, like a little mother. That was the last time I'd spoken to him.

"Hey," I said when Teddy opened the door. "Your dog."

Teddy was gaping at me like we hadn't been neighbors our whole lives. I rolled my eyes a little at his silence.

"He was in our yard," I went on. The dog moved against my hold.

It took Teddy a second to speak, but before he did, I saw him cut a helpless look at my swimsuit top, the exaggerated swell of cleavage. Teddy saw that I had noticed and got more flustered. He scowled at the dog, taking his collar. "Bad Tiki," he said, hustling the animal into the house. "Bad dog."

The thought that Teddy Dutton might be somehow nervous around me was a surprise. Though I hadn't even owned a bikini the last time I'd seen him, and my breasts were bigger now, pleasing even to me. I found his attention almost hilarious. A stranger had once shown Connie and me his dick by the movie theater bathrooms—it had taken a moment to understand why the man was gasping like a fish for air, but then I saw his penis, out of his zipper like an arm out of a sleeve. He'd looked at us like we were butterflies he was pinning to a board. Connie had grabbed my arm, and we'd turned and run, laughing, the Raisinets clutched in my hand starting to melt. We recounted our disgust to each other in strident tones, but there was pride, too. Like the satisfied way Patricia Bell had once asked me after class whether I'd seen how Mr. Garrison had been staring at her, and didn't I think it was **weird**?

"His paws are all wet," I said. "He's gonna mess up the floors."

"My parents aren't home. It doesn't matter." Teddy stayed in the doorway, awkward with an air of expectancy; did he think we were going to hang out?

He stood there, like the unhappy boys who sometimes got erections at the chalkboard for no reason at all—he was obviously under the command of some other force. Maybe the proof of sex was visible on me in a new way.

"Well," I said. I worried I would start laughing—Teddy looked so uncomfortable. "See you."

Teddy cleared his throat, trying to throttle his voice deeper. "Sorry," he said. "If Tiki was bothering you."

How did I know I could mess with Teddy? Why did my mind range immediately to that option? I'd only been to the ranch twice since the solstice party, but I'd already started to absorb certain ways of seeing the world, certain habits of logic. Society was crowded with straight people, Russell told us, people in paralyzed thrall to corporate interests and docile as dosed lab chimps. Those of us at the ranch functioned on a whole other level, fighting against the miserable squall, and so what if you had to mess with the straight people to achieve larger goals, larger worlds? If you checked yourself out of that old contract, Russell told us, refused all the bullshit scare tactics of civics class and prayer books and the principal's office, you'd see there was no such thing as right and wrong. His permissive equations reduced these concepts to hollow relics, like medals from a regime no longer in power.

I asked Teddy for a drink. Lemonade, I figured, soda, anything but what he brought me, his hand shaking nervously when he passed me the glass.

"Do you want a napkin?" he said.

"Nah." The intensity of his attention seemed exposing, and I laughed a little. I was just starting to learn how to be looked at. I took a deep drink. The glass was full of vodka, cloudy with the barest slip of orange juice. I coughed.

"Your parents let you drink?" I asked, wiping at my mouth.

"I do what I want," he said, proud and uncertain at the same time. His eyes gleamed; I watched him decide what to say next. It was strange to watch someone else calibrate and worry over their actions instead of being the one who was worrying. Was this what Peter had felt around me? A limited patience, a sense of power that felt heady and slightly distressing. Teddy's freckled face, ruddy and eager—he was only two years younger than me, but the distance seemed definitive. I took a large swallow from the glass, and Teddy cleared his throat.

"I have some dope if you want it," he said.

Teddy led me to his room, expectant as I glanced around at his boyish novelties. They seemed arranged for viewing, though it was all junk: a captain's clock whose hands were dead, a long-forgotten ant farm, warped and molding. The glassy stipple of a partial arrowhead, a jar of pennies, green and scuzzy as sunken treasure. Usually I'd make some crack to Teddy. Ask him where he got the arrowhead or tell him about the whole one I'd found, the obsidian point sharp enough to draw blood. But I sensed a pressure to preserve a haughty coolness, like Suzanne that day in the park. I was already starting to understand that other people's admiration asked something of you. That you had to shape yourself around it. The weed Teddy produced from under his mattress was brown and crumbled, barely smokable, though he held out the plastic bag with gruff dignity.

I laughed. "It's like dirt or something. No, thanks."

He seemed stung and stuffed the bag deep in his

pocket. It had been his trump card, I understood, and he hadn't expected its failure. How long had the bag been there, crushed by the mattress, waiting for deployment? I suddenly felt sorry for Teddy, the neckline of his striped shirt gone limp with grime. I told myself there was still time to leave. To put down the now empty glass, to say a breezy thank-you and go back to my own house. There were other ways to get money. But I stayed. He eyed me, sitting on his bed, with a bewildered and attentive air, as if looking away would break the rare spell of my presence.

"I can get you some real stuff, if you want," I said. "Good stuff. I know a guy."

His gratitude was embarrassing. "Really?"

"Sure." I saw him notice as I adjusted my swimsuit strap. "You have any money on you?" I asked.

He had three dollars in his pocket, wadded and limp, and didn't hesitate to hand them over. I tucked the bills away, all business. Even possessing that small amount of money tindered an obsessive need in me, a desire to see how much I was worth. The equation excited me. You could be pretty, you could be wanted, and that could make you valuable. I appreciated the tidy commerce. And maybe it was something I already perceived in relationships with men—that creep of discomfort, of being tricked. At least this way the arrangement was put toward some use.

"What about your parents?" I said. "Don't they have money somewhere?"

He cut a quick glance at me.

"They're gone, aren't they?" I sighed, impatient. "So who cares?"

Teddy coughed. Rearranged his face. "Yeah," he said. "Let me check."

The dog banged at our heels while I followed Teddy up the stairs. The dimness of his parents' room, a room that seemed both familiar—the stale glass of water on the nightstand, the lacquered tray of perfume bottles—and foreign, his father's slacks collapsed in the corner, an upholstered bench at the foot of the bed. I was nervous, and I could tell Teddy was, too. It seemed perverse to be in his parents' bedroom in the middle of the day. The sun was hot outside the shades, outlining them brightly.

Teddy went into the closet in the far corner, and I followed. If I stayed close, I was less like an intruder. He reached up on his toes to feel blindly through a cardboard box. While he searched, I shuffled through the clothes hanging from fussy silken hangers. His mother's. Paisley pussy-bow blouses, the grim, tight tweeds. They all seemed like costumes, impersonal and not quite real, until I pinched the sleeve of an ivory blouse. My mother had the same one, and it made me uneasy, the familiar gold of the I. Magnin label like a rebuke. I dropped the shirt back on its hanger. "Can't you hurry up?" I hissed at Teddy, and he made a muffled reply, rummaging farther, until he finally pulled out some new-looking bills.

He shoved the box back onto the high shelf, breathing hard, while I counted.

"Sixty-five," I said. Neatening the stack, folding it to a more substantial thickness.

"Isn't that enough?"

I could tell by his face, the effort of his breathing, that if I demanded more, he would find a way to get it. Part of me almost wanted to. To gorge myself on this new power, see how long I could keep it going. But then Tiki trotted in the doorway, startling us both. The dog panting as he nudged at Teddy's legs. Even the dog's tongue was spotted, I saw, the crimped pink freckled with black.

"This'll be fine," I said, putting the money in my pocket. My damp shorts gave off an itch of chlorine.

"So when will I get the stuff?" Teddy said.

It took a second to understand the significant look he gave me: the dope I'd promised. I'd almost forgotten that I hadn't just demanded money. When he saw my expression, he corrected himself. "I mean, no rush. If it takes time or whatever."

"Hard to say." Tiki was sniffing at my crotch; I pushed his nose away more roughly than I'd meant to, his snout wetting my palm. My desire to get out of the room was suddenly overwhelming. "Pretty soon, probably," I said, starting to back toward the door. "I'll bring it over when I get it."

"Oh, yeah," Teddy said. "Yeah, okay."

...

I had the uncomfortable sense, at the front door, that Teddy was the guest and I was the host. The wind chime over the porch rippling a thin song. The sun and trees and blond hills beyond seemed to promise great freedoms, and I could already start to forget what I'd done, washed over by other concerns. The pleasing meaty rectangle of the folded bills in my pocket. When I looked at Teddy's freckled face, a surge of impulsive, virtuous affection passed through me—he was like a little brother. The gentle way he'd mothered the barn kitten.

"I'll see you," I said, leaning to kiss him on the cheek.

I was congratulating myself for the sweetness of my gesture, the kindness, but then Teddy adjusted his hips, hunching them protectively; when I pulled away, I saw his erection pushing stubbornly against his jeans.

7

I could ride my bike most of the way there. Adobe Road empty of cars, except for the occasional motorcycle or horse trailer. If a car passed, it was usually heading to the ranch, and they'd give me a lift, my bicycle half hanging out a window. Girls in shorts and wood sandals and plastic rings from the dispensers outside the Rexall. Boys who kept losing their train of thought, then coming to with a stunned smile, as if returned from cosmic tourism. The barest of nods we'd give one another, tuned to the same unseen frequencies.

It wasn't that I couldn't remember my life before Suzanne and the others, but it had been limited and expected, objects and people occupying their temperate orbits. The yellow cake my mother made for birthdays, dense and chilly from the freezer. The girls at school eating lunch on the asphalt, sitting on their overturned backpacks. Since I'd met Suzanne, my life had come into sharp, mysterious relief, revealing a world beyond the known world, the hidden passage behind the bookcase. I'd catch myself eating an apple, and even the wet swallow of apple could incite gratitude in me. The arrangement of oak leaves overhead condensing with a hothouse clarity, clues to a riddle I hadn't known you could try to solve.

I followed Suzanne past the motorcycles parked at the front of the main house, as big and heavy looking as cows. Men in denim vests sat on the nearby boulders, smoking cigarettes. The air was prickly from the llamas in their pen, the funny smell of hay and sweat and sunbaked shit.

"Hey, bunnies," one of the men called. Stretching so his belly strained pregnant against his shirt.

Suzanne smiled back but pulled me along. "If you stand around too much, they'll jump on you," she said, though she was pushing her shoulders back to emphasize her breasts. When I cut a glance over my shoulder, the man flicked his tongue at me, quick as a snake.

"Russell can help all kinds of people, though," Suzanne said. "And you know, the pigs don't mess with the motorcycle guys. That's important."

"Why?"

"Because," she said, like it was obvious. "The cops hate Russell. They hate anyone who tries to free people from the system. But they stay away if those guys are here." She shook her head. "The pigs are trapped, too, that's the bullshit. Their fucking shiny black shoes."

I stoked my own righteous agreement: I was in league with truth. I followed her to the clearing beyond the house, toward the campfire hum of voices in chorus. The money was banded tightly in my pocket, and I kept starting to tell Suzanne I'd brought it, then losing my nerve, concerned it was too meager an offering. Finally I stopped her, touching her shoulder before we joined the others.

"I can get more," I said, flustered. I just wanted her to know the money existed, imagining I would be the one to give it to Russell. But Suzanne quickly corrected that idea. I tried not to mind how swiftly she took the bills from my hand, counting them with her eyes. I saw that she was surprised by the amount.

"Good girl."

The sun hit the tin outbuildings and broke up the smoke in the air. Someone had lit a joss stick that kept going out. Russell's eyes moved around each of our faces, the group sitting at his feet, and I flushed when he caught my gaze—he seemed unsurprised by my return. Suzanne's hand touched my back lightly, possessively, and a hush came over me like in a movie theater or church. My awareness of her hand was almost paralyzing. Donna was playing with her orange hair. Weaving sections into tight, lacy braids, using her pinched fingernails to flay split ends.

Russell looked younger when he sang, his mess of hair tied back, and he played the guitar in a funny, mocking way, like a TV cowboy. His voice wasn't the nicest I'd ever heard, but that day—my legs in the sun, the stubble of oat grass—that day, his voice seemed to slide all over me, to saturate the air, so that I felt pinned in place. I couldn't move even if I wanted to, even if I could imagine there was any place I could go.

In the lull that followed Russell's singing, Suzanne got to her feet, her dress already thick with dust, and picked her way to his side. His face changed as she whispered to him, and he nodded. Squeezing her shoulder. I saw her slip him my wad of money, which Russell put in his pocket. Resting his fingers there for a moment as if giving a blessing.

Russell's eyes crinkled. "We've got good news. We've got some resources, sweethearts. Because someone has opened themselves up to us, they've opened their hearts."

A shimmer passed through me. And all at once, it

seemed worth it—trawling my mother's purse. The stillness of Teddy's parents' bedroom. How cleanly that worry had been transmuted into belonging. Suzanne seemed gratified as she hurried to settle back beside me.

"Little Evie's shown us her big heart," Russell said. "She's shown us her love, hasn't she?" And the others turned to look at me, a current of goodwill pulsed in my direction.

The rest of the afternoon passed in a drowsy span of sunlight. The skinny dogs retreating under the house, tongues heaving. We sat alone on the porch steps—Suzanne rested her head on my knees and recounted scraps of a dream she'd had. Pausing to take ripping bites from a length of French bread.

"I was convinced I knew sign language, but it was obvious to me I didn't, that I was just flailing my hands around. But the man understood everything I was saying, like I actually did know sign language. But later it just turned out he was only pretending to be deaf," she said, "in the end. So it was all fake—him, me, the whole train."

Her laugh was an afterthought, a sharp addendum—how happy I was for any news of her interior, a secret meant for me alone. I couldn't say how long we sat there, the two of us cut adrift from the rhythms of normal life. But that's what I wanted—

for even time to feel different and new, washed with special import. Like she and I were occupying the same song.

We were, Russell told us, starting a new kind of society. Free from racism, free from exclusion, free from hierarchy. We were in service of a deeper love. That's how he said it, a deeper love, his voice booming from the ramshackle house in the California grasslands, and we played together like dogs, tumbling and biting and breathless with sun shock. We were barely adults, most of us, and our teeth were still milky and new. We ate whatever was put in front of us. Oatmeal that gummed up in the throat. Ketchup on bread, chipped beef from a can. Potatoes soggy with PAM.

"Miss 1969," Suzanne called me. "Our very own."

And they treated me like that, like their new toy, taking turns hooking their arms through mine, clamoring to braid my long hair. Teasing me about the boarding school I'd mentioned, my famous grandmother, whose name some of them recognized. My clean white socks. The others had been with Russell for months, or years, even. And that was the first worry that the days slowly melted in me. Where were their families, girls like Suzanne? Or baby-voiced Helen—she spoke sometimes of a house in Eugene. A father who gave her enemas every month and rubbed her calves after tennis practice with mentholated balm, among other dubious hygienic practices.

But where was he? If any of their homes had given them what they needed, why would they be here, day after day, their time at the ranch stretching on endlessly?

Suzanne slept late, barely up by noon. Groggy and lingering, her movements at half-speed. Like there would always be more time. By then, I was already sleeping in Suzanne's bed every few nights. Her mattress wasn't comfortable, gritty with sand, but I didn't mind. Sometimes she reached over blindly from sleep to sling her arm around me, a warmth coming off her body like baked bread. I would lie awake, painfully alert to Suzanne's nearness. She turned in the night so she kicked off the sheet, exposing her bare breasts.

Her room was dark and jungly in the mornings, the tar roof of the outbuilding getting bubbly in the heat. I was already dressed but knew we wouldn't join the others for another hour. Suzanne always took a long time to get ready, though preparation was mostly a matter of time and not action—a slow shrug into herself. I liked to watch her from the mattress, the sweet, blank way she studied her reflection with the directionless gaze of a portrait. Her naked body was humble at these moments, even childish, bent at an unflattering angle as she rummaged through the trash bag of clothes. It was comforting to me, her humanness. Noticing how her ankles were gruff with stubble, or the pin dots of blackheads.

Suzanne had been a dancer in San Francisco. The flashing neon snake outside the club, the red apple that cast an alien glow on the passersby. One of the other girls burned off Suzanne's moles backstage with a caustic pencil.

"Some girls hated being up there," she said, tugging a dress over her nakedness. "Dancing, the whole thing. But I didn't think it was so bad."

She assessed the dress in the mirror, cupping her breasts through the fabric. "People can be so prudish," she said. She made a lewd face, laughing a little at herself, and let her breasts drop. She told me, then, how Russell fucked her gently and how sometimes he didn't, and how you could like it either way. "There's nothing sick about that," she said. "The people who act so uptight, who act like it's so evil? They're the real perverts. It's like some of the guys who'd come to see us dance. All mad at us that they were there. Like we'd tricked them."

Suzanne didn't often talk about her hometown or family, and I didn't ask. There was a glossy pucker of scar tissue along one of her wrists that I'd seen her tracing with a tragic pride, and once she slipped and mentioned a humid street outside Red Bluff. But then she caught herself. "That cunt," she called her mother, peaceably. My dizzy solidarity overwhelmed me, the weary justice in her tone—I thought we both knew what it was to be alone, though it seems silly to me now. To think we were so alike, when I had grown up with housekeepers and parents and she told me she had sometimes lived in a car, sleeping in the reclined passenger seat with her mother in the driver's side. If I was hungry, I ate. But we had other things in common, Suzanne and I, a different hunger. Sometimes I wanted to be touched so badly I was scraped by longing. I saw the same thing in Suzanne, too, perking up like an animal smelling food whenever Russell approached.

Suzanne went into San Rafael with Russell to look at a truck. I stayed behind—there were chores, and I threw myself into them with an eagerness born of fear. I didn't want to give them any excuse to make me leave. Feeding the llamas, weeding the garden, scrubbing and bleaching the kitchen floors. Work was just another way to show your love, to offer up the self.

Filling the llamas' trough took a long time, the water pressure sluggish at best, but it was nice to be out in the sun. Mosquitoes hovered around my bare skin and I kept having to shiver them off. They didn't bother the llamas, who just stood there, as sultry and heavy-lidded as screen sirens.

I could see Guy beyond the main house, messing with the bus engine with the low-stakes curiosity of a science fair project. Taking breaks to smoke cigarettes and do downward dog. He went to the main house every once in a while to get another beer from Russell's stash, checking to make sure everyone did their chores. He and Suzanne were like the head counselors, keeping Donna and the others in line with a stray word or glance. Operating as satellite versions of Russell, though Guy's deference was different from Suzanne's. I think he stayed around because Russell was a way to get things he wanted—girls, drugs, a place to crash. He wasn't in love with Russell, didn't cower or pant in his presence—Guy was more like a sidekick, and all his blustery tales of adventure and hardship continued to star himself.

He approached the fence, his beer and cigarette in the same hand, his jeans low on his hips. I knew he was watching me, and I concentrated on the hose, the warm fill of water in the trough.

"The smoke keeps 'em away," Guy said, and I turned as if I'd just noticed his presence. "The mosquitoes," he said, holding out his cigarette.

"Yeah," I said, "sure. Thanks." I took the cigarette over the fence, careful to keep the hose trained on the trough.

"You seen Suzanne?"

Already Guy assumed I'd know her movements. I was flattered to be the keeper of her whereabouts.

"Some guy in San Rafael was selling his truck," I said. "She went with Russell to look at it."

"Hm," Guy said. Reaching to take his cigarette back. He seemed amused by my professionalism, though I'm sure he saw, too, the worship that hijacked my face whenever I spoke of Suzanne. My half-hitch step those times I hurried to her side. Maybe it confused him not to be the focus of all that desire—he was a handsome boy, used to the attention of girls. Girls who sucked in their stomachs when he put his hand down their jeans, girls who believed the jewelry he wore was the pretty evidence of his untapped emotional depths.

"They're probably at the free clinic," Guy said. He mimed scratching his crotch, his cigarette waving around. He was trying to get me to snicker at Suzanne, collude in some way—I didn't respond, beyond a grim smile. He tilted back on the heels of his cowboy boots. Studying me.

"You can go on and help Roos," he said in between the final slugs of his beer. "She's in the kitchen."

I'd already finished my chores for the day, and working with Roos in the hot kitchen would be tedious, but I nodded with a martyr's air.

Roos had been married to a policeman in Corpus Christi, Suzanne had told me, which seemed about right. She floated around the border with the dreamy solicitude of beaten wives, and even my offer of help with the dishes was met with a mild cower. I scrubbed gelatinous fug from their biggest stew pot, the colorless scraps of food gumming up the sponge. Guy was punishing me in his petty fashion, but I didn't care. Any irritation was softened by Suzanne's return. She gusted into the kitchen, breathless.

"The guy gave Russell the truck," Suzanne said, her face bright, casting around for an audience. She opened a cabinet, rooting inside. "It was so perfect," she said, "'cause he wanted, like, two hundred bucks. And Russell said, all calm, You should just give it to us."

She laughed, still residually thrilled, and sat up on the counter. Starting to crack her way through a bag of dusty-looking peanuts. "The guy was real angry, at first, that Russell was just asking for it. For free."

Roos was only half listening, picking through the makings of that night's dinner, but I turned off the faucet, watching Suzanne with my whole body.

"And Russell said, Let's just talk for a minute. Just let me tell you what I'm about." Suzanne spit a shell back into the bag. "We had some tea with the guy, in his weird log cabin house. For an hour or something. Russell gave him the whole vision, laid it all out. And the guy was real interested in what we were doing out here. Showed Russell his old army pictures. Then he said we could just have the truck."

I wiped my hands on my shorts, her giddiness making me so shy I had to turn away. I finished the dishes to the sound of her snapping open peanut after peanut from her perch on the counter, amassing an unruly pile of damp shells until the bag was gone and she went looking for someone else to tell her story to.

The girls would hang out near the creek because it was cooler, the breeze carrying a chill, though the flies were bad. The rocks capped with algae, the sleepy shade. Russell had come back from town in the new truck, bearing candy bars, comic books whose pages grew limp from our hands. Helen ate her candy immediately and looked around at the rest of us with a seethe of jealousy. Though she'd also come from a wealthy family, we weren't close. I found her dull except around Russell, when her brattiness took on a directed aim. Preening under his touch like a cat, she acted younger, even than me, stunted in a way that would later seem pathological.

"Jesus. Stop staring at me," Suzanne said, hunching her candy away from Helen. "You already ate yours." Her shape on the bank next to me, her toes curling into the dirt. Jerking when a mosquito swarmed by her ear.

"Just a bite," Helen whined. "Just the corner."

Roos glanced up from the chambray mess of cloth in her lap. She was mending a work shirt for Guy, her tiny stitches made with absent precision.

"You can have some of mine," Donna said, "if you be quiet." She picked her way to Helen, her chocolate bar craggy with peanuts.

Helen took a bite. When she giggled, her teeth washed with chocolate.

"Candy yoga," she pronounced. Anything could be yoga: doing the dishes, grooming the llamas. Making food for Russell. You were supposed to bliss out on it, to settle into whatever the rhythms were going to teach you.

Break down the self, offer yourself up like dust to the universe.

...

All the books made it sound like the men forced the girls into it. That wasn't true, not all the time. Suzanne wielded her Swinger camera like a weapon. Goading men to drop their jeans. To expose their penises, tender and naked in dark nests of hair. The men smiled shyly in the pictures, paled from the guilty flash, all hair and wet animal eyes. "There isn't any film in the camera," Suzanne would say, though she had stolen a case of film from the store. The boys pretended to believe her. It was like that with lots of things.

I trailed after Suzanne, after all of them. Suzanne letting me draw suns and moons on her naked back with tanning oil while Russell played an idle riff on his guitar, a coy up-and-down fragment. Helen sighing like the lovesick kid she was, Roos joining us with a drifty smile, some teenage boy I didn't know looking at us all with grateful awe, and no one even had to speak—the silence was knit with so much.

I prepared inwardly for Russell's advances, but it only happened after a while. Russell giving me a cryptic nod so I knew to follow him.

I'd been washing windows with Suzanne in the main house—the floor littered with the crumple of newspaper and vinegar, the transistor radio going; even chores took on the delight of truancy. Suzanne singing along, talking to me with happy, fitful distraction. She looked different, those times we worked together, like she forgot herself and relaxed into the girl she was. It's strange to remember she was just nineteen. When Russell nodded at me, I looked at her reflexively. For permission or forgiveness, either one. The ease in her face had drained into a brittle mask. Scrubbing the warped window with new concentration. She shrugged goodbye when I left, like she didn't mind, though I could sense her watchful gaze on my back.

Every time Russell nodded at me like that, my heart contracted, despite the strangeness. I was eager for our encounters, eager to cement my place among them, as if doing what Suzanne did was a way of being with her. Russell never fucked me—it was always other stuff, his fingers moving in me with a technical remove I ascribed to his purity. His aims were elevated, I told myself, unsullied by primitive concerns.

"Look at yourself," he said whenever he sensed shame or hesitance. Pointing me toward the fogged mirror in the trailer. "Look at your body. It's not some stranger's body," he said evenly. When I shied away, goofing some excuse, he took me by the shoulders and pointed me back at the mirror. "It's you," he said. "It's Evie. Nothing in you but beauty."

The words worked on me, even if only temporarily. A trance overtaking me when I saw my reflection—the scooped breasts, even the soft stomach, the legs rough with mosquito bites. There was nothing to figure out, no complicated puzzles—just the obvious fact of the moment, the only place where love really existed.

Afterward he'd hand me a towel to clean myself, and this seemed like a great kindness.

When I returned to her purview, there was always a brief period when Suzanne was cool to me. Even her movements were stiff, as if braced, a lull behind her eyes, like someone asleep at the wheel. I learned quickly how to compliment her, how to ride by her side until she forgot to be aloof and deigned to pass her cigarette to me. It would occur to me later that Suzanne missed me when I left, her formality a clumsy disguise. Though it's hard to tell—maybe that is only a wishful explanation.

The other parts of the ranch flash in and out. Guy's black dog that they called by a rotating series of names. The wanderers who passed through the ranch that summer, crashing for a day or two before leaving. Denizens of the brainless dream, appearing at all hours of the day with woven backpacks and their parents' cars. I didn't see anything familiar in how quickly Russell talked them out of their possessions, put them on the spot so their generosity became a forced theater. They handed over pink slips to cars, bankbooks, once even a gold wedding ring, with the stunned and exhausted relief of a drowning person finally giving in to the tidal suck. I was distracted by their tales of sorrow, both harrowing and banal. Complaints of evil fathers and cruel mothers, a similarity to the stories that made us all feel like victims of the same conspiracy.

It was one of the few days it rained that summer, and most of us were indoors, the old parlor smelling damp and gray like the air outside. Blankets gridded the floor. I could hear a baseball game on the radio in the kitchen, rain dropping into the plastic bucket under a leak. Roos was giving Suzanne a hand massage, their fingers slick with lotion, while I read a years-old magazine. My horoscope from March 1967. An irritated sulk hung between us; we were not used to limitations, to being stuck anywhere.

The kids did better at being indoors. They passed only briefly through our watch, trundling by on their private missions. There was the bang of a fallen chair in the other room, but no one got up to investigate. Besides Nico, I didn't know who most of the other kids belonged to—all of them were thin wristed, like they'd gone to seed, powdered milk glazed around their mouths. I'd watched Nico for Roos a few times, had held him in my arms and felt his sweaty, pleasing weight. I combed his hair with my fingers, untangled his shark-tooth necklace. All those self-consciously maternal tasks, tasks that pleased me more than him and allowed me to imagine I alone had the power to make him calm. Nico was uncooperative with these moments of softness, breaking the spell bluntly, like he'd sensed my good feelings and resented them. Tugging his little penis at me. Demanding juice in a shrieking falsetto. Once hitting me so hard that I bruised. I watched him squat and take a shit out on the concrete by the pool, shits we'd sometimes hose away and sometimes not.

Helen wandered downstairs in a Snoopy T-shirt and too-big socks, the red heels bunched around her ankles.

"Anyone wanna play Liar's Dice?"

"Nah," Suzanne announced. For all of us, it was assumed.

Helen slumped onto a balding armchair stripped of cushions. She glanced at the ceiling. "Still leaking," she said. Everyone ignored her. "Can someone roll a joint?" she said. "Please?"

When no one answered, she joined Roos and Suzanne on the floor. "Please, please, please?" she said, nuzzling her head into Roos's shoulder, draping herself in her lap like a dog.

"Oh, just do it," Suzanne said. Helen jumped up to get the fake ivory box they kept the supplies in, while Suzanne rolled her eyes at me. I smiled back. It wasn't so bad, I thought, being inside. All of us huddled in the same room like Red Cross survivors, water boiling on the stove for tea. Roos working by the window, where the light was alabaster through the scrappy lace curtain.

The calm was cut by Nico's sudden whine, stampeding into the room as he chased a little girl with a bowl cut—she had Nico's shark-tooth necklace, and a yelping scrabble broke out between them. Tears, clawing.

"Hey," Suzanne said without looking up, and the kids got quiet, though they kept staring hotly at each other. Breathing hard, like drunks. Everything seemed fine, quickly handled, until Nico scratched the girl's face, raking her with his overgrown nails, and the screaming doubled. The girl clapped both hands over her cheek, wailing so her baby teeth showed. Sustaining a high note of misery.

Roos got to her feet with effort.

"Baby," she said, holding her arms out, "baby, you gotta be nice." She took a few steps toward Nico, who started screaming, too, sitting down heavy on his diaper. "Get up," Roos said, "come on, baby," trying to hold on to his shoulders, but he'd gone limp and wouldn't be moved. The other girl sobered in the face of Nico's antics, how he wrenched away from his mother and started banging his head against the floor. "Baby," Roos said, droning louder, "no, no, no," but he kept going, his eyes getting dark and buttony with pleasure.

"God." Helen laughed, a strange laugh that persisted. I didn't know what to do. I remembered the helpless panic I'd sometimes felt when babysitting, a realization that this child did not belong to me and was beyond my reach; but even Roos seemed paralyzed with the same worry. Like she was waiting for

Nico's real mother to come home and fix everything. Nico was getting pink with effort, his skull knocking on the floor. Yelling until he heard the footsteps on the porch—it was Russell, and I saw everyone's faces condense with new life.

"What's this?" Russell said. He was wearing one of Mitch's cast-off shirts, big bloody roses embroidered along the yoke. He was barefoot, wet all over from the rain.

"Ask Roos," Helen chirped. "It's her kid."

Roos muttered something, her words going wild at the end, but Russell didn't respond on her level. His voice was calm, seeming to draw a circle around the crying child, the flustered mother.

"Relax," Russell intoned. He wouldn't let anyone's upset in, the jitter in the room deflected by his gaze. Even Nico looked wary in Russell's presence, his tantrum taking on a hollow cast, like he was an understudy for himself.

"Little man," Russell said, "come on up here and talk to me."

Nico glared at his mother, but his eyes were drawn, helpless, to Russell. Nico pushed out his fat bottom lip, calculating.

Russell stayed standing in the doorway, not bending down eager and wet toothed like some grown-ups did with kids, and Nico was mostly quiet, settling into a whimper. Darting another look between his mother and Russell before finally scurrying over to Russell and letting himself be picked up.

"There's the little man," Russell said, Nico's arms clinging tight around his neck, and I remember how strange it was to see Russell's face change as he talked to the boy. His features mutable, turning antic and foolish, like a jester's, though his voice stayed calm. He could do that. Change himself to fit the person, like water taking on the shape of whatever vessel it was poured into. He could be all these things at once: The man who crooked his fingers in me. The man who got everything free. The man who sometimes fucked Suzanne hard and sometimes fucked her gently. The man who whispered to the little boy, his voice grazing his ear.

I couldn't hear what Russell said, but Nico swallowed his crying. His face was thrilled and wet: he seemed happy just to be in someone's arms.

Helen's eleven-year-old cousin Caroline ran away from home and stayed for a while. She'd been living in the Haight, but there had been a police crackdown: she'd hitched to the ranch with a cowhide wallet and a ratty fox fur coat she petted with skittish affection, like she didn't want anyone to see how much she loved it.

The ranch wasn't that far from San Francisco, but we didn't go there very often. I'd gone only once with Suzanne, to pick up a pound of grass from a house she called, jokingly, the Russian Embassy. Some friends of Guy's, I think, the old Satanist hangout. The front door was painted a tarry black—she saw my hesitation and hooked her arm through mine.

"Doomy, huh?" she said. "I thought so too, at first."

When she hitched me closer, I felt the knock of her hipbones. These moments of kindness were never anything but dazzling to me.

Afterward, she and I walked over to Hippie Hill. It was grayed-out, and drizzling, empty, except for the undead stumbling of junkies. I tried hard to squeeze out a vibe from the air, but there was nothing—I was relieved when Suzanne laughed, too, halting any labor for meaning. "Jesus," she said, "this place is a dump." We ended up back in the park, the fog dripping audibly from the eucalyptus leaves.

I spent almost every day at the ranch, except for brief stopovers at my house to change clothes or leave notes on the kitchen table for my mother. Notes that I'd sign, "Your Loving Daughter." Indulging the overblown affection my absence made room for.

I knew I was starting to look different, the weeks at the ranch working me over with a grubby wash. My hair getting light from the sun and sharp at the edges, a tint of smoke lingering even after I shampooed. Much of my clothes had passed into the ranch possession, morphing into garments I often failed to recognize as my own: Helen clowning around in my once precious bib shirt, now torn and spotted with peach juice. I dressed like Suzanne, a raunchy patchwork culled from the communal piles, clothes whose scrappiness announced a hostility to the larger world. I had gone with Suzanne to the Home Market once, Suzanne wearing a bikini top and cutoffs, and we'd watched the other shoppers glare and grow hot with indignation, their sideways glances becoming outright stares. We'd laughed with insane, helpless snorts, like we'd had some wild secret, and we had. The woman who'd seemed about to cry with baffled disgust, clutching for her daughter's arm: she hadn't known her hatred only made us more powerful.

I prepared for possible sightings of my mother with pious ablutions: I showered, standing in the hot water until my skin splotched red, my hair slippery with conditioner. I put on a plain T-shirt and white cotton shorts, what I might have worn when I was younger, trying to appear scrubbed and sexless enough to comfort my mother. Though maybe I didn't need to try so hard—she wasn't looking closely enough to warrant the effort. The times we did have dinner together, a mostly silent affair, she would fuss at her food like a picky child. Inventing reasons to talk about Frank, inane weather reports from her own life. I could have been anyone. One night I didn't bother to change, showing up at the table in a voile halter top that showed my stomach. She didn't say anything, plowing her spoon through her rice with a distracted air until she seemed suddenly to remember my presence. Darting a slanted look at me. "You're getting so skinny," she announced, gripping my wrist and letting it drop in jealous measurement. I shrugged and she didn't bring it up again.

When I finally met him in person, Mitch Lewis was fatter than I expected someone famous to be. Swollen, like there was butter under his skin. His face was furred with sideburns, his feathered golden hair. He brought a case of root beer for the girls and six netted bags of oranges. Stale brownies with German-chocolate frosting, in individual frilled cups like Pilgrims' bonnets. Nougat candy in bright pink tins. The dregs of gift baskets, I assumed. A carton of cigarettes.

"He knows I like this kind," Suzanne said, hugging the cigarettes to her chest. "He remembered."

They all spoke of Mitch with that possessiveness, like he was an idea more than an actual person. They'd preened and prepared for Mitch's visit with girlish eagerness.

"You can see the ocean from his hot tub," Suzanne told me. "Mitch put lights up so the water is all glowy."

"His dick is really big," Donna added. "And like, purple."

Donna was washing her armpits in the sink, and Suzanne rolled her eyes. "Whore's bath," she murmured, but she'd changed into a dress. Even Russell slicked back his hair with water, giving him a polished, urbane air.

Russell introduced me to Mitch, saying, "Our little actress," his hand at my back.

Mitch studied me with a questioning, smug smile. Men did it so easily, that immediate parceling of value. And how they seemed to want you to collude on your own judgment.

"I'm Mitch," he said. As if I hadn't already known. His skin was fresh looking and poreless in the way of wealthy overeaters.

"Give Mitch a hug," Russell said. Nudging me. "Mitch wants a hug, just like the rest of us. He could use a little love."

Mitch looked expectant, opening a present he'd already shaken and identified. Usually, I would have been eaten by shyness. Conscious of my body, some error I could make. But already I felt different. I was one of them, and that meant I could smile back at Mitch, stepping forward to let him mash himself against me.

The long afternoon that followed: Mitch and Russell took turns playing guitar. Helen sitting on Mitch's lap in a bikini top. She kept giggling and ducking her pigtailed head into his neck. Mitch was a much better musician than Russell, but I tried not to notice. I got stoned with a new and furious concentration, passing beyond the point of nervousness and into a blunted state. Smiling almost involuntarily, so my cheeks started to ache. Suzanne sat cross-legged in the dirt beside me, her fingers grazing mine. Our faces cupped and attentive as tulips.

...

It was one of those slurry days we offered up to the shared dream, a violence in our aversion to real life; though it was all about connecting, tuning in, we told ourselves. Mitch had dropped off some acid, sourced from a lab tech at Stanford. Donna mixed it with orange juice in paper cups and we drank it for breakfast, so the trees seemed to thrum with energy, the shadows purpling and wet. It was curious, later, to think of how easily I fell into things. If there were drugs around, I did them. You were in the moment—when everything back then happened. We could talk about **the moment** for hours. Turn it over in conversation: the way the light moved, why someone was silent, dismantling all the layers of what a look had really meant. It seemed like something important, our desire to describe the shape of each second as it passed, to bring out everything hidden and beat it to death.

Suzanne and I were working on the childish bracelets the girls had been trading among ourselves, collecting them up our arms like middle-schoolers. Practicing the V stitch. The candy stripe. I was making one for Suzanne, fat and wide, a poppy-red chevron on a field of peach thread. I liked the calm collection of the knots, how the colors vibrated happily under my fingers. I got up once to get Suzanne a glass of water, and there was a domestic gentleness in that act. I wanted to meet a need, put water in her mouth. Suzanne smiled up at me as she drank, gulping so fast I could see her throat ripple.

Helen's cousin Caroline was hanging around that day. She seemed more knowing than I had ever been at eleven. Her bracelets shook with the kiss of cheap metal. Her terry-cloth shirt was the pale yellow of a lemon slushie and showed her small stomach, though her knees were scraped and ashy like a boy's.

"Far-out," she said when Guy tipped a paper cup of juice to her lips, and like a windup toy, she kept repeating this phrase when the acid began to hit. I'd started to detect the first signs in myself, too, my mouth filling with saliva. I thought of the flooded creeks I'd seen in childhood, the death cold of the rainwater as it came swift over the rocks.

I could hear Guy spinning nonsense on the porch. One of his meaningless stories, the drug making his bluster echo. His long hair pulled into a dark knot at the base of his skull.

"This fella was banging on the door," he was saying, "shouting that he'd come to take what was his, and I was like aw, hell, big fuckin' deal," he droned, "I'm Elvis Presley," and Roos was nodding along. Squinting up at the sun while Country Joe sounded from the house. Clouds drifting across the blue, outlined in neon.

"Check out Orphan Annie," Suzanne said, rolling her eyes at Caroline.

Caroline was overdoing it at first, her stumbling, dopey affect, but soon the drug actually caught up to her and she got wild-eyed and a little scared. She was thin enough that I could see the glandular throb at her throat. Suzanne was watching her, too, and I waited for her to say something, but she didn't. Helen, Caroline's supposed cousin, didn't say anything, either. She was sunstruck, catatonic, stretched out on a piece of old carpet and listing a hand over her eyes. Giggling to no one. I went over to Caroline finally, touching her tiny shoulder.

"How's it going?" I said.

She didn't look up until I said her name. I asked her where she was from; she screwed her eyes tight. It was the wrong thing to say—of course it was, bringing up all that bad shit from the outside, whatever rotten memories were probably doubling right then. I didn't know how to pull her back from the bog.

"You want this?" I said, holding up the bracelet. She peeked at it. "Just have to finish it," I said, "but it's for you."

Caroline smiled.

"It's gonna look real nice on you," I went on. "It'll go good with your shirt."

The electricity in her eyes calmed. She held her own shirt away from her body to study it, softening.

"I made it," she said, fingering the embroidered outline of a peace sign on the shirt, and I saw the hours she'd spent on it, maybe borrowing her mother's sewing box. It seemed easy: to be kind to her, to put the finished bracelet around her wrist, burning the knot with a match so she'd have to cut it off.

I didn't notice Suzanne eyeing us, her own bracelet ignored in her lap.

"Beautiful," I said, lifting Caroline's wrist. "Nothing but beauty."

As if I were an occupant of that world, someone who could show the way to others. Such grandiosity mixed up in my feelings of kindness; I was starting to fill in all the blank spaces in myself with the certainties of the ranch. The cool glut of Russell's words—no more ego, turn off the mind. Pick up the cosmic wind instead. Our beliefs as mild and digestible as the sweet rolls and cakes we hustled from a bakery in Sausalito, stuffing our faces with the easy starch.

In the days after, Caroline followed me like a stray dog. Hovering, in the doorway of Suzanne's room, asking if I wanted one of the cigarettes she'd cadged from the bikers. Suzanne stood up and clasped her elbows behind her back, stretching.

"They just gave you them?" Suzanne said archly. "For free?"

Caroline glanced at me. "The cigarettes?"

Suzanne laughed without saying anything else. I was confused, in these moments, but translated them into further proof: Suzanne was prickly with other people because they didn't understand her like I did.

I didn't say it out loud to myself or even think about it too much. Where things were heading with

Suzanne. The dredge of discomfort I got when she disappeared with Russell. How I didn't know what to do without her, seeking out Donna or Roos like a lost kid. The time she came back smelling of dried sweat and roughly wiped herself between the legs with a washcloth, like she didn't care I was watching.

I got up when I saw how nervously Caroline fingered the bracelet I'd given her.

"I'll take a cigarette," I said, smiling at Caroline.

Suzanne hooked her arm in mine.

"But we're gonna feed the llamas," Suzanne said. "Don't want them to starve, do you? Waste away?"

I hesitated, and Suzanne reached out to play with a part of my hair. She was always doing that: picking burrs off my shirt, once wedging a fingernail between my front teeth to dislodge a bit of food. Breaching the boundaries to let me know they didn't exist.

Caroline's desire to be invited was so blatant that I felt almost ashamed. But it didn't stop me from following Suzanne outside, shrugging an apology at Caroline. I could feel her watching us go. The hooded attentions of a child, that wordless understanding. I saw that disappointment was already something familiar to Caroline.

I was scanning the contents of my mother's refrigerator, the glass jars mortared with dried spills. The fumes of cruciferous vegetables, roiling in plastic bags. Nothing to eat, as usual. Little things like this reminded me why I'd rather be somewhere else. When I heard my mother shuffling in the front door, the razzle of her heavy jewelry, I tried to slink off without crossing paths.

"Evie," she called, coming into the kitchen. "Wait up a minute."

I was out of breath from the bike ride from the ranch and at the tail end of being stoned. I tried to blink an ordinary number of times, to present a blank face that would give her nothing.

"You're getting so tan," she said, lifting my arm, and I shrugged. She idly brushed the hair on my arm back and forth, then paused. There was an uncomfortable moment between us. It occurred to me: she'd finally caught on to the trickle of money that had been disappearing. The thought of her anger didn't scare me. The act had been so preposterous that it took on the safety of the unreal. I'd almost started to believe that I had never really lived here, so strong was the feeling of disassociation as I crept through the house on my errands for Suzanne. My excavation of my mother's underwear drawer, sifting through the tea-colored silks and pilly lace until I closed in on a roll of bills banded with a hair tie.

My mother furrowed her brows. "Listen," she said. "Sal saw you out on Adobe Road this morning. Alone."

I tried to keep my face blank, but I was relieved—it was just one of Sal's bovine observations. I'd been telling my mother I'd been at Connie's house. And

I was still home some nights, trying to keep the balance in check.

"Sal said there's some very strange people out there," my mother said. "Some kind of mystic or something, but he sounds"—her face screwed up.

Of course—she would love Russell if he lived in a mansion in Marin, had gardenias floating in his pool, and charged rich women fifty dollars for an astrology reading. How transparent she seemed to me then, always on constant guard against anything lesser than, even as she opened the house up to anyone who smiled at her. To Frank and his shiny-buttoned shirts.

"I've never met him," I said, my voice impassive. So my mother would know I was lying. The fact of the lie hovered there, and I watched her till for a response.

"I just wanted to warn you," she said. "So you know that this guy is out there. I expect you and Connie to take care of each other, understand?"

I could see how badly she wanted to avoid a fight, how she strained for this middle ground. She'd warned me, so she had done what she was supposed to do. It meant she was still my mother. Let her feel this was true—I nodded and she relaxed. My mother's hair was growing out. She was wearing a new tank top with knit straps, and the skin of her shoulders was loose, showing a tan line from a swimsuit—I had no idea when or where my mother had been swimming. How quickly we'd become strangers to each other, like nervous roommates encountering each other in the halls.

"Well," she said.

I saw, for a moment, my old mother, the cast of weary love in her face, but it disappeared when her bracelets made a tinny sound, falling down her arms.

"There's rice and miso in the fridge," she said, and I made a noise in my throat like I might eat it, but we both knew I wouldn't.

8

The police photos of Mitch's house make it look cramped and spooky, as if destined for its fate. The fat splintered beams along the ceiling, the stone fireplace, its many levels and hallways, like something in the Escher lithographs Mitch collected from a gallery in Sausalito. The first time I encountered the house, I remember thinking it was as spare and empty as a coastal church. There was very little furniture, the big windows in the shape of chevrons. Herringbone floors, wide and shallow steps. From the front door, you could already see the black plane of bay spreading past the house, the dark, rocky bank. The houseboats knocking peaceably against each other, like cubes of ice.

Mitch poured us drinks while Suzanne opened

his refrigerator. Humming a little song as she peered at the shelves. Making noises of approval or disapproval, lifting tinfoil off a bowl to sniff at something. I was in awe of her at moments like that. How boldly she acted in the world, in someone else's house, and I watched our reflections wavering in the black windows, our hair loose on our shoulders. Here I was, in this famous man's kitchen. The man whose music I'd heard on the radio. The bay out the door, shining like patent leather. And how glad I was to be there with Suzanne, who seemed to call these things into being.

Mitch had a meeting with Russell earlier that afternoon—I remember noticing it was strange that Mitch had been late for it. Two o'clock had passed, and we were still waiting for Mitch. I was silent, like they all were, the quiet between us expanding. A horsefly bit at my ankle. I didn't want to shoo it away, conscious of Russell a few feet away, perched on his chair with his eyes closed. I could hear him humming under his breath. Russell had decided it would be best for Mitch to come upon him sitting there, his girls surrounding him, Guy at his side, the troubadour with his audience. He was ready to perform, guitar laid across his knees. His bare foot jiggling.

There was something in the way Russell was fingering the guitar, pressing silently on the strings—he was nervous in a way I didn't know how to decipher yet. Russell didn't look up when Helen started whispering to Donna, just a low whisper. Something about Mitch, probably, or some stupid thing Guy had said, but when Helen kept talking, Russell got to his feet. He took a moment to lay the guitar against his chair, pausing to make certain it was stable, then walked over swiftly and slapped Helen in the face.

She gave an involuntary yip, a strange burble of sound. Her wide-eyed hurt draining quickly into apology, blinking fast so the tears wouldn't fall.

It was the first time I had ever seen Russell react that way, the cut of anger aimed at one of us. He couldn't have hit her—the stupid blare of sun made that impossible, the hour of afternoon. The idea was too ludicrous. I looked around for confirmation of the frightening breach, but everyone was staring pointedly away or had arranged their faces into disapproving masks, like Helen had brought this on herself. Guy scratched behind an ear, sighing. Even Suzanne seemed bored by what had happened, like it was no different from a handshake. The vinegar in my throat, my sudden, despairing shock, seemed like a failing.

And soon enough, Russell was petting Helen's hair, tightening her lopsided pigtails. Whispering something in her ear that made her smile and nod, like a goopy-eyed baby doll.

...

When Mitch finally showed up at the ranch, an hour late, he was bearing much-needed supplies: a cardboard flat of canned beans, some dried figs, and chocolate spread. Rock-hard Packham pears, individually wrapped in pink tissue paper. He let the kids clamber up his legs, though normally he shook them off.

"Hi, Russell," Mitch said. A lace of sweat on his face.

"Long time no see, brother," Russell said. He kept his grin steady, though he didn't get up from his chair. "How goes the Great American Dream?"

"Things are good, man," he said. "Sorry I'm late."

"Haven't heard from you in a while," Russell said. "Breaking my heart, Mitch."

"Been busy," Mitch said. "A lot going on."

"There's always a lot going on," Russell said. Looking around at us, making long eye contact with Guy. "Don't you think? Seems like there's a lot going on and that's what life is. Think it only stops when you die."

Mitch laughed, like everything was fine. Passing out the cigarettes he'd brought, the food, like a sweating Santa. The books would identify this as the day things turned between Russell and Mitch, though I didn't know any of this at the time. Didn't pick up on any meaning in the tension between them, Russell's fury muffled by a calm, indulgent exterior. Mitch had come to give Russell the bad news that there would be no record deal for Russell, after all: the cigarettes, the food, all of it meant as a consolation. Russell had been hounding Mitch for weeks about the supposed record deal. Pushing and pushing, wearing Mitch down. Sending Guy to deliver cryptic messages to Mitch that could oscillate between threatening and benign. Russell was trying to get what he believed he deserved.

We smoked some grass. Donna made peanut-butter sandwiches. I sat in the circle of shade cast by an oak. Nico was running around with one of the other kids, chins crusted with remnants of breakfast. He snapped a stick at a bag of trash, the garbage spilling everywhere—nobody noticed but me. Guy's dog was out in the meadow, the llamas high-stepping in agitation. I was stealing looks at Helen, who seemed, if anything, insistently happy, like the exchange with Russell fulfilled a comforting pattern.

The slap should have been more alarming. I wanted Russell to be kind, so he was. I wanted to be near Suzanne, so I believed the things that allowed me to stay there. I told myself there were things I didn't understand. I recycled the words I'd heard Russell speak before, fashioned them into an explanation. Sometimes he had to punish us in order to show his love. He hadn't wanted to do it, but he had to keep us moving forward, for the good of the group. It had hurt him, too.

Nico and the other kid had abandoned the trash pile, squatting in the grass with their heavy diapers sagging. They spoke rapidly to each other in serious Asiatic voices, with sober, rational inflection, like the conversation of two little sages. Breaking into sudden hysterical laughter.

It was late in the day. We drank the dirty wine they sold by the gallon in town, sediment staining our tongues, a nauseous heat. Mitch had gotten to his feet, ready to head home.

"Why don't you go with Mitch?" Russell suggested. Squeezing my hand in submerged code.

Had a look passed between him and Mitch? Or maybe I am imagining that I witnessed that exchange. The logistics of the day were shrouded in confusion, so that somehow it was dusk and Suzanne and I were driving Mitch back to his house, hurtling along the back roads of Marin in his car.

Mitch was sitting in the backseat, Suzanne driving. I was up front. I kept catching sight of Mitch in the mirror, lost in an aimless fog. Then he'd jolt back into himself, staring at us with wonderment. I didn't fully understand why we'd been chosen to take Mitch home. Information passed through selectively, so all I knew was that I got to be with Suzanne. All the windows open to the smell of summer earth and the secret flash of other driveways, other lives, along that narrow road in the shadow of Mount Tam. The loops of garden hoses, the pretty magnolia. Suzanne drove in the wrong lane sometimes, and we shrieked with happy and confused terror, though there was a flatness to my yelling: I did not believe anything bad could ever happen, not really.

Mitch changed into a white pajama-like suit, a souvenir from a three-week sojourn in Varanasi. He handed us each a glass—I caught the medical whiff of gin and something else, too, a tinge of bitterness. I drank it easily. I was almost pathologically stoned, and I kept swallowing, my nose getting stuffy. I laughed a little to myself. It seemed so odd to be in Mitch Lewis's house. Among his cluttered shrines and new-looking furniture.

"The Airplane lived here for a few months," he said. He blinked heavily. "With one of those dogs," he continued, staring around at his house. "The big white ones. What are they called? Newfoundlands? It tore up the lawn."

He didn't seem to care that we were ignoring him. He was out of it, glazing over with silence. Abruptly he got to his feet, putting a record on. Turning the volume up so loud I startled, but Suzanne laughed, urging him to make it louder. It was his own music, which embarrassed me. His heavy belly pressed against his long shirt, as flowing as a dress.

"You're fun girls," he said dimly. Watching Suzanne start to dance. Her dirty feet on the white carpet. She'd found chicken in the refrigerator and had torn off a piece with her fingers, chewing while she moved her hips.

"Kona chicken," Mitch remarked. "From Trader Vic's." The banality of this remark—Suzanne and I caught each other's eyes.

"What?" Mitch said. When we kept laughing, he did, too. "This is fun," he repeated over the music. He kept saying how much some actor he knew liked the song. "He really got it," he said. "Wouldn't stop playing it. Tuned-in guy."

It was new to me, that you could treat someone famous like they weren't that special, that you could see all the ways they were disappointing and regular or notice the way his kitchen smelled of trash that hadn't been taken out. The phantom squares on the wall where photographs had once hung, the gold records leaned against the baseboard, still wrapped in plastic. Suzanne acted like it was really only she and I that mattered, and this was all a little game we were playing with Mitch. He was the background to the larger story, which was our story, and we pitied him and felt grateful to him, at the same time, for how he sacrificed himself for our enjoyment.

Mitch had a little coke, and it was almost painful to watch him shake it out carefully onto a book about TM, staring at his own hands with a queer distance, like they didn't belong to him. He cut three lines, then peered at them. He fussed around until one was markedly bigger and snorted it quickly, breathing hard.

"Ahh," he said, leaning back, his throat raw and pricked with golden stubble. He held out the book to Suzanne, who danced over, sniffing up a line, and I did the last one.

The coke made me want to dance, so I did. Suzanne grabbing my hands, smiling at me. It was a strange moment: we were dancing for Mitch, but I was eaten up by her eyes, how she urged me on. She watched me move with pleasure.

Mitch was trying to talk, telling us some story about his girlfriend. How lonesome he'd been since she'd left for Marrakesh, on some tear about needing more space.

"Baloney," he kept saying. "Ah, baloney."

We were indulging him: I took my lead from Suzanne, who nodded when he spoke but rolled her eyes at me or loudly urged him to tell us more. He was talking about Linda that night, though her name meant nothing to me. I was barely listening: I'd picked up a small wooden box rattling with tiny silver balls and tipped it, trying to get the balls to drop into holes painted to look like the mouths of dragons.

Linda would be his ex-girlfriend by the time of the murders, only twenty-six, though that age seemed vague to me then, like a knock on a faraway door. Her son, Christopher, was five years old but had already been to ten countries, bundled along on his mother's travels like the pouch of her scarab jewelry. The ostrich-skin cowboy boots she stuffed with rolled-up magazines so they'd keep their shape. Linda was beautiful, though I'm sure her face would've grown bawdy or cheap. She slept in bed with her golden-haired little boy, like a teddy bear.

I was so lulled into feeling that the world had winnowed itself around Suzanne and me, that Mitch was just the comic fill—I didn't even consider other possibilities. I'd gone to the bathroom, used Mitch's strange black soap and peeked in his cabinet, loaded with bottles of Dilaudid. The enamel shine of the bathtub, the cut of bleach in the air so I could tell he had a cleaning lady.

I had just finished peeing when someone opened the bathroom door without knocking. I was startled, reflexively trying to cover myself. I saw the man sliver a glance toward my exposed legs before he ducked back into the hallway.

"Apologies," I heard him say from the other side of the door. A chain of stuffed marigold birds swung gently from where they hung by the sink.

"My deepest apologies," the man said. "I was looking for Mitch. Sorry to bother you."

I sensed him hesitate on the other side of the door, then tap the wood lightly before he walked away. I pulled up my shorts. The adrenaline that spread through me lessened but didn't disappear. It was probably just a friend of Mitch's. I was jumpy from the coke, but I wasn't frightened. Which made sense:

nobody thought until later that strangers might be anything but friends. Our love for one another boundless, the whole universe an extended crash pad.

I'd realize a few months after that this must have been Scotty Weschler. The caretaker who lived in the back house, a tiny white-paneled cabin with a hot plate and a space heater. The man who cleaned the hot tub filters and watered the lawn and checked that Mitch hadn't overdosed in the night. Prematurely balding, with wire glasses: Scotty had been a cadet at a military academy in Pennsylvania before dropping out, moving west. He never shook his cadet idealism: he wrote letters to his mother about the redwoods, the Pacific Ocean, using words like "majestic" and "grandeur."

He'd be the first. The one who tried to fight back, to run.

I wish I could squeeze more out of our brief encounter. To believe, when he opened the door, that I had felt a shiver of what was coming. But I'd made out nothing but the flash of a stranger, and I thought of it very little. I didn't even ask Suzanne who the man was.

The living room was empty when I came back. The music blaring, a cigarette leaching smoke in the ashtray. The glass door that led out to the bay was open.

I was surprised by the suddenness of the water when I went out on the porch, the wall of woolly lights: San Francisco in the fog.

No one was out on the bank. Then I heard, over the water, a distorted echo. And there they were, both of them, splashing in the waves, the water foaming around their legs. Mitch flapping around in his white outfit, now like soggy bedsheets, Suzanne in the dress she called her Br'er Rabbit dress. My heart lurched—I wanted to join them. But something held me in place. I kept standing on the stairs that led to the sand, smelling the sea-softened wood. Did I know what was coming? I watched Suzanne shed her dress, shrugging it off with drunken difficulty, and then he was on her. His head lowering to lick at her bare breast. Both of them unsteady in the water. I watched for longer than seemed right. I was buzzy and adrift by the time I turned my back and wandered into the house.

I turned the music down. Shut the refrigerator door, which Suzanne had left open. The picked-over carcass of the chicken. Kona chicken, as Mitch had insisted: the sight made me a little nauseous. The too-pink flesh emanating a chill. I would always be like this, I thought, the person who closed the refrigerator. The person who watched from the steps like a spook while Suzanne let Mitch do whatever he wanted. Jealousy started to oscillate in my gut. The strange gnaw when I imagined his fingers inside her, how she'd taste of salt water. Confusion, too—how quickly things had changed and I was the one on the outside again.

The chemical pleasure in my head had already faded, so all I recognized anymore was the lack of it. I wasn't tired, but I didn't want to sit on the couch, waiting for them to come inside. I found an unlocked bedroom that looked like a guest room: no clothes in the closet, a bed with slightly mussed sheets. They smelled like someone else, and there was a single gold earring on the nightstand. I thought of my own home, the weight and feel of my own blankets—then a sudden desire to sleep at Connie's house. Curled up against her back in our familiar, ritual arrangement, her sheets printed with chubby cartoon rainbows.

I lay in the bed, listening for the sound of Suzanne and Mitch in the other room. Like I was Suzanne's thick-necked boyfriend, the same ratchet of righteous anger. It wasn't aimed at her, not exactly—I hated Mitch with a fierceness that kept me wide-awake. I wanted him to know how she'd been laughing at him earlier, to know the exact degree of pity I had for him. How impotent my anger was, a surge with no place to land, and how familiar that was: my feelings strangled inside me, like little half-formed children, bitter and bristling.

...

I was almost certain, later, that this was the same bedroom that Linda and her little boy were sleeping in. Though I know there were other bedrooms, other possibilities. Linda and Mitch were broken up by the night of the murder, but they were still friends, Mitch delivering an oversize stuffed giraffe on Christopher's birthday the week before. Linda was only staying at Mitch's because her apartment in the Sunset was crawling with mold—she'd planned on being at his house for two nights. Then she and Christopher would stay in Woodside with her boyfriend, a man who owned a series of seafood restaurants.

After the murders, I had seen the man on a talk show: face red, pressing a handkerchief to his eyes. I wondered if his fingernails were manicured. He told the host he'd been planning to propose to Linda. Though who knows if that was true.

Around three in the morning, there was a knock on my door. It was Suzanne, stumbling inside without waiting for an answer. She was naked, bringing a gusty smell of brine and cigarette smoke.

"Hi," she said, pulling at my blankets.

I'd been half-asleep, lulled by the sameness of the dark ceiling, and she was like a creature from a dream, storming into the room, smelling as she did. The sheets getting damp when she crawled in beside me. I believed she had come for me. To be with me, a gesture of apology. But how quickly that thought disappeared when I took in her urgency, her stoned, glassy focus—I knew this was for him.

"Come on," Suzanne said, and laughed. Her face new in the strange blue light. "It's beautiful," she said, "you'll see. He's gentle."

Like that was the most you could hope for. I sat back, grabbing the covers.

"Mitch is a creep," I said. It was clear to me that we were in a stranger's house. The oversize, empty guest room, with its unsavory off-gassing of other bodies.

"Evie," she said. "Don't be like that."

Her nearness, the dart of her eyes in the dark. How easily she pressed her mouth to mine, then, edging her tongue past my lips. Running the tip along the ridges of my teeth, smiling into my mouth, and saying something I couldn't hear.

I could taste the cocaine drip in her mouth, the brackish sea. I went to kiss her again, but she had already drifted away, smiling like this was a game, like we'd done something funny and unreal. Playing lightly with my hair.

I was happy to twist the meanings, willfully misread the symbols. Doing what Suzanne asked seemed like the best gift I could give her, a way to unlock her own reciprocal feelings. And she was trapped, in her way, just like I was, but I never saw that, shifting easily in the directions she prompted for me. Like the wooden toy, clattering with the silver ball I'd tilted and urged into the painted holes, trying for the winning drop.

Mitch's room was big, and the tile floor was cold. The bed was on a raised platform, carved with Balinese figures. He grinned when he saw me behind Suzanne, showing a quick flash of teeth, and opened his arms to us, his bare chest foaming with hair. Suzanne went right to him, but I sat on the edge of the bed, hands folded in my lap. Mitch raised up on his elbows.

"No," he said, patting the mattress. "Here. Come here."

I scooted over to lie beside him. I could feel Suzanne's impatience, how she sidled to him like a dog.

"I don't want you yet," Mitch said to her. I couldn't see Suzanne's face, but I could imagine the swift hurt.

"Can you take these off?" Mitch tapped at my underwear with his hand.

I was ashamed: they were full-seated and childish, the elastic limp. I lowered them down my hips until they were around my knees.

"Oh God," Mitch said, sitting up. "Can you open your legs a little?"

I did. He crouched over me. I could feel his face close to my childish mound. His snout had the wet heat of an animal.

"I'm not going to touch you," Mitch said, and I

knew he was lying. "Jesus," he breathed. He gestured Suzanne over. Murmuring low, placing us like dolls. Announcing fussy asides to no one in particular. Suzanne looked to me like a stranger in that strange room, like the part of her I recognized had retreated.

He sucked my tongue into his mouth. I could stay still, mostly, while Mitch kissed me, and accept his probing tongue with a hollow distance, even his fingers inside me like something curious and without meaning. Mitch lifted himself and pushed inside me, groaning a little when it was difficult. He spit on his hand and rubbed me, then tried again, and how sudden it was, his jacking between my legs, and how I kept thinking to myself with some surprise and disbelief that it was actually happening, and then I felt Suzanne's hand snake over and grab mine.

Maybe Mitch nudged Suzanne in my direction, but I didn't see. When Suzanne kissed me again, I was lulled into thinking she was doing it for me, that this was our way to be together. That Mitch was just the background noise, the necessary excuse that allowed for her eager mouth, the curl of her fingers. I could smell myself and smell her, too. A sound deep in her throat that I believed was meant for me, as if her pleasure were at some pitch Mitch couldn't hear. She moved my hand to her breast, shivering when I touched the nipple. Closing her eyes like I had done something good.

Mitch rolled off me in order to watch. Kneading

the wet head of his dick, the mattress slanting toward his weight.

I kept kissing Suzanne, so different from kissing a man. Their forceful mash getting across the idea of a kiss, but not this articulation. I pretended Mitch wasn't there, though I could feel his gaze, his mouth as slack as the open trunk of a car. I was skittish when Suzanne tried to push apart my legs, but she smiled up at me, so I let her. Her tongue was tentative, first, then she used her fingers, too, and I was embarrassed at how wet I was, the noises I made. My mind fritzing from a pleasure so foreign I didn't know how to name it.

Mitch fucked us both after that, like he could correct our obvious preference for each other. Sweating hard, his eyes crimping with effort. The bed moving away from the wall.

When I woke up in the morning and saw the soiled twist of my underwear on Mitch's tile floor, such helpless embarrassment bubbled up in me that I almost cried.

Mitch drove us back to the ranch. I was silent, looking out the windows. The passing houses seemed long dormant, the fancy cars shrouded in their putty-colored covers. Suzanne was sitting in the front. She turned around to smile at me from time to time. An apology, I could tell, but I was stone-faced, my heart a tight fist. A grief that I didn't fully indulge.

I was shoring up the bad feelings, I suppose, like I could preempt sorrow with my bravado, with the careless way I thought about Suzanne to myself. And I'd had sex: so what? It was no big deal, another working of the human body. Like eating, something rote and accessible to everyone. All the pious and pastel urgings to wait, to make yourself into a present for your future husband: there was relief in the plainness of the actual act. I watched Suzanne from the backseat, watched her laugh at something Mitch said and roll down the window. Her hair lifting in the rush.

Mitch pulled up at the ranch.

"Later, girls," he said, raising a pink palm. Like he'd taken us for ice cream, some innocent outing, and was returning us to the cradle of our parents' house.

Suzanne had gone immediately in search of Russell, cleaving from me without a word. I realized later that she must have been giving Russell a report. Letting him know how Mitch had seemed, whether we'd made him happy enough to change his mind. At the time, I only noticed the abandonment.

I tried to busy myself, peeling garlic in the kitchen with Donna. Smashing cloves between the flat blade of a knife and the counter like she showed me. Donna slid the radio knob from one end of the dial to the other and back, getting varying degrees of static and alarming strains of Herb Alpert. She gave up finally and returned to jabbing at a mess of black dough.

"Roos put Vaseline in my hair," Donna said. She gave a shake and her hair barely moved. "It's gonna be real soft when I wash it."

I didn't answer. Donna could tell I was distracted and catted her eyes over at me.

"Did he show you the fountain in the backyard?" she said. "He got it from Rome. Mitch's place has high vibes," she went on, "all the ions, 'cause of the ocean."

I reddened, trying to concentrate on separating the garlic from its woody husks. The buzz of the radio suddenly seemed nasty, polluting, the announcer talking too fast. They'd all been there, I understood, to Mitch's strange house by the sea. I'd enacted some pattern, been defined, neatly, as a girl, providing a known value. There was something almost comforting about it, the clarity of purpose, even as it shamed me. I didn't understand that you could hope for more.

I hadn't seen the fountain. I did not say so.

Donna's eyes were bright.

"You know," she said, "Suzanne's parents are actually real rich. Propane or something. She never was homeless or anything, either." She was working the dough on the counter as she spoke. "Didn't end up in any hospital. Any of that shit she says. Just scratched herself up with a paper clip, on some freaky jag."

I was queasy from the stench of food scraps softening in the sink. I shrugged like I didn't much care either way.

Donna went on. "You don't believe me," she said. "But it's true. We were up in Mendocino. Crashing with an apple farmer. She'd done too much acid, just started working away at herself with that clip until we made her quit. She didn't even bleed, though."

When I didn't respond, Donna slammed the dough into a bowl. Punching it down. "Think whatever you want," she said.

Suzanne came into her bedroom later, while I was changing. I hunched myself protectively over my naked chest: Suzanne noticed and seemed ready to mock me but stopped herself. I saw the scars on her wrist but didn't indulge the uneasy questions—Donna was just jealous. Never mind Donna and her stiff Vaseline hair, shanky and foul as a muskrat's.

"Last night was a trip," Suzanne said.

I pulled away when she tried to sling her arm around me.

"Oh, come on, you were into it," she said. "I saw."

I made a sick face—she laughed. I occupied myself with tidying the sheets, as if the bed could ever be anything but a dank nest.

"Aw, it's fine," Suzanne said. "I got something to cheer you up."

I thought she was going to apologize. But then it occurred to me—she was going to kiss me again.

The dim room got airless. I almost felt it happen, an imperceptible lean—but Suzanne just hefted her bag onto the bed, the fringe pooling on the mattress. The bag was full of a strange weight. She gave me a triumphant look.

"Go on," she said. "Look inside."

Suzanne huffed at my stubbornness and opened it herself. I didn't understand what was inside, the odd metallic flash. The sharp corners.

"Take it out," Suzanne said, impatient.

It was a gold record framed in glass, much heavier than expected.

She nudged me. "We got him, huh?"

Her expectant look—was this meant to explain something? I stared at the name, engraved on a small plaque: Mitch Lewis. The **Sun King** album.

Suzanne started laughing.

"Man, you should see your face right now," she said. "Don't you know I'm on your side?"

The record glinted dully in the dark room, but even its pretty Egyptian gleam failed to stir me—it was just an artifact of that strange house, nothing so valuable. Already the weight was making my arms tired.

9

The clatter on the porch startled me, followed by the sound of my mother's dissolving laughter, Frank's heavy steps. I was in the living room, stretched out in my grandfather's chair and reading one of my mother's **McCall's.** Its pictures of genitally slick hams, wreathed with pineapple. Lauren Hutton lounging on a rocky cliff in her Bali brassieres. My mother and Frank were loud, coming into the living room, but stopped talking when they caught sight of me. Frank in his cowboy boots, my mother swallowing whatever she'd been saying.

"Sweetheart." Her eyes were filmy, her body swaying just enough so I knew she was drunk and trying to hide it, though her pink neck—exposed in a chiffon shirt—would have given it away.

"Hi," I said.

"Whatcha doing home, sweetheart?" My mother came over to wrap her arms around me, and I let her, despite the metallic smell of alcohol on her, the wilt of her perfume. "Is Connie sick?"

"Nah." I shrugged. Turning back to my magazine. The next page: a girl in a butter-yellow tunic, kneeling on a white box. An advertisement for Moon Drops.

"You're usually in and out so quick," she said.

"I just felt like being home," I said. "Isn't it my house, too?"

My mother smiled, smoothing my hair. "Such a pretty girl, aren't you? Of course it's your house. Isn't she a pretty girl?" she said, turning to Frank. "Such a pretty girl," she repeated to no one.

Frank smiled back but seemed restless. I hated that unwilling knowledge, how I'd started to notice each tiny shift of power and control, the feints and jabs. Why couldn't relationships be reciprocal, both people steadily accruing interest at the same rate? I snapped the magazine shut.

"Good night," I said. I didn't want to imagine what would happen later, Frank's hands in the chiffon. My mother aware enough to turn out the lights, eager for the forgiving dark.

These were the fantasies I goaded: that by leaving the ranch for a while, I could provoke Suzanne's sudden appearance, her demand that I return to her. The loneliness I could gorge myself on, like the saltines I ate by the sleeve, relishing the cut of sodium in my mouth. When I watched **Bewitched,** I had new irritation for Samantha. Her priggish nose, how she made a fool of her husband. The desperation of his doltish love turning him into the punch line. I paused one night to study the studio photo of my grandmother that hung in the hall, her shellacked cap of curls. She was pretty, awash in health. Only her eyes were sleepy, as if just woken from flowery dreams. The realization was bracing—we looked nothing alike.

I smoked a little bit of grass out the window, then fingered myself to tiredness, reading a comic book or a magazine, it didn't matter which. It was just the form of bodies, my brain let loose on them. I could look at an advertisement for a Dodge Charger, a smiling girl in a snow-white cowboy hat, and furiously project her into obscene positions. Her face slack and swollen, sucking and licking, her chin wet with saliva. I was supposed to understand the night with Mitch, be easy with things, but I had only my stiff and formal anger. That stupid gold record. I tried hard to mash up new meaning, like I'd missed some important sign, a weighted look Suzanne had given me behind Mitch's back. His goatish face, dripping sweat onto me so I had to turn my head.

...

The next morning I'd been pleased to find the kitchen empty, my mother taking a shower. I tipped sugar in my coffee, then settled at the table with a sleeve of saltines. I liked to crumble a saltine in my mouth, then flood the starchy mess with coffee. I was so absorbed in this ritual that Frank's sudden presence startled me. He scraped out the other chair, hitching it close as he sat down. I saw him take in the debris of saltines, inciting my vague shame. I was about to slither away, but he spoke before I could.

"Big plans for today?" he asked me.

Trying to pal around. I twisted the sleeve of crackers closed and wiped my hands of crumbs, suddenly fastidious. "Dunno," I said.

How quickly the veneer of patience drained away. "You just going to mope around the house?" he asked.

I shrugged; that's exactly what I'd do.

A muscle in his cheek jumped. "At least go outside," he said. "You stay in that room like you're locked in there."

Frank wasn't wearing his boots, just his blaring white socks. I swallowed a helpless snort; it was ridiculous to see a grown man's socked feet. He noticed my mouth twitch and got flustered.

"Everything's funny to you, huh?" he said. "Doing whatever you want. You think your mom doesn't notice what's going on?"

I stiffened but didn't look up. There were so many

things he could be talking about: the ranch, what I'd done with Russell. Mitch. The ways I thought about Suzanne.

"She got real confused the other day," Frank went on. "She's missing some money. Gone right from her purse."

I knew my cheeks had flushed, but I stayed quiet. Narrowing my eyes at the table.

"Give her a break," Frank said. "Hm? She's a nice lady."

"I'm not stealing." My voice was high and false.

"Borrowing, let's say. I'm not gonna tell. I get it. But you should stop. She loves you a lot, you know?"

No more noise from the shower, which meant my mother would appear soon. I tried to gauge whether Frank really wouldn't say anything—he was trying to be nice, I understood, not getting me in trouble. But I didn't want to be grateful. Imagine him trying to be fatherly with me.

"The town party is still happening," Frank said. "Today and tomorrow, too. Maybe you could go on down there, have some fun. I'm sure that would make your mother happy. You staying busy."

When my mother entered, toweling the ends of her hair, I immediately brightened, arranging my face like I was listening to Frank.

"Don't you think so, Jeanie?" Frank said, gazing at my mother.

"Think what?" she said.

"Shouldn't Evie go check out that carnival?" Frank said. "That centennial thing? Keep busy?"

My mother took up this pet notion like it was a flash of brilliance. "I don't know if it's the centennial, exactly—" she said.

"Well, town party," Frank broke in, "centennial, whatever it is."

"But it's a good idea," she said. "You'll have a great time."

I could feel Frank watching me.

"Yeah," I said, "sure."

"Nice to see you two having a good talk," my mother added shyly.

I made a face, collecting my mug and crackers, but my mother didn't notice: she had already bent to kiss Frank. Her robe falling open so I saw a triangle of shadowy, sun-spotted chest and had to look away.

The town was celebrating 110 years, after all, not 100, the awkward number setting the tone for the meager affair. To even call it a carnival seemed overly generous, though most of the town was there. There had been a box social in the park and a play about the town's founding in the high school amphitheater, the student council members sweating in theater department costumes. They'd closed the road to street traffic, so I found myself in a bobbing press of people, pushing and grabbing at the promise of leisure and fun. Husbands whose faces were tight with aggrieved duty, flanked by kids and wives who needed stuffed animals. Who needed pale, sour lemonade and hot dogs and grilled corn. All the proof of a good time. The river was already clotted with litter, the slow drift of popcorn bags and beer cans and paper fans.

My mother had been impressed by Frank's miraculous ability to get me to leave the house. Just as Frank wanted her to be. So she could imagine the neat way he'd slot into a father shape. I was having exactly as much fun as I'd expected to have. I ate a snow cone, the paper cup weakening until the syrup leaked out over my hands. I threw the rest away, but my hands scudded with the residue, even after I wiped them on my shorts.

I moved among the crowd, in and out of shade. I saw kids I knew, but they were the background fill from school, no one I had ever spent concentrated time with. Still, I incanted their first and last names helplessly in my head. Norm Morovich. Jim Schumacher. Farm kids, mostly, whose boots smelled of rot. Their soft-spoken answers in class, speaking only when specifically called upon, the humble ring of dirt I saw in the upturned cowboy hats on their desks. They were polite and virtuous, the trace of milk cows and clover fields and little sisters on them. Nothing at all like the ranch population, who would pity boys who still respected their father's authority or wiped their boots before entering their mother's kitchen. I wondered what Suzanne was doing—swimming in the creek, maybe, or lying around with Donna or Helen or maybe even Mitch, a thought that made me bite my lip, working a ruff of dry skin with my teeth.

I'd have to stay at the carnival only a little while longer and then I could go back home, Frank and my mother satisfied with my healthy dose of sociable activity. I tried to make my way toward the park, but it was packed—the parade had started, the pickup beds heavy with crepe-paper models of town hall. Bank employees and girls in Indian costumes waving from floats, the noise of the marching band violent and oppressive. I weaved out of the crowd, scuttling along the periphery. Sticking to the quieter side streets. The sound of the marching band grew louder, the parade winding down East Washington. The laughter I heard, pointed and performative, cut through my focus: I knew, before I looked up, that it was aimed at me.

It was Connie, Connie and May, a netted bag stretching from Connie's wrist. I could make out a can of orange soda and other groceries straining inside, the line of a swimsuit under Connie's shirt. Encoded within was their whole simple day—the boredom of the heat, the orange soda going flat. The bathing suits drying on the porch.

My first feeling was relief, like the familiarity of

turning into my own driveway. Then came an uneasiness, the clicking together of the facts. Connie was mad at me. We were not friends anymore. I watched Connie move past her initial surprise. May's bloodhound eyes squinted, eager for drama. Her braces thickening her mouth. Connie and May exchanged a few whispered words, then Connie edged forward.

"Hey," she said cautiously. "What's going on?"

I had expected anger, derision, but Connie was acting normal, even a little glad to see me. We hadn't spoken in almost a month. I looked at May's face for a clue, but it was insistently blank.

"Nothing much," I said. I should have been fortified by the last few weeks, the existence of the ranch lessening the stakes of our familiar dramas, and yet how quickly the old loyalties return, the pack animal push. I wanted them to like me.

"Us either," Connie said.

My sudden gratitude for Frank—it was good that I had come, good to be around people like Connie who were not complicated or confusing like Suzanne, but just a friend, someone I'd known beyond daily changes. How she and I had watched television until we got blinky headaches and popped pimples on each other's backs in the harsh light of the bathroom.

"Lame, huh?" I said, gesturing in the direction of the parade. "A hundred and ten years."

"There's a bunch of freaky people around." May sniffed, and I wondered if she was somehow implicating me. "By the river. They stunk."

"Yeah," Connie said, kinder. "The play was really stupid, too. Susan Thayer's dress was pretty much see-through. Everyone saw her underwear."

They shot each other a look. I was jealous of their shared memory, how they must have sat together in the audience, bored and restless in the sun.

"We might go swimming," Connie said. This statement seemed vaguely hilarious to both of them, and I joined in, tentative. Like I understood the joke.

"Um." Connie seemed to silently confirm something with May. "Do you want to come with us?"

I should have known that it wouldn't end well. That it was happening too easily, that my defection wouldn't be tolerated. "To swim?"

May stepped up, nodding. "Yeah, at the Meadow Club. My mom can drive us. You wanna come?"

The thought that I might go with them was such a ludicrous anachronism, as if an alternate universe were unfolding where Connie and I were still friends and May Lopes was inviting us to the Meadow Club to swim. You could get milkshakes there and grilled cheese sandwiches with lacy frills of burnt cheese. Simple tastes, food for children, everything paid for by signing your parent's name. I allowed myself to feel flattered, remembering an easy familiarity with Connie. Her house so known to me that I didn't even think about where each bowl went in the cabinet, each plastic cup, their rims eaten by the dishwasher. How nice that seemed, how uncomplicated, the cogent march of our friendship.

That was the moment May stepped toward me, pitching the can of orange soda forward: the soda inside hit my face at an angle, so it didn't douse me so much as dribble. Oh, I thought, my stomach dropping. Oh, of course. The parking lot tilted. The soda was tepid and I could smell the chemicals, the unsavory drip on the asphalt. May dropped the mostly empty can. It rolled a ways and then stopped. Her face was as shiny as a quarter, and she looked spooked by her own audacity. Connie was more uncertain, her face a flickering bulb, coming to full-watt attention when May rattled her bag like a warning bell.

The liquid had barely grazed me. It could have been worse, a real soaking instead of this meager attempt, but somehow I longed for the soaking. I wanted the event to be as big and ruthless as the way my humiliation felt.

"Have a fun summer," May trilled, linking arms with Connie.

And then they were walking away, their bags jostling and their sandals loud on the sidewalk. Connie turned to glance back at me, but I saw May tug her, hard. The bleed of surf music carried across the road from an open car window—I thought I saw Peter's friend Henry at the wheel, but maybe that was my imagination. Projecting a larger net of conspiracy onto my childish humiliation, as if that were an improvement.

...

I kept a lunatic calm on my face, afraid someone might be watching me, alert for signs of weakness. Though I'm sure it was obvious—a tightness in my features, a wounded insistence that I was fine, everything was fine, that it was just a misunderstanding, girlish high jinks between friends. **Ha ha ha,** like the laugh track on **Bewitched** that drained the look of horror on Darrin's marzipan face of any meaning.

It had only been two days without Suzanne, but already I had slipped back so easily into the dull stream of adolescent life—Connie and May's idiot dramas. My mother's cold hands, sudden on my neck, like she was trying to startle me into loving her. This awful carnival and my awful town. My anger at Suzanne was hard to access, an old sweater packed away and barely remembered. I could think of Russell slapping Helen and it surfaced as a little glitch at the back of certain thoughts, a memory of wariness. But there were always ways I made sense of things.

I was back at the ranch the next day.

I found Suzanne on her mattress, bent intently over a book. She never read, and it was odd to see her stilled in concentration. The cover was half-torn and had a futuristic pentagram on it, some blocky white type.

"What's that about?" I asked from the doorway.

Suzanne looked up, startled.

"Time," she said. "Space."

The sight of her brought flashes of the night with

Mitch, but they were unfocused, like a secondhand reflection. Suzanne didn't say anything about my absence. About Mitch. All she did was sigh and toss the book down. She lay back on the bed, studying her nails. Pinching the skin of her upper arm.

"Flabby," she declared, waiting for me to protest. As she knew I would.

I had a hard time sleeping that night, shifting on the mattress. I was returned to her. So alert to every cue in her face that I made myself sick, watching her, but happy, too.

"I'm glad I'm back," I whispered, the darkness allowing me to say the words.

Suzanne laughed a little, half-asleep. "But you can always go home."

"Maybe I never will."

"Free Evie."

"I'm serious. I don't ever want to leave."

"That's what all the kids say when summer camp is over."

I could see the whites of her eyes. Before I could say anything, she let out a sudden heavy breath.

"I'm too hot," she announced. Kicking off the sheet and turning from me.

10

The clock was loud in the Dutton house. The apples in the netted basket looked waxy and old. I could see photos on the mantel: the familiar faces of Teddy and his parents. His sister who'd married an IBM salesman. I kept waiting for the front door to open, for someone to identify our intrusion. The sun lit a folded paper star in the window so it went bright. Mrs. Dutton must have taken the time to tape that up, make her home nice.

Donna disappeared into another room, then reappeared. I heard the shudder of drawers, of things being moved.

I saw the Dutton house that day as if for the first time. Noticing that the living room was carpeted. That the rocking chair had a cross-stitched pillow on the seat that looked handmade. The wonky antennae of the television, a smell like stale potpourri in the air. Everything was waterlogged by the knowledge of the family's absence: the arrangement of papers on the low table, an uncapped aspirin bottle in the kitchen. None of it made any sense without the animation of the Duttons' presence, like the blurry glyphs of 3-D pictures before the glasses knocked them into clarity.

Donna kept reaching to bump something out of its place: little things. A blue glass of flowers moved four inches to the left. A penny loafer kicked away from its mate. Suzanne didn't touch anything, not at first. She was picking things up with her eyes, ingesting it all—the framed photos, the ceramic cowboy. The cowboy made Donna and Suzanne weaken into giggles, me smiling, too, but I did not get the joke; only a queer feeling in my stomach, the starkness of the hollow sunlight.

The three of us had gone on a garbage run earlier that afternoon, in a borrowed car, a Trans Am, possibly Mitch's. Suzanne turned up the radio, KFRC, K. O. Bayley on the big 610. Both Suzanne and Donna seemed energized, and so was I. Happy to be back among them. Suzanne pulled into a glass-fronted Safeway that was familiar to me, the cant of its green roof. Where my mother shopped occasionally.

"Grubby grub time," Donna announced, making herself laugh.

Donna hoisted herself over the lip of the dumpster, avid as an animal, knotting her skirt around her hips so she could dig deep. She got off on it, happy to muck around in the trash, the wet squelch.

On the way back to the ranch, Suzanne made an announcement.

"Time for a little trip," she said, loudly recruiting Donna into the plan.

I liked knowing she was thinking of me, trying to placate me. I noticed a new desperation around her after Mitch. I was more conscious of her attentions, of how to keep her eyes on me.

"Where?" I asked.

"You'll see," Suzanne said, catching Donna's gaze. "It's like our medicine, like a little cure for what ails you."

"Ooh," Donna said, leaning forward. She seemed to have understood immediately what Suzanne was talking about. "Yes, yes, yes."

"We need a house," Suzanne said. "That's the first thing. An empty house." She flashed a look at me. "Your mom's gone, right?"

I didn't know what they were going to do. But I recognized a tinge of alarm, even then, and had the sense to spare my own home. I shifted in the seat. "She's there all day."

Suzanne made a disappointed hum. But I was already thinking of another house that might be empty. And I offered it up to them, easily.

I gave Suzanne directions, watching the roads grow

more and more familiar. When Suzanne stopped the car and Donna got out and smeared mud on the first two numbers of the license plate, I only worried a little. I gathered an unfamiliar braveness, a sense of pushing past limitations, and tried to give myself up to the uncertainty. I was locked into my body in a way that was unfamiliar. It was the knowledge, perhaps, that I would do whatever Suzanne wanted me to do. That was a strange thought—that there was just this banal sense of being moved along the bright river of whatever was going to happen. That it could be as easy as this.

Suzanne was driving erratically, rolling through a stop sign and gazing away from the road for long stretches of time, caught in a private daydream. She turned onto my own road. The gates like a familiar string of beads, one following the other.

"There," I said, and Suzanne slowed the car.

The windows of the Dutton house were plain with curtains, the flagstone path cutting a line to the front door. No car in the carport, just a glisten of oil on the asphalt. Teddy's bike wasn't in the yard—he was gone, too. The house looked empty.

Suzanne parked the car down the road a little bit, mostly out of sight, while Donna went briskly to the side yard. I trailed Suzanne, but I was hanging back slightly, shuffling my sandals through the dirt.

Suzanne turned to me. "Are you coming or what?"

I laughed, but I'm sure she saw the effort it took. "I just don't understand what we're doing."

She cocked her head and smiled. "Do you really care?"

I was scared and couldn't say why. I mocked myself for letting my mind range furiously to the very worst thing. Whatever they were going to do—steal, probably. I didn't know.

"Hurry up," Suzanne said. She was getting annoyed, I could tell, though she was still smiling. "We can't just stand here."

Afternoon shadows were starting to slant through the trees. Donna reemerged from the wooden side gate. "The back door's open," she said. My stomach sank—there was no way to stop whatever was about to happen. And then there was Tiki, scrambling in our direction, barking in wretched alarm. Yips shook his whole body, his skinny shoulders twitching.

"Fuck," Suzanne muttered. Donna backed off, too.

The dog could have been enough of an excuse, I suppose, and we could've piled back into the car and gone back to the ranch. A part of me wanted that. But another part wanted to fulfill the sick momentum in my chest. The Dutton family seemed like perpetrators, too, just like Connie and May and my parents. All quarantined by their selfishness, their stupidity.

"Wait," I said. "He knows me."

I squatted, holding out my hand. Keeping my eyes on the dog. Tiki approached, sniffing my palm.

"Good Tiki," I said, petting him, scratching under his jaw, and then the barking stopped and we went inside.

I couldn't believe nothing happened. That no cop cars were whining after us. Even after shifting so easily into the Dutton domain, crossing the invisible boundaries. And why had we done that? Jarred the inviolate grid of a home for no reason? Just to prove we could? The calm mask of Suzanne's face as she touched the Duttons' things confused me, her odd remove, even as I fluoresced with a strange, unreadable thrill. Donna was looking over some treasure from the house, a bauble of milky ceramic. I peered closer and saw it was a little figure of a Dutch girl. How bizarre, the detritus of people's lives removed from their context. It made even things that were precious seem like junk.

The lurch in me made me think of an afternoon when I was younger, my father and I hunched over the shoreline at Clear Lake. My father squinting in the harshness of midday, the fish white of his thighs in his swimming shorts. How he pointed out a leech in the water, quivering and tight with blood. He was pleased, poking at the leech with a stick to make it move, but I was frightened. The inky leech caused some drag on my insides that I sensed again, there, in the Dutton house, Suzanne's eyes meeting mine across the living room.

"You like?" Suzanne said. Smiling a little. "Wild, right?"

Donna came out into the entryway. Her forearms shone with sticky juice, and she held a triangle of watermelon in her hand, the spongy pink of an organ.

"Greetings and salutations," she said, chewing wetly. There was an almost feral percolation emanating from Donna like a bad smell, her dress whose hem was ratty from being stepped on: how out of place she looked next to the polished coffee table, the tidy curtains. Drops of watermelon juice fell on the floor.

"There's more in the sink," she said. "It's real good."

Donna picked a black seed from her mouth with a delicate little pinch, then flicked it off into the corner of the room.

We were there only a half hour or so, though it seemed much longer. Snapping the TV on and off. Paging through the mail on the side table. I followed Suzanne up the stairs, wondering where Teddy was now, where his parents were. Was Teddy still waiting for me to bring him his drugs? Tiki banged around in the hallway. I realized with a start that I'd known the Dutton family my whole life. Under the hanging photographs, I could make out the line of wallpaper, just starting to peel, the tiny pink flowers. The smear of fingerprints.

I would often think of the house. How innocent

I told myself it was: harmless fun. I was reckless, wanting to win back Suzanne's attention, to feel like we were arranged again against the world. We were ripping a tiny seam in the life of the Dutton family, just so they'd see themselves differently, even if for a moment. So they'd notice a slight disturbance, try to remember when they'd moved their shoes or put their clock in the drawer. That could only be good, I told myself, the forced perspective. We were doing them a favor.

Donna was in the parents' bedroom, a long silk slip pulled over her dress.

"I'll need the Rolls at seven," she said, swishing the watery fabric, the color of champagne.

Suzanne snorted. I could see a cut-glass bottle of perfume tipped on the nightstand and the golden tubes of lipstick like shell casings in the carpet. Suzanne was already sifting through the bureau, stuffing her hand inside the flesh-tone nylons, creating obscene bulges. The brassieres were heavy and medical looking, stiff with wire. I lifted one of the lipsticks and uncapped it, smelling the talcum scent of the orangy red.

"Oh, yeah," Donna said, seeing me. She grabbed a lipstick, too, and made a cartoonish pucker, pretending to apply it. "We should leave a little message," she said. Looking around.

"On the walls," Suzanne said. The idea excited her, I could tell.

I wanted to protest: leaving a mark seemed almost violent. Mrs. Dutton would have to scrub the wall clean, though it would probably always have a phantom nap, the receipt of all the scrubbing. But I stayed quiet.

"A picture?" Donna said.

"Do the heart," Suzanne added, coming over. "I'll do it."

I had a startling vision of Suzanne then. The desperation that showed through, the sudden sense of a dark space yawning in her. I didn't think of what that dark space might be capable of, only a doubling of my desire to be near it.

Suzanne took the lipstick from Donna but hadn't yet pressed the tip to the ivory wall when we heard a noise in the driveway.

"Shit," Suzanne said.

Donna's eyebrows were raised in mild curiosity: What would happen next?

The front door opened. I tasted my own stale mouth, the rancid announcement of fear. Suzanne seemed scared, too, but her fear was distant and amused, like this was a game of sardines and we were just hiding until the others found us. I knew it was Mrs. Dutton when I heard high heels.

"Teddy?" she called. "You home?"

They'd parked the ranch car down the road, but

still: I'm sure Mrs. Dutton took note of the unfamiliar car. Maybe she thought it was a friend of Teddy's, some older neighborhood pal. Donna was giggling, her hand pressed over her mouth. Eyes bulged in mirth. Suzanne made an exaggerated shushing face. My pulse was loud in my ears. Tiki clattered through the rooms downstairs and I heard Mrs. Dutton cooing to him, the heaving sighs he made in response.

"Hello?" she called.

The wake of silence that followed seemed obviously uneasy. She'd come upstairs soon enough, and then what?

"Come on," Suzanne whispered. "Let's sneak out the back."

Donna was laughing silently. "Shit," she said, "shit."

Suzanne dropped the lipstick on the bureau, but Donna kept the slip on, hitching the straps.

"You go first," she said to Suzanne.

There was no way out but to pass Mrs. Dutton in the kitchen.

She was probably wondering at the pink mess of watermelon in the sink, the sticky patches on the floor. Maybe just starting to pick up the disturbance in the air, the itch of strangers in the house. A nervous hand fluttering at her throat, a sudden wish for her husband at her side.

Suzanne took off down the stairs, Donna and I

hustling behind. The racket of our footsteps as we plowed past Mrs. Dutton, barreling at full speed through the kitchen. Donna and Suzanne were laughing their heads off, Mrs. Dutton shrieking in fright. Tiki came barking after us, quick and hectic, his nails skittering on the floor. Mrs. Dutton backed up, nakedly afraid.

"Hey," she said, "stop," but her voice wavered.

She bumped against a stool and lost her balance, sitting down hard on the tile. I looked back as we banged past—there was Mrs. Dutton splayed on the floor. Recognition tightened her face.

"I see you," she called from the floor, struggling to right herself, her breath going wild. "I see you, Evie Boyd."

PART THREE

JULIAN RETURNED FROM HUMBOLDT with a friend who wanted a ride to L.A. The friend's name was Zav. It seemed vaguely Rastafarian, how he pronounced it, though Zav was fishy white with a bog of orange hair held back by a woman's elastic. He was much older than Julian, maybe thirty-five, but dressed like an adolescent: the same too-long cargo shorts, the T-shirt worn to a pulp. He walked around Dan's house with an appraising squint, picking up a figurine of an ox, carved from bone or ivory, then putting it down. He peered at a photo of Julian in his mother's arms on the beach, then replaced the frame on the shelf, chuckling to himself.

"It's cool if he stays here tonight, right?" Julian asked. As if I were the den mother.

"It's your house."

Zav came over to shake my hand. "Thanks," he said, pumping away, "that's real decent of you."

Sasha and Zav seemed to know each other, and soon all three were talking about a gloomy bar near Humboldt owned by a gray-haired grower. Julian had his arm around Sasha with the adult air of a man returning from the mines. It was hard to imagine him harming a dog, or harming anyone, Sasha so obviously pleased to be near him. She'd been girlish and veiled with me all day, no hint of our conversation the night before. Zav said something that made her laugh, a pretty, subdued laugh. Half covering her mouth, like she didn't want to expose her teeth.

I'd planned to walk to town for dinner, leave them alone, but Julian noticed me heading for the door.

"Hey, hey, hey," he said.

They all turned to look at me.

"I'm gonna go into town for a bit," I said.

"You should eat with us," Julian said. Sasha nodded, scooting into his side. Giving me the sloppy half attention of someone in the orbit of her beloved.

"We got a bunch of food," she said.

I made the usual smiling excuses, but finally I took off my jacket. Already getting used to attention.

...

They'd stopped for groceries on the way back from Humboldt: a giant frozen pizza, some discount ground beef in a Styrofoam tray.

"A feast," Zav said. "You've got your protein, your calcium." He pulled a pill bottle from his pocket. "Your vegetables."

He started rolling a joint on the table, a process that involved multiple papers and much fussing over the construction. Zav eyed his work from a distance, then pinched a little more from the pill bottle, the room marinating in the stench of damp weed.

Julian was cooking the beef on the stove, the meat losing its sheen. He poked at the crude patties with a butter knife, prodding and sniffing. Dorm-room cookery. Sasha slid the pizza in the oven, balling up the plastic wrap. Setting out paper towels at each chair, a suburban memory of chores, of setting the table for dinner. Zav drank a beer and watched Sasha with amused contempt. He hadn't lit the joint yet, though he twirled it in his fingers with obvious pleasure.

I listened while he and Julian talked about drugs with the intensity of professionals, exchanging stats like bond traders. Greenhouse yield vs. sun-grown. Comparing THC levels in varying strains. This was nothing like the hobby drugs of my youth, pot grown alongside tomato plants, passed around in mason jars. You could pick out seeds from a bud and plant them yourself, if you felt like it. Trade a lid for enough gas to get to the city. It was strange to hear drugs flattened to a matter of numbers, a knowable commodity instead of a mystic portal. Maybe Zav and Julian's way was better, cutting out all the woozy idealism.

"Fuck," Julian said. The kitchen smelled of ashes and burning starch. "Damn, damn, damn." He opened the oven and pulled the pizza out with his bare hands, swearing as he tossed it on the counter. It was black and smoky.

"Man," Zav said, "that was the good kind, too. Expensive."

Sasha was frantic. Hurrying over to consult the back of the pizza box. "Preheat to four fifty," she droned. "I did that. I don't understand."

"What time did you put it in?" Zav asked.

Sasha's eyes moved to the clock.

"The clock's frozen, idiot," Julian said. He grabbed the box and stuffed it in the garbage. Sasha looked like she might cry. "Whatever," he said with disgust. Picking at the burnt shell of cheese, then rubbing his fingers clean. I thought of the professor's dog. The poor animal, limping in circles. Vascular system slushy with poison. All the other things Sasha had probably not told me.

"I can make something else," I said. "There's some pasta in the cabinet."

I tried to catch Sasha's eye. Willing some combination of warning and sympathy to pass from me to her. But Sasha was unreachable, stung by her failure.

The room got quiet. Zav fussing the joint between his fingers, waiting to see what would happen.

"There's a lot of beef, I guess," Julian said finally, his anger slipping from sight. "No big thing."

He rubbed Sasha's back, roughly, I thought, though the movement seemed to comfort her, returning her to the world. When he kissed her, she closed her eyes.

We drank a bottle of Dan's wine at dinner, the sediment settling in the cracks of Julian's teeth. Beer after that. Alcohol cut the fat on our breath. I didn't know what time it was. The windows black, the squeeze of wind through the eaves. Sasha was corralling wet pieces of the wine label into a meticulous pile. I could feel her glance at me from time to time, Julian's hand working the back of her neck. He and Zav maintained a constant patter all through dinner, Sasha and I fading into a silence familiar from adolescence: the effort to break through Zav and Julian's alliance wasn't worth the return. It was simpler to watch them, to watch Sasha, who acted like just sitting there was enough.

"'Cause you're a good guy," Zav kept saying. "You're a good guy, Julian, and that's why I don't make you pay up front with me. You know I have to do that with McGinley, Sam, all those retards."

They were drunk, the three of them, and maybe I was, too, the ceiling drab with expired smoke. We'd shared a burly joint, a sexual droop descending on

Zav. A pleased, overcome squint. Sasha had drawn further into herself, though she'd unzipped her sweatshirt, her chest sunless and crossed with faint blue veins. Her eye makeup was heavier than it had been: I didn't know when she'd put more on.

I got to my feet when we finished eating. "I've got to do a few things," I said.

They made halfhearted efforts to get me to stay, but I waved them off. I closed the door to the bedroom, though bits of their conversation slipped through.

"I respect you," Julian was saying to Zav, "I always have, man, ever since Scarlet was like, You have to meet this guy." Performing an extravagant admiration, the stoned person's tendency toward optimistic summary.

Zav responded, resuming their practiced volley. I could hear Sasha's silence.

When I passed through later, nothing had really changed. Sasha was still listening to their conversation like she'd be tested someday. Julian's and Zav's intoxication had passed into a strenuous state, their hairlines wet with sweat.

"Are we being too loud?" Julian asked. That weird politeness again, how easily it clicked in.

"Not at all," I said. "Just getting some water."

"Sit with us," Zav said, studying me. "Talk."

"That's okay."

"Come on, Evie," Julian said. The odd intimacy of my name in his mouth surprised me.

The table was stamped with rings from the bottles, the litter of dinner. I started to clear the dishes.

"You don't have to do that," Julian said, scooting back so I could reach his plate.

"You cooked," I said.

Sasha made a peep of thanks when I added her plate to the stack. Zav's phone lit up, shivering across the surface of the table. Someone was calling: a blurry photograph of a woman in underwear flashed on the screen.

"Is that Lexi?" Julian asked.

Zav nodded, ignoring the call.

A look passed between Julian and Zav: I didn't want to notice it. Zav belched. They both laughed. I could smell the memory of chewed meat.

"Benny is doing computer shit now," Zav said, "you know that?"

Julian hit the table. "No fucking way."

I walked the dishes to the sink, gathering the balled paper towels from the counter. Sweeping crumbs into my hand.

"He's fat as fuck," Zav said, "it's hilarious."

"Is Benny the guy from your high school?" Sasha asked.

Julian nodded. I let the sink fill with water. Watching Julian swivel his body to mirror Sasha's, knocking his knees into hers. He kissed her on the temple.

"You guys are too fucking much," Zav said.

His tone had a tricky bite. I sank the dishes in the water. A scummy network of grease formed on the surface.

"I just don't get it," Zav went on, addressing Sasha, "why you stay with Julian. You're too hot for him."

Sasha giggled, though I glanced back and saw her labor to calculate a response.

"I mean, she's a babe," Zav said to Julian, "am I right?"

Julian smiled what I thought of as the smile of an only son, someone who believed he would always get what he wanted. He probably always had. The three of them were lit like a scene from a movie I was too old to watch.

"But Sasha and I know each other, don't we?" Zav smiled at her. "I like Sasha."

Sasha held a basic smile on her face, her fingers tidying the pile of torn label.

"She doesn't like her tits," Julian said, pulsing the back of her neck, "but I tell her they're nice."

"Sasha!" Zav affected upset. "You have great tits."

I flushed, hurrying to finish the dishes.

"Yeah," Julian said, his hand still on her neck. "Zav would tell you if you didn't."

"I always tell the truth," Zav said.

"He does," Julian said. "That's true."

"Show me," Zav said.

"They're too small," Sasha said. Her mouth was tight like she was making fun of herself, and she shifted in her seat.

"They'll never sag, so that's good," Julian said. Tickling her shoulder. "Let Zav see."

Sasha's face reddened.

"Do it, babe," Julian said, a harshness in his voice making me glance over. I caught Sasha's eye—I told myself the look in her face was pleading.

"Come on, you guys," I said.

The boys turned with amused surprise. Though I think they were tracking where I was all along. That my presence was a part of the game.

"What?" Julian said, his face snapping into innocence.

"Just cool it," I told him.

"Oh, it's fine," Sasha said. Laughing a little, her eyes on Julian.

"What exactly are we doing?" Julian said. "What exactly should we 'cool'?"

He and Zav snorted—how quickly all the old feelings came back, the humiliating interior fumble. I crossed my arms, looking to Sasha. "You're bothering her."

"Sasha's fine," Julian said. He tucked a strand of her hair behind her ear—she smiled faintly and with effort. "Besides," he went on, "are you really someone who should be lecturing us?"

My heart tightened.

"Didn't you, like, kill someone?" Julian said.

Zav sucked his teeth, then let loose a nervous laugh.

My voice sounded strangled. "Of course not."

"But you knew what they were going to do," Julian said. Grinning with the thrill of capture. "You were there with Russell Hadrick and shit."

"Hadrick?" Zav said. "Are you shitting me?"

I tried to rein in the hysterical lean coming into my voice. "I was barely around."

Julian shrugged. "That's not what it sounded like."

"You don't really believe that." But there was no entry point in any of their faces.

"Sasha said you told her so," Julian went on. "Like you could have done it, too."

I inhaled sharply. The pathetic betrayal: Sasha had told Julian everything I'd said.

"So show us," Zav said, turning back to Sasha. I was already invisible again. "Show us the famous tits."

"You don't have to," I said to her.

Sasha flicked her eyes in my direction. "It isn't a big deal or anything," she said, her tone dripping with cool, obvious disdain. She plucked her neckline away from her chest and looked pensively down her shirt.

"See?" Julian said, smiling hard at me. "Listen to Sasha."

I had gone to one of Julian's recitals when Dan and I were still close. Julian must have been nine years old or so. He was good at the cello, I remembered, his tiny arms going about their mournful adult work.

His nostrils rimed with snot, the instrument in careful balance. It didn't seem possible that the boy who had called forth those sounds of longing and beauty was the same almost-man who watched Sasha now, a cold varnish on his eyes.

She pulled her shirt down, her face flushed but mostly dreamy. The impatient, professional tug she gave when the neckline caught on her bra. Then both pale breasts were exposed, her skin marked by the line of her bra. Zav exclaimed approvingly. Reaching to thumb a rosy nipple while Julian looked on.

I had long outlived whatever usefulness I had here.

1969

11

I got caught; of course I did.

Mrs. Dutton on her kitchen floor, calling my name like a right answer. And I hesitated for just a moment—a stunned, bovine reaction to my own name, the knowledge that I should help the fallen Mrs. Dutton—but Suzanne and Donna were far ahead, and by the time I jarred back into that realization, they had almost disappeared. Suzanne turned back just long enough to see Mrs. Dutton clamp a trembling hand on my arm.

My mother's pained and baffled declarations: I was a failure. I was pathological. She wore the air of crisis like a flattering new coat, the stream of her anger performed for an invisible jury. She wanted to know who had broken into the Dutton house with me.

"Judy saw two girls with you," she said. "Maybe three. Who were they?"

"Nobody." I tended my rigid silence like a suitor, full of honorable feelings. Before she and Donna disappeared, I tried to flash Suzanne a message: I would take responsibility. She didn't have to worry. I understood why they'd left me behind. "It was just me," I said.

Anger made her words garbled. "You can't stay in this house and spout lies."

I could see how rattled she was by this confusing new situation. Her daughter had never been a problem before, had always zipped along without resistance, as tidy and self-contained as those fish that clean their own tanks. And why would she bother to expect otherwise or even prepare herself for the possibility?

"You told me you were going to Connie's all summer," my mother said. Almost shouting. "You said it so many times. Right to my face. And guess what? I called Arthur. He says you haven't been there in months. Almost two months."

My mother looked like an animal then, her face made strange with rage, a gaspy run of tears.

"You're a liar. You lied about that. You're lying about this, too." Her hands were clenched hard. She kept lifting them, then dropping them at her sides.

"I was seeing friends," I snapped. "I have other friends besides Connie."

"Other friends. Sure. You were out screwing some boyfriend, God knows what. Nasty little liar." She was barely looking at me, her words as compulsive and fevered as the muttered obscenities of a pervert. "Maybe I should take you down to the juvenile detention center. Is that what you want? It's clear to me I just can't control you anymore. I'll let them have you. See if they can straighten you out."

I wrenched away, but even in the hallway, even with my door closed, I could still hear my mother at her bitter chant.

Frank was called in as reinforcement: I watched from the bed as he took my bedroom door off its hinges. He was careful and quiet, though it took him a while, and he eased the door out of the frame as if it were made of glass instead of cheapo hollow-core. He placed it against the wall gently. Then hovered for a moment in the now empty doorway. Rattling the screws in his hands like dice.

"Sorry about this," he said, like he was just the hired help, the maintenance man carrying out my mother's wishes.

I didn't want to have to notice the actual kindness in his eyes, how immediately it drained my hateful narration of Frank of any real heat. I could picture him in Mexico for the first time, slightly sunburned so the hair on his arm turned platinum. Sipping a lemon soda while overseeing his gold mine—I pictured a cave whose interior was cobblestoned in stony growths of gold.

I kept expecting Frank to tell my mother about the stolen money. Pile on more problems to the list. But he didn't. Maybe he'd seen that she was already angry enough. Frank kept up a silent vigil at the table during her many phone calls with my father while I listened from the hallway. Her high-pitched complaints, all her questions squeezed to a panicked register. What kind of person breaks into a neighbor's house? A family I'd known my whole life?

"For no reason," she added shrilly. A pause. "You think I haven't asked her? You think I haven't tried?"

Silence.

"Oh, sure, right, I bet. You want to try?"

And so I was sent to Palo Alto.

I spent two weeks at my father's apartment. Across from a Denny's, the Portofino Apartments as blocky and empty as my mother's house was sprawling and dense. Tamar and my father had moved into the biggest unit, and everywhere were the still lifes of adulthood she had so obviously arranged: a bowl of waxed fruit on the counter, the bar cart with its unopened bottles of liquor. The carpet that held the bland tracks of the vacuum.

Suzanne would forget me, I thought, the ranch would hurtle on without me and I'd have nothing. My sense of persecution gobbled up and grew fat off these worries. Suzanne was like a soldier's hometown sweetheart, made gauzy and perfect by distance. But maybe part of me was relieved. To take some time away. The Dutton house had spooked me, the blank cast I'd seen in Suzanne's face. These were little bites, little inward shifts and discomforts, but even so, they were there.

What had I expected, living with my father and Tamar? That my father would try to sleuth out the source of my behavior? That he would punish me, act like a father? He seemed to feel punishment was a right he'd relinquished and treated me with the courtly politeness you'd extend to an aging parent.

He startled when he first saw me—it had been over two months. He seemed to remember that he should hug me and made a lurching step in my direction. I noticed a new bunching at his ears, and his cowboy shirt was one I had never seen before. I knew I looked different, too. My hair was longer and wild at the edges, like Suzanne's. My ranch dress was so worn I could hook my thumb through the sleeve. My father made a move to help me with my bag, but I'd already hefted it into the backseat before he reached me.

"Thanks, though," I said, trying to smile.

His hands spread at his sides, and when he smiled back, it was with the helpless apology of a foreigner who needed directions repeated. My brain, to him, was a mysterious magic trick that he could only wonder at. Never bothering to puzzle out the hidden compartment. As we took our seats, I could sense that he was gathering himself to invoke the parental script.

"I don't have to lock you in your room, do I?" he said. His halting laugh. "No breaking in to anyone's house?"

When I nodded, he visibly relaxed. Like he'd gotten something out of the way.

"It's a good time for you to visit," he went on, as if this were all voluntary. "Now that we're settled. Tamar's real particular about the furniture and stuff." He started the ignition, already beyond any mention of trouble. "She went all the way to the flea market in Half Moon Bay to get this bar cart."

There was a brief moment I wanted to reach for him across the seat, to draw a line from myself to the man who was my father, but the moment passed.

"You can pick the station," he offered, seeming as shy to me as a boy at a dance.

The first few days, all three of us had been nervous. I got up early to make the bed in the guest room, trying to heft the decorative pillows back into completion. My life was limited to my drawstring purse and my duffel of clothes, an existence I tried to keep as neat and invisible as possible. Like camping, I thought, like a little adventure in self-reliance. The first night, my father brought home a cardboard tub of ice cream, striated with chocolate, and scooped free heroic amounts. Tamar and I just picked at ours, but my father made a point of eating another bowl. He kept glancing up, as if we could confirm his own pleasure. His women and his ice cream.

Tamar was the surprise. Tamar in her terry shorts and shirt from a college I had never heard of. Who waxed her legs in the bathroom with a complicated device that filled the apartment with the humidity of camphor. Her attendant unguents and hair oils, the fingernails whose lunar surfaces she studied for signs of nutritional deficiencies.

At first, she seemed unhappy with my presence. The awkward hug she offered, like she was grimly accepting the task of being my new mother. And I was disappointed, too. She was just a girl, not the exotic woman I'd once imagined—everything I'd thought was special about her was actually just proof of what Russell would call a straight world trip. Tamar did what she was supposed to. Worked for my father, wore her little suit. Aching to be someone's wife.

But then her formality quickly melted away, the veil of adulthood she wore as temporarily as a costume. She let me rummage through the quilted pouch that held her makeup, her blowsy perfume bottles, watching with the pride of a true collector. She pushed a blouse of hers, with bell sleeves and pearl buttons, onto me.

"It's just not my style anymore." She shrugged, picking at a loose thread. "But it'll look good on you, I know. Elizabethan."

And it did look good. Tamar knew those things. She knew the calorie count of most foods, which she recited in sarcastic tones, like she was making fun of her own knowledge. She cooked vegetable vindaloo. Pots of lentils coated with a yellow sauce that gave off an unfamiliar brightness. The roll of powdery antacids my father swallowed like candy. Tamar held out her cheek for my father to kiss but swatted him away when he tried to hold her hand.

"You're all sweaty," she said. When my father saw that I had noticed, he laughed a little but seemed embarrassed.

My father was amused at our collusion. But it sometimes shook out so we were laughing at him. Once Tamar and I were talking about Spanky and Our Gang, and he chimed in. Like the Little Rascals, he figured. Tamar and I looked at each other.

"It's a band," she said. "You know, that rock-and-roll music the kids like." And my father's confused, orphaned face set us off again.

They had a fancy turntable that Tamar often spoke of moving to another corner or room for varying acoustic or aesthetic reasons. She constantly mentioned future plans for oak flooring and crown moldings and even different dish towels, though the planning itself seemed to satisfy. The music she played was more slick than the ranch racket. Jane Birkin and her froggy old-man husband, Serge.

"She's pretty," I said, studying the record cover. And she was, tan as a nut with a delicate face, those rabbit teeth. Serge was disgusting. His songs about Sleeping Beauty, a girl who seemed most desirable because her eyes were always closed. Why would Jane love Serge? Tamar loved my father, the girls loved Russell. These men who were nothing like the boys I'd been told I would like. Boys with hairless chests and mushy features, the flocking of blemishes along their shoulders. I didn't want to think of Mitch because it made me think of Suzanne—that night had happened somewhere else, in a little dollhouse in Tiburon with a tiny pool and a tiny green lawn. A dollhouse I could look onto from above, lifting the roof to see the rooms segmented like chambers of the heart. The bed the size of a matchbox.

Tamar was different from Suzanne in a way that was easier. She was not complicated. She didn't track my attention so closely, didn't prompt me to shore up her declarations. When she wanted me to move over, she said so. I relaxed, which was unfamiliar. Even so, I missed Suzanne—Suzanne, who I remembered like dreams of opening a door on a forgotten room. Tamar was sweet and kind, but the world she moved around in seemed like a television set: limited and straightforward and mundane, with the notations and structures of normality. Breakfast, lunch, and dinner. There wasn't a frightening gap between the life she was living and the way she thought about that life, a dark ravine I often sensed in Suzanne, and maybe in my own self as well. Neither of us could fully participate in our days, though later Suzanne would participate in a way she could never take back. I mean that we didn't quite believe it was enough, what we were offered, and Tamar seemed to accept the world happily, as an end point. Her planning wasn't actually about making anything different—she was just rearranging the same known quantities, puzzling out a new order like life was an extended seating chart.

Tamar made dinner while we waited for my father. She looked younger than usual—her face washed with the cleanser she'd explained had actual milk proteins in it, to prevent wrinkles. Her hair wet and darkening the shoulders of the big T-shirt she wore, her lace-edged cotton shorts. She belonged in a dorm room somewhere, eating popcorn and drinking beer.

"Hand me a bowl?"

I did, and Tamar set aside a portion of lentils. "Without spices." She rolled her eyes. "For the tender heart's stomach."

I had a bitter flash of my mother doing that for my father: little consolations, little adjustments, making the world mirror my father's wants. Buying him ten pairs of the same socks so he never mismatched.

"It's almost like he's a kid sometimes, you know?" Tamar said, pinching out a measure of turmeric. "I left him for a weekend, and there was nothing to eat when I came back but beef jerky and an onion. He'd die if he had to take care of himself." She looked at me. "But I probably shouldn't tell you this, huh?"

Tamar wasn't being mean, but it surprised me—her ease in dismantling my father. It hadn't occurred to me before, not really, that he could be a figure of fun, someone who could make mistakes or act like a child or stumble helplessly around the world, needing direction.

Nothing terrible happened between me and my father. There was not a singular moment I could look back on, no shouting fight or slammed door. It was just the sense I got, a sense that seeped over everything until it seemed obvious, that he was just a normal man. Like any other. That he worried what other people thought of him, his eyes scatting to the mirror by the door. How he was still trying to teach himself French from a tape and I heard him repeating words to himself under his breath. The way his belly, which was bigger than I remembered, sometimes showed through the gap in his shirts. Exposing segments of skin, pink as a newborn's.

"And I love your father," Tamar said. Her words were careful, like she was being archived. "I do. He asked me to dinner six times before I said yes, but he was so nice about it. Like he knew I would say yes even before I did."

She seemed to catch herself—both of us were thinking it. My father had been living at home. Sleeping in bed with my mother. Tamar flinched, obviously waiting for me to say as much, but I couldn't muster any anger. That was the strange thing—I didn't hate my father. He had wanted something. Like I wanted Suzanne. Or my mother wanted Frank. You wanted things and you couldn't help it, because there was only your life, only yourself to wake up with, and how could you ever tell yourself what you wanted was wrong?

Tamar and I lay on the carpet, knees bent, heads angled toward the turntable. My mouth was still buzzing from the tartness of the orange juice we'd walked four blocks to buy from a stand. The wood heels of my sandals slapping the sidewalk, Tamar chatting happily in the warm summer dark.

My father came in and smiled, but I could tell he was annoyed by the music, the way it skittered on purpose. "Can you turn that down?" he asked.

"Come on," Tamar said. "It's not that loud."

"Yeah," I echoed, thrilled by the unfamiliarity of an ally.

"See?" Tamar said. "Listen to your daughter." She reached blindly to pat at my shoulder. My father left without saying anything, then returned a minute later and lifted the needle, the room abruptly silent.

"Hey!" Tamar said, sitting up, but he was already stalking away and I heard the shower start in the bathroom. "Fuck you," Tamar muttered. She got to her feet, the backs of her legs printed with the nub of the carpet. Glancing at me. "Sorry," she said absently.

I heard her talking in low tones in the kitchen. She was on the phone, and I watched her fingers piercing the loops of the cord, over and over. Tamar laughed, covering her mouth as she did, cupping the receiver close. I had the uncomfortable certainty that she was laughing at my father.

I don't know when I understood that Tamar would leave him. Not right away, but soon. Her mind was already somewhere else, writing a more interesting life for herself, one where my father and I would be the scenery to an anecdote. A detour from a larger, more correct journey. The redecoration of her own story. And who would my father have then, to make money for, to bring dessert home to? I imagined him opening the door on the empty apartment after a long day at work. How the rooms would be as he'd left them, undisturbed by another person's living. And how there would be a moment, before he flicked on the light, when he might imagine a different life revealed within the darkness, something besides the lonely borders of the couch, the cushions still holding the shape of his own sleepy body.

...

A lot of young people ran away: you could do it back then just because you were bored. You didn't even need a tragedy. Deciding to go back to the ranch wasn't difficult. My other house wasn't an option anymore, the ludicrous possibility of my mother dragging me to the police station. And what was there at my father's? Tamar, the way she insisted on my youthful alliance. The chocolate pudding after dinner, cold from the refrigerator, like our daily allotment of pleasure.

Maybe before the ranch, that life would have been enough.

But the ranch proved that you could live at a rarer pitch. That you could push past these petty human frailties and into a greater love. I believed, in the way of adolescents, in the absolute correctness and superiority of my love. My own feelings forming the definition. Love of that kind was something my father and even Tamar could never understand, and of course I had to leave.

While I had been watching television all day in the stuffy, overheated dark of my father's apartment, the ranch was going sour. Though I wasn't aware to what degree until later. The problem was the record deal—it wasn't going to happen, and that was not something Russell could accept. His hands were tied, Mitch told Russell; he could not force the record company to change their minds. Mitch was a successful musician, a talented guitar player, but he did not have that kind of power.

This was true—my night with Mitch seems piteous for that reason, a groundless whir of wheels. But Russell didn't believe Mitch, or it didn't matter anymore. Mitch became the convenient host for a universal sickness. The pacing rants that increased in frequency and length, Russell pinning it all on Mitch, that overfed Judas. The .22s traded for Buntlines, the frenzy of betrayal Russell worked in the others. Russell wasn't even bothering to hide his anger anymore. Guy was bringing speed around, he and Suzanne running to the pump house, coming back with eyes black as berries. The target practice in the trees. The ranch had never been of the larger world, but it grew more isolated. No newspapers, no televisions, no radio. Russell began to turn away visitors and send Guy out with the girls on every garbage run. A shell hardening around the place.

I can imagine Suzanne waking up, those mornings, with no sense of the days passing. The food situation getting dire, everything tinted with mild decay. They didn't eat much protein, their brains motoring on simple carbohydrates and the occasional peanut-butter sandwich. The speed that scraped Suzanne of feeling—she must have moved through the filtery electricity of her own numbness like moving through deep ocean.

Everyone, later, would find it unbelievable that anyone involved in the ranch would stay in that situation. A situation so obviously bad. But Suzanne had nothing else: she had given her life completely over to Russell, and by then it was like a thing he could hold in his hands, turning it over and over, testing its weight. Suzanne and the other girls had stopped being able to make certain judgments, the unused muscle of their ego growing slack and useless. It had been so long since any of them had occupied a world where right and wrong existed in any real way. Whatever instincts they'd ever had—the weak twinge in the gut, a gnaw of concern—had become inaudible. If those instincts had ever been detectable at all.

They didn't have very far to fall—I knew just being a girl in the world handicapped your ability to believe yourself. Feelings seemed completely unreliable, like faulty gibberish scraped from a Ouija board. My childhood visits to the family doctor were stressful events for that reason. He'd ask me gentle questions: How was I feeling? How would I describe the pain? Was it more sharp or more spread out? I'd just look at him with desperation. I needed to be **told**, that was the whole point of going to the doctor. To take a test, be put through a machine that could comb my insides with radiated precision and tell me what the truth was.

Of course the girls didn't leave the ranch: there is a lot that can be borne. When I was nine, I'd broken my wrist falling from a swing. The shocking crack, the blackout pain. But even then, even with my wrist swelling with a cuff of trapped blood, I insisted I was fine, that it was nothing, and my parents believed me right up until the doctor showed them the X-ray, the bones snapped clean.

12

As soon as I'd packed my duffel, the guest room already looked like no one had ever stayed there—my absence quickly absorbed, which was maybe the point of rooms like that. I'd figured Tamar and my father had already left for work, but when I came into the living room, my father grunted from the couch.

"Tamar's buying orange juice or some stupid thing," he said.

We sat together and watched television. Tamar was gone a long time. My father kept rubbing his freshly shaven jaw, his face seeming undercooked. The commercials embarrassed me with their strident feeling, how they seemed to mock our awkward quiet. My father's nervous measurement of the silence. How I would have been, a month ago, tense with expectation. Dredging my life for some gem of experience to present to him. But I couldn't summon that effort anymore. My father was both more knowable to me than he had ever been, and at the same time, more of a stranger—he was just a man, sensitive to spicy foods, guessing at his foreign markets. Plugging away at his French.

He stood up the moment he heard Tamar's keys fussing in the door.

"We should have left thirty minutes ago," he said.

Tamar glanced at me, reshouldered her purse. "Sorry." She cut him a tight smile.

"You knew when we had to go," he said.

"I said I was sorry." She seemed, for a moment, genuinely sorry. But then her eyes drifted helplessly to the television, still on, and though she tried to click back to attention, I knew my father had noticed.

"You don't even have any orange juice," he said, his voice flickering with hurt.

A young couple was the first to pick me up. The girl's hair was the color of butter, a blouse knotted at her waist, and she kept turning to smile and offer me pistachios from a bag. Kissing the boy so I could see her darting tongue.

I hadn't hitchhiked before, not really. It made me

nervous to have to be whatever strangers expected from a girl with long hair—I didn't know what degree of outrage to show about the war, how to talk about the students who threw bricks at police or took over passenger planes, demanding to be flown to Cuba. I'd always been outside all that, like I was watching a movie about what should have been my own life. But it was different, now that I was heading to the ranch.

I kept imagining the moment when Tamar and my father, home from the office, would realize I was actually gone. They would understand slowly, Tamar probably coming to the conclusion faster than my father. The apartment empty, no trace of my things. And maybe my father would call my mother, but what could either of them do? What punishment could they possibly pass down? They didn't know where I'd gone. I had moved beyond their purview. Even their concern was exciting, in its way: there would be a moment when they'd have to wonder why I'd left, some murky guilt rising to the surface, and they would have to feel the full force of it, even if it was only for a second.

The couple took me as far as Woodside. I waited in the parking lot of the Cal-Mart until I got a ride from a man in a rattly Chevrolet, on his way to Berkeley to drop off a motorcycle part. Every time he went over a pothole, his duct-taped glove compartment clattered. The shaggy trees flashed past the window, thick with sun, the purple stretch of the bay beyond. I held my purse on my lap. His name was Claude, and he seemed ashamed of how it jarred with his appearance. "My mother liked that French actor," he mumbled.

Claude made a point of flipping through his wallet, showing me pictures of his own daughter. She was a chubby girl, the bridge of her nose pink. Her unfashionable sausage curls. Claude seemed to sense my pity, suddenly grabbing the wallet back.

"None of you girls should be doing this," he said.

He shook his head and I saw how his face moved a little with concern for me, an acknowledgment, I thought, of how brave I was. Though I should have known that when men warn you to be careful, often they are warning you of the dark movie playing across their own brains. Some violent daydream prompting their guilty exhortations to "make it home safe."

"See, I wish I'd been like you," Claude said. "Free and easy. Just traveling around. I always had a job."

He slid his eyes to me before turning them back to the road. The first twinge of discomfort—I'd gotten good at deciphering certain male expressions of desire. Clearing the throat, an assessing nip in the gaze.

"None of you people ever work, huh?" he said.

He was teasing, probably, but I couldn't tell for sure. There was sourness in his tone, a sting of real resentment. Maybe I should have been frightened of him. This older man who saw that I was alone, who felt like I owed him something, which was the worst thing a man like that could feel. But I wasn't afraid. I was protected, a hilarious and untouchable giddiness overtaking me. I was going back to the ranch. I would see Suzanne. Claude seemed barely real to me: a paper clown, innocuous and laughable.

"This good?" Claude said.

He'd pulled over near the campus in Berkeley, the clock tower and stair-step houses thickening the hills behind. He turned off the ignition. I felt the heat outside, the close wend of traffic.

"Thanks," I said, gathering my purse and duffel.

"Slow down," he said as I started to open the door. "Just sit with me a second, hm?"

I sighed but sat back in the seat. I could see the dry hills above Berkeley and remembered, with a start, that brief time in winter when the hills were green and plump and wet. I hadn't even known Suzanne then. I could feel Claude looking at me sideways.

"Listen." Claude scratched at his neck. "If you need some money—"

"I don't need money." I was unafraid, shrugging a quick goodbye and opening the door. "Thanks again," I said. "For the ride."

"Wait," he said, grabbing my wrist.

"Fuck off," I said, wrenching my arm away from the bracelet of his grasp, an unfamiliar heat in my voice. Before I slammed the door, I saw Claude's weak and sputtering face. I was walking away, breathless. Almost laughing. The sidewalk radiating even heat, the pulse of the abrupt sunshine. I was buoyed by the exchange, as if suddenly allowed more space in the world.

"Bitch," Claude called, but I didn't turn back to look.

Telegraph was packed: people selling tables of incense or concho jewelry, leather purses hung from an alley fence. The city of Berkeley was redoing all the roads that summer, so piles of rubble collected on the sidewalks, trenches cracking through the asphalt like a disaster movie. A group in floor-length robes fluttered pamphlets at me. Boys with no shirts, their arms pressed with faint bruising, looked me up and down. Girls my age lugged carpetbags that banged against their knees, wearing velvet frock coats in the August heat.

Even after what had happened with Claude, I wasn't afraid of hitchhiking. Claude was just a harmless floater in the corner of my vision, drifting peacefully into the void. Tom was the sixth person I approached, tapping his shoulder as he ducked into his car. He seemed flattered by my request for a ride, like it was an excuse I'd made up to be near him. He hurriedly brushed off the passenger seat, raining silent crumbs onto the carpet.

"It could be cleaner," he said. Apologetic, as if I might possibly be picky.

Tom drove his small Japanese car at exactly the speed limit, looking over his shoulder before changing lanes. His plaid shirt was thinning at the elbows but clean and tucked, a boyishness to his slim wrists that moved me. He took me all the way to the ranch, though it was an hour from Berkeley. He'd claimed to be visiting friends at the junior college in Santa Rosa, but he was a bad liar: I could see his neck get pink. He was polite, a student at Berkeley. Premed, though he liked sociology, too, and history.

"LBJ," he said. "Now there was a president."

He had a large family, I learned, and a dog named Sister, and too much homework: he was in summer school, trying to get through prereqs. He'd asked me what my major was. His mistake excited me—he must have thought I was eighteen, at least.

"I don't go to college," I said. I was about to explain I was only in high school, but Tom immediately got defensive.

"I was thinking of doing that, too," he said, "dropping out, but I'm gonna finish the summer classes. I already paid fees. I mean, I wish I hadn't, but—" He trailed off. Gazing at me until I realized he wanted my forgiveness.

"That's a bummer," I said, and this seemed like enough.

He cleared his throat. "So do you have a job or something? If you're not in school?" he said. "Gee, unless that's a rude question. You don't have to answer."

I shrugged, affecting ease. Though maybe I was feeling easy on that car ride, like my occupation of the world could be seamless. These simple ways I could meet needs. Talking to strangers, dealing with situations.

"The place I'm going now—I've been staying there," I said. "It's a big group. We take care of each other."

His eyes were on the road, but he was listening closely as I explained the ranch. The funny old house, the kids. The plumbing system Guy had rigged in the yard, a knotty mess of pipes.

"Sounds like the International House," he said. "Where I live. There are fifteen of us. There's a chore board in the hall, we all take turns with the bad ones."

"Yeah, maybe," I said, though I knew the ranch was nothing like the International House, the squinty philosophy majors arguing over who'd left the dinner dishes unwashed, a girl from Poland nibbling black bread and crying for a faraway boyfriend.

"Who owns the house?" he said. "Is it like a center or something?"

It was odd to explain Russell to someone, to remember that there were whole realms in which Russell or Suzanne did not figure.

"His album's gonna come out around Christmas, probably," I remember saying.

I kept talking about the ranch, about Russell. The way I tossed free Mitch's name, like Donna had that day on the bus, with studied, careful deployment. The closer we got, the more worked up I became. Like horses that bolt with barn sickness, forgetting their rider.

"It sounds nice," Tom said. I could tell my stories had charged him, a dreamy excitement in his features. Mesmerized by bedtime tales of other worlds.

"You could hang out for a while," I said. "If you wanted."

Tom brightened at the offer, gratitude making him shy. "Only if I'm not intruding," he said, a blush clotting his cheeks.

I imagined Suzanne and the others would be happy with me for bringing this new person. Expanding the ranks, all the old tricks. A pie-faced admirer to raise his voice with ours and contribute to the food pool. But it was something else, too, that I wanted to extend: the taut and pleasant silence in the car, the stale heat raising vapors of leather. The warped image of myself in the side mirrors, so I caught only the quantity of hair, the freckled skin of my shoulder. I took on the shape of a girl. The car crossed the bridge, passing through the shit-stench veil of the landfill. I could see the span of another distant highway, sided by water, and the marshy flats before the sudden drop into the valley, the ranch hidden in its hills.

By that time, the ranch I'd known was a place that no longer existed. The end had already arrived: each interaction its own elegy. But there was too much hopeful momentum in me to notice. The leap in me when Tom's car had first turned down the ranch drive: it had been two weeks, not long at all, but the return was overwhelming. And only when I saw everything still there, still alive and strange and half-dreamy as ever, did I understand I'd worried it might be gone. The things I loved, the miraculous house—like the one in **Gone with the Wind**, I'd realized, coming upon it again. The silty rectangle of pool, half-full, with its teem of algae and exposed concrete: it could all pass back into my possession.

As Tom and I walked from the car, I had a flash of hesitation, noticing how Tom's jeans were too clean. Maybe the girls would tease him, maybe it had been a bad idea to invite him along. I told myself it would be fine. I watched him absorbing the scene—I read his expression as impressed, though he must have been noticing the disrepair, the junked-out skeletons of cars. The crispy package of a dead frog, drifting on the surface of the pool. But these were details that no longer seemed notable to me, like the sores on Nico's legs that stuck with bits of gravel. My eyes were already habituated to the texture of decay, so I thought that I had passed back into the circle of light.

13

Donna stopped when she caught sight of us. A nest of laundry in her arms, smelling like the dusty air.

"Trou-ble," she hooted. "Trouble," a word from a long-forgotten world. "That lady just nabbed you, huh?" she said. "Man. Heavy."

Dark circles made crescents under her eyes, a hollow sink to her features, though these details were overshadowed by the swell of familiarity. She seemed happy enough to see me, but when I introduced Tom, she zipped a look at me.

"He gave me a ride," I supplied helpfully.

Donna's smile teetered, and she hitched the laundry higher in her arms.

"Is it cool that I'm here?" Tom whispered to me, as if I had any power at all. The ranch had always welcomed visitors, putting them through their jokey gauntlet of attention, and I couldn't imagine why that would have changed.

"Yeah," I said, turning to Donna. "Right?"

"Well," Donna said. "I don't know. You should talk to Suzanne. Or Guy. Yeah."

She giggled absently. She was being odd, though to me it was just the usual Donna rap—I could even feel affection for it. Some movement in the grass caught her attention: a lizard, scuttling in search of shade.

"Russell saw a mountain lion a few days ago," she remarked to no one in particular. Widening her eyes. "Wild, huh?"

"Look who's back," Suzanne said, a flounce of anger in her greeting. Like I had disappeared on a little vacation. "Figured you'd forgotten how to get here."

Even though she'd seen Mrs. Dutton stop me, she kept glancing at Tom like he was the reason I'd left. Poor Tom, who wandered the grassy yard with the hesitant shuffle of museumgoers. His nose pricking from the animal smells, the backed-up outhouse. Suzanne's face was shuttered with the same distant confusion as Donna's: they could no longer conceive of a world where you could be punished. I was suddenly guilty for the nights with Tamar, the whole afternoons when I didn't even think of Suzanne. I tried to make my father's apartment sound worse than it had been, as if I'd been watched at every moment, suffered through endless punishments.

"Jesus," Suzanne snorted. "Dragsville."

The shadow of the ranch house stretched along the grass like a strange outdoor room, and we occupied this blessing of shade, a line of mosquitoes hovering in the thin afternoon light. The air crackled with a carnival sheen—the familiar bodies of the girls jostling against mine, knocking me back into myself. The quick metal flash through the trees—Guy was bumping a car through the back ranch, calls echoing and disappearing. The drowsy shape of the children, mucking around a network of shallow puddles: someone had forgotten to turn off the hose. Helen had a blanket around herself, pulled up to her chin like a woolly ruff, and Donna kept trying to snap it away and expose the homecoming queen body underneath, the hematoma on Helen's thigh. I was aware of Tom, sitting awkwardly in the dirt, but mostly I thrilled to Suzanne's familiar shape beside me. She was talking quickly, a glaze of sweat on her face. Her dress was filthy, but her eyes were shining.

Tamar and my father weren't even home yet, I realized, and how funny it was to already be at the ranch when they didn't even know I was gone. Nico was riding a tricycle that was too small for him, the bike rusted and clanging as he pedaled hard.

"Cute kid," Tom said. Donna and Helen laughed.

Tom wasn't sure what he'd said that was funny, but he blinked like he was willing to learn. Suzanne plucked at a stalk of oat grass, sitting in an old winged chair pulled from the house. I was keeping an eye out for Russell but didn't see him anywhere.

"He went to the city for a bit," Suzanne said.

We both turned at the sound of screeching: it was just Donna, trying to do a handstand on the porch, the flail of her kicking feet. She'd knocked over Tom's beer, though he was the one apologizing, looking around as if he'd find a mop.

"Jesus," Suzanne said. "Relax."

She wiped her sweating hands on her dress, her eyes pinging a little—speed made her stiff as a china cat. The high school girls used it to stay skinny, but I'd never done it: it seemed at odds with the droopy high I associated with the ranch. It made Suzanne harder to reach than usual, a change I didn't want to acknowledge to myself. I assumed she was just angry. Her gaze never exactly focusing, stopping at the brink.

We were talking like we always did, passing a joint that made Tom cough, but I was noticing other things at the same time with a slight drift of unease—the ranch was less populated than before, no strangers milling around with empty plates, asking what time dinner would be ready. Shaking back their hair and invoking the long car ride to L.A. I didn't see Caroline anywhere, either.

"She was weird," Suzanne said when I asked about

Caroline. "Like you could see her insides through her skin. She went home. Some people came and picked her up."

"Her parents?" The thought seemed ludicrous, that anyone at the ranch even had parents.

"It's cool," Suzanne said. "A van was heading north, I think Mendocino or something. She knew them from somewhere."

I tried to picture Caroline back at her parents' house, wherever that was. I didn't push much further than those thoughts, Caroline safe and elsewhere.

Tom was clearly uncomfortable. I was sure he was used to college girls with part-time jobs and library cards and split ends. Helen and Donna and Suzanne were raw, a sour note coming off them that struck me, too, returned from two weeks with miraculous plumbing and proximity to Tamar's obsessive grooming, the special nylon brush she used only on her fingernails. I didn't want to notice the hesitation in Tom, the shade of a cower whenever Donna addressed him directly.

"So what's new with the record?" I asked loudly. Expecting the reassuring invocation of success to shore up Tom's faith. Because it was still the ranch, and everything I'd said was true—he just had to open himself to it. But Suzanne gave me a strange look. The others watching for her to set a tone. Because it hadn't gone well, that was the point of her stare.

"Mitch is a fucking traitor," she said.

I was too shocked to fully take in the ugly cast of Suzanne's hatred: how could Russell really not have gotten his deal? How could Mitch not have seen it on him, the aura of strange electricity, the air around him murmuring? Was it specific to this place, whatever power Russell had? But Suzanne's gaudy anger recruited me back in, too.

"Mitch freaked, who knows why. He lied. These people," Suzanne said. "These fucking dopes."

"You can't fuck with Russell," Donna said, nodding along. "Saying one thing, then going back on it. Mitch doesn't know how Russell is. Russell wouldn't even have to lift a finger."

Russell had slapped Helen, that time, like it was nothing. The uncomfortable rearranging I had to do, the mental squint in order to see things differently.

"But Mitch could change his mind, right?" I asked. When I finally looked toward Tom, he wasn't paying attention, his gaze trained beyond the porch.

Suzanne shrugged. "I don't know. He told Russell not to call him anymore." She let out a snort. "Fuck him. Just disappearing like he didn't make promises."

I was thinking about Mitch. His desire, that night, making him brutish so he didn't care when I winced, my hair caught under his arm. His fogged-over gaze that kept us indistinct, our bodies just the symbol of bodies.

"But it's cool," Suzanne said, forcing a smile. "It's not—"

She was cut off by the sudden surprise of Tom, surging to his feet. He clattered down from the porch and sprinted in the direction of the pool. Shouting something I couldn't make out. His shirt coming untucked, the naked, vulnerable holler.

"What's his problem?" Suzanne said, and I didn't know, flushing with desperate embarrassment that morphed into fear: Tom was still shouting, scrambling down the steps into the pool.

"The kid," he said, "the boy."

Nico: I flashed on the silent shape of his body in the water, his little lungs sloshing and full. The porch tilted. By the time we hurried over to the pool, Tom already slogging the kid out of the slimy water, it was immediately clear that he was okay. Everything was fine. Nico sat down on the grass, dripping, an aggrieved look on his face. Fisting at his eyes, pushing Tom away. He was crying more because of Tom than anything else, the strange man who'd yelled at him, who'd dragged him from the pool when he was just having fun.

"What's the big idea?" Donna said to Tom. Patting Nico on the head roughly, like a good dog.

"He jumped in." Tom's panic was reverberating through his whole body, his pants and shirt sopping. The wet suck of his shoes.

"So?"

Tom was wide-eyed, not understanding that trying to explain would make it worse.

"I thought he'd fallen into the pool."

"But there's water in there," Helen said.

"That wet stuff," Donna said, sniggering.

"The kid's fine," Suzanne said. "You scared him."

"Glug glug glug." A fit of giggling overtook Helen. "You thought he was dead or something?"

"He still could have drowned," Tom said, his voice going high. "No one was watching him. He's too young to really swim."

"Your face," Donna said. "God, you're all freaked, aren't you?"

The sight of Tom wringing the biological stink of pool water from his shirt. The junk in the yard catching the light. Nico got to his feet, shaking out his hair. Sniffing a little with his weird childish dignity. The girls were laughing, all of them, so Nico trundled off easily, no one noticing his departure. And I pretended I hadn't worried, either, that I'd known everything was fine, because Tom seemed pathetic, his panic right on the surface with no place to retreat, and even the kid was mad at him. I was ashamed for bringing him around, for how he'd caused such a fuss, and Suzanne was staring at me, so I knew exactly what a stupid idea it had been. Tom looked at me for help, but he saw the distance in my face, the way I slid my eyes back to the ground.

"I just think you should be careful," Tom said.

Suzanne snorted. "We should be careful?"

"I was a lifeguard," he said, his voice cracking. "People can drown even in shallow water." But Suzanne wasn't listening, making a face at Donna.

Their shared disgust including me, I thought. I couldn't bear it.

"Relax," I said to Tom.

Tom looked wounded. "This is an awful place."

"You should leave, then," Suzanne said. "Doesn't that sound like a good idea?" The rattle of speed in her, the vacant, vicious smile—she was being meaner than she needed to be.

"Can I talk to you for a second?" Tom said to me.

Suzanne laughed. "Oh, man. Here we go."

"Just for a second," he said.

When I hesitated, Suzanne sighed. "Go talk to him," she said. "Christ."

Tom walked away from the others and I followed him with halting steps, as if distance could prevent contagion. I kept glancing back to the group, the girls heading to the porch. I wanted to be among them. I was furious with Tom, his silly pants, his thatchy hair.

"What?" I said. Impatient, my lips tight.

"I don't know," Tom said, "I just think—" He hesitated, darting a look at the house, pulling at his shirt. "You can come back with me right now, if you want. There's a party tonight," he said. "At the International House."

I could picture it. The Ritz crackers, earnest groups crammed around bowls of watery ice. Talking SDS and comparing reading lists. I half shrugged, the barest shift of a shoulder. He seemed to understand this gesture for the falsehood it was.

"Maybe I should write down my number for you," Tom said. "It's the hall phone, but you can just ask for me."

I could hear the stark billow of Suzanne's laughter carrying in the air.

"That's okay," I said. "There's no phone here, anyway."

"They aren't nice," Tom said, catching my eyes. He looked like a rural preacher after a baptism, the wet pants clinging to his legs, his earnest stare.

"What do you know?" I said, an alarming heat rising in my cheeks. "You don't even know them."

Tom made an abortive gesture with his hands. "It's a trash heap," he said, sputtering, "can't you see that?"

He indicated the crumbling house, the tangle of overgrown vegetation. All the junked-out cars and oil drums and picnic blankets abandoned to the mold and the termites. I saw it all, but I didn't absorb anything: I'd already hardened myself to him and there was nothing else to say.

Tom's departure allowed the girls to deepen into their natures without the fracture of an outsider's gaze. No more peaceful, sleepy chatter, no balmy stretches of easy silence.

"Where's your special friend?" Suzanne said. "Your old pal?" Her hollow affect, her leg jiggling even though her expression was blank.

I tried to laugh like they did, but I didn't know why I got unnerved at the thought of Tom returning to Berkeley. He was right about the junk in the yard, there was more of it, and maybe Nico really could have been hurt, and what then? I noticed all of them had gotten skinnier, not just Donna, a brittle quality to their hair, a dull drain behind the eyes. When they smiled, I glimpsed the coated tongues seen on the starving. Without consciously doing so, I pinned a lot of hope on Russell's return. Wanting him to weigh down the flapping corners of my thoughts.

"Heartbreaker," Russell catcalled when he caught sight of me. "You run off all the time," he said, "and it breaks our hearts when you leave us behind."

I tried to convince myself, seeing the familiarity of Russell's face, that the ranch was the same, though when he hugged me, I saw something smeared at his jawline. It was his sideburns. They were not stippled, like hair, but flat. I looked closer. They were drawn on, I saw, with some kind of charcoal or eyeliner. The thought disturbed me; the perverseness, the fragility of the deception. Like a boy I'd known in Petaluma who shoplifted makeup to cover his pimples. Russell's hand worked my neck, passing along a fritter of energy. I couldn't tell if he was angry or not. And how immediately the group jolted to attention at his arrival, trooping in his wake like ragged ducklings. I tried to pull Suzanne aside, hook my arm through hers like the old days, but she just smiled, low burning and unfocused, and shook herself loose, intent on following Russell.

I learned that Russell had been harassing Mitch for the last few weeks. Showing up unannounced at his house. Sending Guy to knock over his trash cans, so Mitch came home to a lawn junked with flattened cereal boxes and shredded wax paper and tinfoil slick with food scraps. Mitch's caretaker had seen Russell there, too, just once—Scotty told Mitch he'd seen some guy parked at the gate, just staring, and when Scotty had asked him to leave, Russell had smiled and told him he was the house's previous owner. Russell had also shown up at the recording engineer's house, trying to cadge the tapes from his session with Mitch. The man's wife was home. Later she'd recall being irritated at the sound of the doorbell: their newborn was asleep in the back bedroom. When she opened the door, there was Russell in his grubby Wranglers, his squinty smile.

She'd heard stories of the session from her husband, so she knew who Russell was, but she wasn't afraid. Not really. He was not a frightening man when first encountered, and when she told him her husband wasn't home, Russell shrugged.

"I could just grab the tapes real quick," he said, straining to look past her. "In and out, just like that." That's when she got a little uneasy. Plowing her feet deeper into her old slippers, the fussing of the baby drifting down the hall.

"He keeps all that at work," she said, and Russell believed her.

The woman remembered she heard a noise in the yard later that night, a thrash in the roses, but when she looked out the window, she didn't see anything except the pebbled driveway, the stubble of the moonlit lawn.

My first night back was nothing like the old nights. The old nights had been alive with a juvenile sweetness in our faces—I'd pet the dog, who'd nose around for love, give him a hearty scratch behind his ears, my coursing hand urging me into a happy rhythm. And there had been strange nights, too, when we'd all taken acid or Russell would have to get in some drunk motorcycle guy's face, using all his flip-flop logic on him. But I had never felt scared. That night was different, by the ring of stones with the barest of fires going. No one paid any attention when the flames dissolved to nothing, everyone's roiling energy directed at Russell, who moved like a rubber band about to snap.

"This right here," Russell said. He was pacing, dinking out a quick song. "I just made it up and it's already a hit."

The guitar was out of tune, twanging flat notes—

Russell didn't seem to notice. His voice rushed and frantic.

"And here's another one," he said. He fussed with the tuning pegs before letting loose a jangle of strums. I tried to catch Suzanne's eye, but she was trained on Russell. "This is the future of music," he said over the din. "They think they know what's good 'cause they got songs on the radio, but that's not shit. They don't have true love in their hearts."

No one seemed to notice his words unraveling around the borders: they all echoed what he said, their mouths twisting in shared feeling. Russell was a genius, that's what I'd told Tom—and I could picture how Tom's face would have moved with pity if he were there to see Russell, and it made me hate Tom, because I could hear it, too, all the space in the songs for you to realize they were rough, not even rough, just bad: sentimental treacle, the words about love as blunt as a grade-schooler's, a heart drawn by a chubby hand. Sunshine and flowers and smiles. But I could not fully admit it, even then. The way Suzanne's face looked as she watched him—I wanted to be with her. I thought that loving someone acted as a kind of protective measure, like they'd understand the scale and intensity of your feelings and act accordingly. That seemed fair to me, as if fairness were a measure the universe cared anything about.

...

There were dreams I had sometimes, and I'd wake from the tail end assuming some image or fact to be true, carrying forward this assumption from the dreamworld into my waking life. And how jarring it would be to realize that I was not married, that I had not cracked the code to flight, and there would be a real sorrow.

The actual moment Russell told Suzanne to go to Mitch Lewis's house and teach him a lesson—I kept thinking I had witnessed it: the black night, the cool flicking chirps of crickets, and all those spooky oaks. But of course I hadn't. I'd read about it so much that I believed I could see it clearly, a scene in the exaggerated colors of a childhood memory.

I'd been waiting in Suzanne's room at the time. Irritable, desperate for her return. I'd tried to talk to her at multiple points that night, tugging at her arm, tracking her gaze, but she kept brushing me off. "Later," she said, and that was all it took for me to imagine her promise fulfilling itself in the darkness of her room. My chest tightened when I heard footsteps enter the room, mind swelling with the thought—Suzanne was here—but then I felt the soft glancing hit and my eyes flew open—it was just Donna. She'd thrown a pillow at me.

"Sleeping Beauty," she said, sniggering.

I tried to settle back into pretty repose; the sheet overheated from the nervous shuffle of my body, ears suggestible for any sound of Suzanne's return. But she didn't come to the room that night. I waited as long as I could, alert to every creak and jar, before passing into the drowsy patchwork of unwilling sleep.

In fact, Suzanne had been with Russell. The air of his trailer probably going stuffy from their fucking, Russell unraveling his plan for Mitch, he and Suzanne staring up at the ceiling. I can imagine how he got right up to the edge before swerving around the details, so maybe Suzanne would start to think she'd had the same idea, that it was hers, too.

"My little hellhound," he had cooed to her, his eyes pinwheeling from a mania that could be mistaken for love. It was strange to think Suzanne would be flattered in this moment, but certainly she was. His hand scratching her scalp, that same agitated pleasure men like to incite in dogs, and I can imagine how the pressure started to build, a desire to move along the larger rush.

"It should be big," Russell had said. "Something they can't ignore." I see him twisting a lock of Suzanne's hair around a finger and pulling, the barest tug so she wouldn't know if the throb she felt was pain or pleasure.

The door he opened, urging Suzanne through.

Suzanne was distracted the whole next day. Going off by herself, face announcing her hurry, or having urgent, whispered conferences with Guy. I was jealous, desperate that I couldn't compete with the fraction of her that was deeded to Russell. She'd folded herself up and I was a distant concern.

I nursed my own confusion, tending hopeful explanations, but when I smiled at her, she blinked with delayed recognition, like I was a stranger returning her forgotten pocketbook. I kept noticing a soldered look in her eyes, a grim inward turning. Later I'd understand this was preparation.

Dinner was some reheated beans that tasted of aluminum, the burned scrapings of the pot. Stale chocolate cake from the bakery with a hoary pack of frost. They wanted to eat indoors, so we sat on the splintered floor, plates crooked on our laps. Forcing a primitive caveman hunch—no one seemed to eat very much. Suzanne pressed a finger to the cake and watched it crumb. Their looks at one another across the room were bursting with suppressed hilarity, a surprise-party conspiracy. Donna handing Suzanne a rag with a significant air. I didn't understand anything, a pitiful dislocation keeping me blind and eager.

I'd steeled myself to force a talk on Suzanne. But I looked up from the nasty slop of my plate and saw she was already getting to her feet, her movements informed by information invisible to me.

They were going somewhere, I realized when I caught up to her, following the play of her flashlight beam. The lurch, the gag of desperation: Suzanne was going to leave me behind.

"Let me come too," I said. Trying to keep up, following the swift rupture she cut through the grass.

I couldn't see Suzanne's face. "Come where?" she said, her voice even.

"Wherever you're going," I said. "I know you're going somewhere."

The teasing lilt. "Russell didn't ask you to go."

"But I want to," I said. "Please."

Suzanne didn't say yes, exactly. But she slowed enough so I could match her stride, a pace new to me, purposeful.

"You should change," Suzanne said.

I looked down, trying to discern what had offended her: my cotton shirt, my long skirt.

"Into dark clothes," she said.

14

The car ride was as slurred over and unbelievable as a long illness. Guy at the wheel, Helen and Donna beside him. Suzanne sat in the backseat, staring out the window, and I was right next to her. The night had dropped deep and dark, the car passing under the streetlights. Their sulfur glow gliding across Suzanne's face, a stupor occupying the others. Sometimes it seemed like I never really left the car. That a version of me is always there.

Russell stayed at the ranch that night. Which didn't even register with me as strange. Suzanne and the others were his familiars, loosed out into the world—it had always been that way. Guy like his second in a duel, Suzanne and Helen and Donna not hesitating. Roos was supposed to have gone, too, but she didn't—she claimed, later, that she'd gotten a bad feeling and stayed behind, but I don't know if that is true. Did Russell hold her back, sensing a stubborn virtue in her that might yoke her to the real world? Roos with Nico, a child of her own. Roos, who did become the main witness against the others, taking the stand in a white dress with her hair parted straight down the middle.

I don't know if Suzanne told Russell I was coming—no one ever answered that question.

The car radio was on, playing the laughably foreign soundtrack to other people's lives. Other people who were getting ready to sleep, mothers who were scraping the last shreds of chicken dinner into the garbage. Helen was jawing away about a whale beaching down in Pismo and did we think it was true that it was a sign a big earthquake was gonna happen? Getting up on her knees then, like the idea thrilled her.

"We'd have to go to the desert," she said. No one was taking her bait: a hush had fallen over the car. Donna muttered something, and Helen set her jaw.

"Can you open the window?" Suzanne said.

"I'm cold," Helen whined in her baby voice.

"Come on," Suzanne said, pounding the back of the seat. "I'm fucking melting."

Helen rolled the window down and the car filled with air, flavored with exhaust. The salt of the nearby ocean.

And there I was among them. Russell had changed,

things had soured, but I was with Suzanne. Her presence corralled any stray worries. Like the child who believes that her mother's bedtime vigil will ward off monsters. The child who cannot decipher that her mother might be frightened, too. The mother who understands she can do nothing for protection except offer up her own weak body in exchange.

Maybe some part of me had known where things were headed, a sunken glimmer in the murk: maybe I had a sense of the possible trajectory and went along anyway. Later that summer, and at various points throughout my life, I would sift through the grain of that night, feeling blindly.

All Suzanne said was that we were paying Mitch a visit. Her words were spiked with a cruelty I hadn't heard before, but even so, this was the furthest my mind ranged: we were going to do what we'd done at the Dutton house. We'd perform an unsettling psychic interruption so Mitch would have to be afraid, just for a minute, would have to reorder the world anew. Good—Suzanne's hatred for him allowed and inflamed my own. Mitch, with his fat, probing fingers, the halting, meaningless chatter he kept up while looking us over. As if his mundane words would fool us, keep us from noticing how his glance dripped with filth. I wanted him to feel weak. We would occupy Mitch's house like tricky spirits from another realm.

Because I did feel that, it's true. A sense that something united all of us in the car, the cool whiff of other worlds on our skin and hair. But I never thought, even once, that the other world might be death. I wouldn't really believe it until the news gathered its stark momentum. After which, of course, the presence of death seemed to color everything, like an odorless mist that filled the car and pressed against the windows, a mist we inhaled and exhaled and that shaped every word we spoke.

We had not gone very far, maybe twenty minutes from the ranch, Guy easing the car along the tight dark curves of the hills, emerging into the long empty stretches of the flat land and picking up speed. The stands of eucalyptus we passed, the chill of fog beyond the window.

My alertness held everything in precise amber. The radio, the shuffle of bodies, Suzanne's face in profile. This is what they had all the time, I imagined, this net of mutual presence like something too near to identify. Just a sense of being buoyed along the fraternal rush, the belonging.

Suzanne rested her hand on the seat between us. The familiar sight stirred me, remembering how she'd grabbed for me in Mitch's bed. The spotty surface of her nails, brittle from poor diet.

I was sick with foolish hope, believing I would ever stay in the blessed space of her attention. I tried to reach for her hand. A tap of her palm, like I had a note to pass. Suzanne startled a little and jarred from a haze I had not noticed until it broke.

"What?" she snapped.

My face dropped all ability to costume itself. Suzanne must have seen the needy swarm of love. Must have taken the measure, like a stone dropped in a well—but there was no sound marking the end. Her eyes went dull.

"Stop the car," Suzanne said.

Guy kept driving.

"Pull over," Suzanne said. Guy glanced back at us, then pulled into the shoulder of the right lane.

"What's the matter—," I said, but Suzanne cut me off.

"Get out," she said, opening the door. Moving too fast for me to stop her, the reel snapping ahead, the sound lagging behind.

"Come on," I said, trying to sound bright with the joke. Suzanne was already out of the car, waiting for me to leave. She wasn't joking.

"But there's nothing here," I said, circling a desperate look at the highway. Suzanne was shifting, impatient. I glanced to the others for help. Their faces were lit by the dome light, leaching their features so they seemed as cold and inhuman as bronze figures. Donna looked away, but Helen watched me with a medical curiosity. Guy shifted in the driver's seat, adjusting the mirror. Helen said something under her breath—Donna shushed her.

"Suzanne," I said, "please," the powerless tilt in my voice.

She said nothing. When I finally shuffled along the seat and got out, Suzanne didn't even hesitate. Ducking back inside the car and closing the door, the dome light snapping off and returning them to darkness.

And then they drove away.

I was alone, I understood, and even as I tended some naïve wish—they would return, it was only a joke, Suzanne would never leave me like that, not really—I knew that I had been tossed aside. I could only zoom away, to hover up somewhere by the tree line, looking down on a girl standing alone in the dark. Nobody I knew.

15

There were all kinds of rumors those first days. Howard Smith reported, erroneously, that Mitch Lewis had been killed, though this would be corrected more swiftly than the other rumors. David Brinkley reported six victims had been cut up and shot and left on the lawn. Then the number was amended to four people. Brinkley was the first to claim the presence of hoods and nooses and Satanic symbols, a confusion that started because of the heart on the wall of the living room. Drawn with the corner of a towel, soaked in the mother's blood.

The mix-up made sense—of course they'd read a ghoulish meaning in the shape, assume some cryptic, doomy scrawl. It was easier to imagine it was the leftover of a black mass than believe the actual truth:

it was just a heart, like any lovesick girl might doodle in a notebook.

A mile up the road, I came upon an exit and nearby Texaco station. I went in and out of the sulfur lights, the sound they made like bacon frying. I rocked on my toes, watching the road. When I finally gave up on anyone coming for me, I called my father's number from the pay phone. Tamar answered. "It's me," I said.

"Evie," she said. "Thank God. Where are you?" I could picture her twining the cord in the kitchen, gathering the loops. "I knew you'd call soon. I told your dad you would."

I explained where I was. She must have heard the crack in my voice.

"I'll leave now," she said. "You stay right there."

I sat on the curb to wait, leaning on my knees. The air was cool with the first news of autumn, and the constellation of brake lights was going along 101, the big trucks rearing as they picked up speed. I was reeling with excuses for Suzanne, some explanation for her behavior that would shake out. But there wasn't anything but the awful, immediate knowledge—we had never been close. I had not meant anything.

I could sense curious eyes on me, the truckers who bought bags of sunflower seeds from the gas station and spit neat streams of tobacco on the ground.

Their fatherly gaits and cowboy hats. I knew they were assessing the facts of my aloneness. My bare legs and long hair. My furious shock must have sent out some protective scrum, warning them off—they left me alone.

Finally I caught sight of a white Plymouth approaching. Tamar didn't turn off the ignition. I got into the passenger side, gratitude for Tamar's familiar face making me fumble. Her hair was wet. "I didn't have time to dry it," she said. The look she gave me was kind but mystified. I could tell she wanted to ask questions, but she must have known that I wouldn't explain. The hidden world that adolescents inhabit, surfacing from time to time only when forced, training their parents to expect their absence. I was already disappeared.

"Don't worry," she said. "He didn't tell your mom you took off. I told him that you'd show up and then she'd just be worried for no reason."

Already my grief was doubling, absence my only context. Suzanne had left me, for good. A frictionless fall, the shock of missing a step. Tamar searched her purse with one hand until she found a small gold box, overlaid with pink stamped leather. Like a card case. There was a single joint inside, and she nodded to the glove compartment—I found a lighter.

"Don't tell your dad?" She inhaled, eyes on the road. "He might ground me, too."

...

Tamar was telling the truth: my father hadn't called my mother, and though he was shaky with rage, he was sheepish, too, his daughter a pet he'd forgotten to feed.

"You could've been hurt," he said, like an actor guessing at his lines.

Tamar calmly patted his back on her way to the kitchen, then poured herself a Coke. Leaving me with his hot, nervous breath, his blinky, frightened face. He regarded me across the living room, his upset trailing off. Everything that had happened—I was unafraid of this, my father's neutered anger. What could he do to me? What could he take away?

And then I was back in my bland room in Palo Alto, the light from the lamp the featureless light of the business traveler.

The apartment was empty by the time I emerged the next morning, my father and Tamar already at work. One of them—probably Tamar—had left a fan going, and a fake-looking plant shivered in the wake of air. There was only a week before I had to leave for boarding school, and seven days seemed too long to be in my father's apartment, seven dinners to soldier through, but, at the same time, unfairly brief—I wouldn't have time for habits, for context. I just had to wait.

I turned on the television, the chatter a comforting soundtrack as I foraged in the kitchen. The box of Rice Krispies in the cabinet had a barest coating of cereal left: I ate it by the handful, then flattened the empty box. I poured a glass of iced tea, balanced a stack of crackers with the pleasing quantity and thickness of poker chips. I ferried the food to the couch. Before I could settle back, the screen stopped me.

The crowd of images, doubling and spreading.

The search for the perpetrator or perpetrators still unsuccessful. The newscaster said Mitch Lewis was not available for comment. The crackers crimped into shards by my wet hands.

Only after the trial did things come into focus, that night taking on the now familiar arc. Every detail and blip made public. There are times I try to guess what part I might have played. What amount would belong to me. It's easiest to think I wouldn't have done anything, like I would have stopped them, my presence the mooring that kept Suzanne in the human realm. That was the wish, the cogent parable. But there was another possibility that slouched along, insistent and unseen. The bogeyman under the bed, the snake at the bottom of the stairs: maybe I would have done something, too.

Maybe it would have been easy.

They'd gone straight to Mitch's after leaving me by the side of the road. Another thirty minutes in the car, thirty minutes that were maybe energized by my dramatic dismissal, the consolidation of the group into the true pilgrims. Suzanne leaning on folded arms over the front seat, giving off an amphetamine fritz, that lucid surety. Guy turning off the highway and onto the two-lane road, crossing the lagoon. The low stucco motels by the off-ramp, the eucalyptus loomy and peppering the air. Helen claimed, in her court testimony, that this was the first moment she expressed reservations to the others. But I don't believe it. If anyone was questioning themselves, it was all under the surface, a filmy bubble drifting and popping in their brains. Their doubt growing weak as the particulars of a dream grow weak. Helen realized she'd left her knife at home. Suzanne shouted at her, according to trial documents, but the group dismissed plans to go back for it. They were already coasting, in thrall to a bigger momentum.

They parked the Ford along the road, not even bothering to hide it. As they made their way to Mitch's gate, their minds seemed to hover and settle on the same movements, like a single organism.

I can imagine that view. Mitch's house, as seen from the gravel drive. The calm fill of the bay, the prow of the living room. It was familiar to them. The month they'd spent living with Mitch before I'd known them, running up delivery bills and catching molluscum from dank towels. But still. I think that night they might have been newly struck by the house, faceted and bright as rock candy. Its inhabitants already doomed, so doomed the group could feel an almost preemptive sorrow for them. For how completely helpless they were to larger movements, their lives already redundant, like a tape recorded over with static.

They'd expected to find Mitch. Everyone knows this part: how Mitch had been called to Los Angeles to work on a track he'd made for **Stone Gods,** the movie that was never released. He'd taken the last TWA flight of the night out of SFO, landing in Burbank, leaving his house in the hands of Scotty, who had cut the grass that morning but not yet cleaned the pool. Mitch's old girlfriend calling in a favor, asking if she and Christopher could crash for two nights, just two nights.

Suzanne and the others had been surprised to find strangers in the house. No one they had ever met. And that could have been the abortive moment, a glance of agreement passing between them. The return to the car, their deflated silence. But they didn't turn back. They did what Russell had told them to do.

Make a scene. Do something everyone would hear about.

...

The people in the main house were preparing to go to bed, Linda and her little boy. She'd made him spaghetti for dinner and had snuck a forkful from his bowl but not bothered to make anything for herself. They were sleeping in the guest bedroom—her quilted weekend bag leaking clothes on the floor. Christopher's grimy stuffed lizard with its jet button eyes.

Scotty had invited his girlfriend, Gwen Sutherland, to listen to records and use Mitch's hot tub while Mitch was away. She was twenty-three, a recent graduate of the College of Marin, and she'd met Scotty at a barbecue in Ross. Not particularly attractive, but Gwen was kind and friendly, the kind of girl that boys are forever asking to sew on buttons or trim their hair.

They had both had a few beers. Scotty smoked some weed, though Gwen had not. They passed the evening in the tiny caretaker's cottage Scotty kept to military standards of cleanliness—the sheets on his futon tight with hospital corners.

Suzanne and the others came across Scotty first. Nodding off on the couch. Suzanne cleaved away to investigate the sound of Gwen in the bathroom, while Guy nodded at Helen and Donna to go search the main house. Guy nudged Scotty awake. He snorted, jolting back from a dream. Scotty didn't have his glasses on—he'd rested them on his chest as he fell asleep—and he must have thought Guy was Mitch, returning early.

"Sorry," Scotty said, thinking about the pool, "sorry." Blindly tapping for his glasses.

Then Scotty fumbled them on and saw the knife smiling up from Guy's hand.

Suzanne had gotten the girl from the bathroom. Gwen was bent over the sink, splashing water on her face. When Gwen straightened, she saw a shape in the corner of her eye.

"Hi," Gwen said, her face dripping. She was a girl who had been well raised. Friendly, even when surprised.

Maybe Gwen thought it was a friend of Mitch's or Scotty's, though within seconds it must have been obvious that something was wrong. That the girl who smiled back (because Suzanne did, famously, smile back) had eyes like a brick wall.

Helen and Donna collected the woman and the boy in the main house. Linda was upset, her hand fluttering at her throat, but she went with them. Linda in her underpants, her big T-shirt—she must have thought that as long as she was quiet and polite, she'd be fine. Trying to reassure Christopher with her eyes. The chub of his hand in hers, his untrimmed fingernails. The boy didn't cry until later; Donna said he seemed interested at first, like it was a game. Hide and go seek, red rover, red rover.

I try to imagine what Russell was doing while all this was happening. Maybe they'd made a fire at the ranch and Russell was playing guitar in its darty light. Or maybe he'd taken Roos or some other girl to his trailer, and maybe they were sharing a joint and watching the smoke drift and hover against the ceiling. The girl would have preened under his hand, his singular attention, though of course his mind would have been far away, in a house on Edgewater Road with the sea out the door. I can see his tricky shrug, the inward coiling of his eyes that made them polished and cold as doorknobs. "They wanted to do it," he'd say later. Laughing in the judge's face. Laughing so hard he was choking. "You think I made them do anything? You think these hands did a single thing?" The bailiff had to remove him from the courtroom, Russell was laughing so hard.

They brought everyone to the living room of the main house. Guy made them all sit on the big couch. The glances between the victims that did not know, yet, that they were victims.

"What are you gonna do to us?" Gwen kept asking.

Scotty rolled his eyes, miserable and sweating, and Gwen laughed—maybe she could see, suddenly, that Scotty could not protect her. That he was just a young man, his glasses fogged, his lips trembling, and that she was far from her own home.

She started to cry.

“Shut up,” Guy said, “Christ.”

Gwen tried to halt her sobs, shaking silently. Linda attempted to keep Christopher calm, even as the girls tied everyone up. Donna knotting a towel around Gwen’s hands. Linda squeezing Christopher one last time before Guy nudged them apart. Gwen sat on the couch with her skirt hitched up her legs, keening with abandon. The exposed skin of her thighs, her still wet face. Linda murmuring to Suzanne that they could have all the money that was in her purse, all of it, that if they just took her to the bank, she could get some more. Linda’s voice was a calm monotone, a shoring up of control, though of course she had none.

Scotty was the first. He’d struggled when Guy put a belt around his hands.

“Just a second,” Scotty said, “hey.” Bristling at the rough grasp.

And Guy lost it. Slamming the knife with such force that the handle had splintered in two. Scotty struggled but could only flop onto the floor, trying to roll over and protect his stomach. A bubble of blood appearing from his nose and mouth.

...

Gwen's hands had been tied loosely—as soon as the blade sank into Scotty, she jerked free and ran out the front door. Screaming with a cartoon recklessness that sounded fake. She was almost to the gate when she tripped and fell on the lawn. Before she could get to her feet, Donna was already on her. Crawling over her back, stabbing until Gwen asked, politely, if she could die already.

They killed the mother and son last.

"Please," Linda said. Plainly. Even then, I think, hoping for some reprieve. She was very beautiful and very young. She had a child.

"Please," she said, "I can get you money." But Suzanne didn't want money. The amphetamines tightening her temples, an incantatory throb. The beautiful girl's heart, motoring in her chest—the narcotic, desperate rev. How Linda must have believed, as beautiful people do, that there was a solution, that she would be saved. Helen held Linda down—her hands on Linda's shoulders were tentative at first, like a bad dance partner, but then Suzanne snapped at Helen, impatient, and she pressed harder. Linda's eyes closed because she knew what was coming.

Christopher had started to cry. Crouching behind the couch; no one had to hold him down. His underwear saturated with the bitter smell of urine. His cries were shaped by screams, an emptying out of all feeling. His mother on the carpet, no longer moving.

Suzanne squatted on the floor. Holding out her hands to him. "Come here," she said. "Come on."

This is the part that isn't written about anywhere, but the part I imagine most.

How Suzanne's hands must have already been sprayed with blood. The warm medical stink of the body on her clothes and hair. And I can picture it, because I knew every degree of her face. The calming mystic air on her, like she was moving through water.

"Come on," she said one last time, and the boy inched toward her. Then he was in her lap, and she held him there, the knife like a gift she was giving him.

By the time the news report was finished, I was sitting down. The couch seemed sheared off from the rest of the apartment, occupying airless space. Images blistered and branched like nightmare vines. The indifferent sea beyond the house. The footage of policemen in shirtsleeves, stepping from Mitch's front door. There was no reason for them to hurry, I saw—it was over. Nobody would be saved.

I understood this news was much bigger than me. That I was only taking in the first glancing flash. I careened toward an exit, a trick latch: maybe Suzanne had broken off from the group, maybe she wasn't involved. But all these frantic wishes carried their own echoed response. Of course she had done it.

The possibilities washed past. Why Mitch hadn't been home. How I could have intersected with what was coming. How I could have ignored all the warnings. My breath was squeezed from the effort of trying not to cry. I could imagine how impatient Suzanne would be with my upset. Her cool voice.

Why are you crying? she'd ask.

You didn't even do anything.

It's strange to imagine the stretch of time when the murders were unsolved. That the act ever existed separately from Suzanne and the others. But for the larger world, it did. They wouldn't get caught for many months. The crime—so close to home, so vicious—sickened everyone with hysteria. Homes had been reshaped. Turned suddenly unsafe, familiarity flung back in their owners' faces, as if taunting them—see, this is your living room, your kitchen, and see how little it helps, all that familiarity. See how little it means, at the end.

The news blared through dinner. I kept turning at a jump of motion in the corner of my eye, but it was just the stream of television or a headlight glinting past the apartment window. My father scratched his neck as we watched, the expression on his face unfamiliar to me—he was afraid. Tamar wouldn't leave it alone.

"The kid," she said. "It wouldn't be so bad if they didn't kill the kid."

I had a numb certainty they would see it on me. A rupture in my face, the silence obvious. But they didn't. My father locked the apartment door, then checked again before he went to bed. I stayed awake, my hands limp and clammy in the lamplight. Was there the merest slip between the outcomes? If the bright faces of planets had orbited in another arrangement, or a different tide had eaten away at the shore that night—was that the membrane that separated the world where I had or had not done it? When I tried to sleep, the inward reel of violence made me open my eyes. And something else, too, chiding in the background—even then, I missed her.

The logic of the killings was too oblique to unravel, involving too many facets, too many false clues. All the police had were the bodies, the scattered scenes of death like note cards out of order. Was it random? Was Mitch the target? Or Linda, or Scotty, or even Gwen? Mitch knew so many people, had a celebrity's assortment of enemies and resentful friends. Russell's name was brought up, by Mitch and by others, but it was one of many. By the time the police finally checked out the ranch, the group had already abandoned the house, taking the bus to campgrounds up and down the coast, hiding out in the desert.

I didn't know how stalled the investigation was, how the police got caught up following trivia—a key fob on the lawn that ended up belonging to a housekeeper, Mitch's old manager under surveillance. Death imbued the insignificant with forced primacy, its scrambled light turning everything into evidence. I knew what had happened, so it seemed the police must know, too, and I waited for Suzanne's arrest, the day the police would come looking for me—because I'd left my duffel behind. Because that Berkeley student Tom would put together the murders and Suzanne's hissing talk of Mitch and contact the police. My fear was real, but it was unfounded—Tom knew only my first name. Maybe he did speak to the police, good citizen that he was, but nothing came of it—they were inundated with calls and letters, all kinds of people claiming responsibility or some private knowledge. My duffel was just an ordinary duffel, and it had no identifying feature. The things inside: clothes, a book about the Green Knight. My tube of Merle Norman. The possessions of a child pretending at an adult's accrual. And of course the girls probably had gone through it, tossing the useless book, keeping the clothes.

I had told many lies, but this one colonized a bigger silence. I thought of telling Tamar. Telling my father. But then I'd picture Suzanne, imagine her picking at a fingernail, the sudden cut of her gaze turning to me. I didn't say anything to anyone.

The fear that followed the wake of the murders is not hard to call up. I was barely alone the week before boarding school, trailing Tamar and my father from room to room, glancing out windows for the black bus. Awake all night, as if my labored vigil would protect us, my hours of suffering a one-to-one offering. It seemed unbelievable that Tamar or my father didn't notice how pale I was, how suddenly desperate for their company. They expected life would march on. Things had to be done, and I got shunted along their logistics with the numbness that had taken the place of whatever had made me Evie. My love of cinnamon hard candies, what I dreamed—that had all been exchanged for this new self, the changeling who nodded when spoken to and rinsed and dried the dinner plates, hands reddening in the hot water.

I had to pack up my room at my mother's house before I went to boarding school. My mother had ordered me the Catalina uniform—I found two navy skirts and a middy blouse folded on my bed, the fabric stinking of industrial cleaner, like rental tablecloths. I didn't bother to try on the clothes, shoving them into a suitcase on top of tennis shoes. I didn't know what else to pack, and it didn't seem to matter. I stared at the room in a trance. All my once beloved things—a vinyl diary, a birthstone charm, a book of pencil drawings—seemed valueless and defunct, drained of an animating force. It was impossible to picture what type of girl would ever have liked those things. Ever worn a charm around her wrist or written accounts of her day.

"You need a bigger suitcase?" my mother said from my doorway, startling me. Her face looked rumpled, and I could smell how much she'd been smoking. "You can take my red one, if you want."

I thought that she'd notice the change in me even if Tamar or my father couldn't. The baby fat in my face disappeared, a hard scrape to my features. But she hadn't mentioned anything.

"This is fine," I said.

My mother paused, surveying my room. The mostly empty suitcase. "The uniform fits?" she asked.

I hadn't even tried it on, but I nodded, wrung into a new acquiescence.

"Good, good." When she smiled, her lips cracked and I was suddenly overcome.

I was shoving books into the closet when I found two milky Polaroids, hidden under a stack of old magazines. The sudden presence of Suzanne in my room: her hot feral smile, the pudge of her breasts. I could call up disgust for her, hopped up on Dexedrine and sweating from the effort of butchery, and at the same time be pulled in by a helpless drift—here was Suzanne. I should get rid of the photo, I knew, the image already charged with the guilty air of evidence. But I couldn't. I turned the picture over, burying it in a book I'd never read again. The second photo was of the smeary back of someone's head, turning away, and I stared at the image for a long moment before I realized the person was me.

PART FOUR

SASHA AND JULIAN AND ZAV left early, and then I was alone. The house looked as it had always looked. Only the bed in the other room, the sheets scrabbled and smelling of sex, indicated anyone else had ever been here. I would wash the sheets in the machine in the garage. Fold and slot them on the closet shelves, sweep the room back to its previous blankness.

I walked along the cold sand that afternoon, stippled with broken bits of shell, the shifting holes where sand crabs burrowed. I liked the rush of wind in my ears. The wind drove people off—students from the junior college yelping while their boyfriends chased down the ripple of a blanket. Families finally giving up and heading toward their cars, toting folding chairs, the poky splay of a cheap kite, already broken. I was wearing two sweatshirts and the bulk made me feel protected, my movements slower. Every couple of feet, I'd come across the giant, ropy seaweed, tangled and thick as a fireman's hose. The purging of an alien species, seemingly not of this world. It was kelp, someone had told me, bull kelp. Knowing its name didn't make it any less strange.

Sasha had barely said goodbye. Burrowing into Julian's side, her face set like a preventative against my pity. She had already absented herself, I knew, gone to that other place in her mind where Julian was sweet and kind and life was fun, or if it wasn't fun, it was **interesting,** and wasn't that valuable, didn't that mean something? I tried to smile at her, to speed her a message on an invisible thread. But it had never been me she wanted.

The fog had been denser in Carmel, descending over the campus of my boarding school like a blizzard. The spire of the chapel, the nearby sea. I had started school that September, just as I was supposed to. Carmel was an old-fashioned place, and my classmates seemed much younger than they were. My roommate with her collection of mohair sweaters arranged by color. The dormitory walls softened with tapestries, the after-curfew creeping. The Tuck Shop, run by seniors, which sold chips and soda and candy, and how all the girls acted like this was the height of sophistication and freedom, being allowed to eat in the Tuck Shop from nine to eleven thirty on weekends. For all their talk, their bluster and crates of records, my classmates seemed childish, even the ones from New York. Occasionally, when the fog obscured the spires of the chapel, some girls could no longer orient themselves and got lost.

For the first few weeks, I watched the girls, shouting to one another across the quad, their backpacks turtled on their backs or slung from their hands. They seemed to move through glass, like the well-fed and well-loved scamps of detective series, who tied ribbons around their ponytails and wore gingham shirts on weekends. They wrote letters home and spoke of beloved kittens and worshipful younger sisters. The common rooms were the domain of slippers and housecoats, girls who ate Charleston Chews cold from miniature refrigerators and huddled by the television until they seemed to have psychologically absorbed the cathode rays. Someone's boyfriend died in a rock-climbing accident in Switzerland: everyone gathered around her, on fire with tragedy. Their dramatic shows of support underpinned with jealousy—bad luck was rare enough to be glamorous.

I worried I was marked. A fearful undercurrent made visible. But the structure of the school—its particularities, its almost municipal quality—seemed to cut through the dim. To my surprise, I made friends. A girl in my poetry class. My roommate, Jessamine.

My dread appeared to others as a rarefied air, my isolation the isolation of weary experience.

Jessamine was from a cattle town near Oregon. Her older brother sent her comic books where female superheroes burst out of their costumes and had sex with octopuses or cartoon dogs. He got them from a friend in Mexico, Jessamine said, and she liked the silly violence, reading them with her head hung over the side of the bed.

"This one's nuts," she'd snort, tossing a comic to me. I'd try to hide a vague queasiness incited by the starbursting blood and heaving breasts.

"I'm on a diet where I just share all my food," Jessamine had explained, giving me one of the Mallomars she kept in her desk drawer. "I used to throw half of everything away, but then the dorms got a mice infestation and I couldn't."

She reminded me of Connie, the same shy way she plucked her shirt away from her belly. Connie, who'd be at the high school in Petaluma. Crossing the low steps, eating lunch at the splintered picnic tables. I had no idea how to think of her anymore.

Jessamine was hungry for my stories of home, imagining I lived in the shadow of the Hollywood sign. In a house the sherbet pink of California money, a gardener sweeping the tennis court. It didn't matter that I was from a dairy town and told her so: other facts were bigger, like who my grandmother had been. The assumptions Jessamine made about the source of my silence at the beginning of the year, all of it—I let myself step into the outline. I talked about a boyfriend, just one in a series of many. "He was famous," I said. "I can't say who. But I lived with him for a while. His dick was purple," I said, snorting, and Jessamine laughed, too. Casting a look in my direction all wrapped up in jealousy and wonder. The way I had looked at Suzanne, maybe, and how easy it was to keep up a steady stream of stories, a wishful narrative that borrowed the best of the ranch and folded it into a new shape, like origami. A world where everything turned out as I'd wanted.

I took French class from a pretty, newly engaged teacher who let the popular girls try on her engagement ring. I took art class from Miss Cooke, earnest with first-job anxiety. The line of makeup I could sometimes see along her jaw made me pity her, though she tried to be kind to me. She didn't comment when she noticed me staring into space or resting my head on my folded arms. Once she took me off campus for malteds and a hot dog that tasted of warm water. She told me how she had moved from New York to take her job, how the city asphalt would reflect sheets of sun, how her neighbor's dog shit all over the apartment stairs, how she'd gone a little crazy.

"I would eat just the corners of my roommate's food. Then it would all be gone, and I would get sick." Miss Cooke's glasses pinched her eyes. "I've never felt so sad, and there was no real reason for it, you know?"

She waited, obviously for me to match the story

with one of my own. Expecting a sad, manageable tale of the defection of a hometown boyfriend or a mother in the hospital, the cruel whispers of a bitchy roommate. A situation she could make heroic sense of for me, cast in older and wiser perspective. The thought of actually telling Miss Cooke the truth made my mouth tighten with unreal hilarity. She knew about the still-unsolved murders—everyone did. People locked doors and installed dead bolts, bought guard dogs at a markup. The desperate police got nothing from Mitch, who had fled in fear to the South of France, though his house wouldn't be razed until the following year. Pilgrims had started driving past the gate, hoping to pick up horror like a vapor in the air. Idling in their cars until weary neighbors shooed them off. In his absence, detectives were following leads from drug dealers and schizophrenics, bored housewives. Even enlisting a psychic to walk the rooms of Mitch's house, straining to pick up vibes.

"The killer is a lonely, middle-aged man," I'd heard the psychic say on a call-in show. "He was punished as a youth for something he hadn't done. I'm getting the letter K. I'm getting the town Vallejo."

Even if Miss Cooke would believe me, what would I tell her? That I had not slept well since August because I'd been too afraid of the unmonitored territory of dreams? That I woke certain that Russell was in the room—taking soggy gasps for breath, the still air like a hand over my mouth? That the cringe of contagion was on me: there was some concurrent realm where that night had not happened, where I insisted Suzanne leave the ranch. Where the blond woman and her teddy-bear son were pushing a cart down a grocery store aisle, planning a Sunday dinner, snippy and tired. Where Gwen was wrapping her damp hair in a towel, smoothing lotion on her legs. Scotty clearing the hot tub filters of debris, the silent arc of the sprinkler, a song floating into the yard from a nearby radio.

The letters I wrote my mother were willful acts of theater, at first. Then true enough.

Class was interesting.

I had friends.

Next week we would go to the aquarium and watch the jellyfish gape and parry in their illuminated tanks, suspended in the water like delicate handkerchiefs.

By the time I'd walked the farthest spit of land, the wind had picked up. The beach empty, all the picnickers and dog walkers gone. I stepped my way over th
boulders, heading back to the main stretch of
Following the line between cliff and wa
this walk many times. I wondered h
Julian and Zav had gotten by t
hour from L.A. Without havi
knew Julian and Zav were sitti
and Sasha was in the back. I could

ing forward from time to time, asking for a joke to be repeated or pointing out some funny road sign. Trying to campaign for her own existence, before finally giving up and lying back on the seat. Letting their conversation thicken into meaningless noise while she watched the road, the passing orchards. The branches flashing with the silver ties that kept away birds.

I was passing by the common room with Jessamine, on our way to the Tuck Shop, when a girl called, "Your sister's looking for you downstairs." I didn't look up; she couldn't be talking to me. But she was. It took me a moment to understand what might be happening.

Jessamine seemed hurt. "I didn't know you had a sister."

I suppose I had known Suzanne would come for me.

The cottony numbness I occupied at school wasn't unpleasant, in the same way a limb falling asleep isn't unpleasant. Until that arm or leg wakes up. Then the prickles come, the sting of return—seeing Suzanne leaning in the shade of the dorm entrance. Her hair uncombed, her lips bristling—her presence knocked he plates of time ajar.

Everything was returned to me. My heart strobed, less, with the tinny cut of fear. But what could ne do? It was daytime, the school filled with witnesses. I watched her notice the fuss of landscaping, teachers on their way to tutoring appointments, girls crossing the quad with tennis bags and chocolate milk on their breath, walking proof of the efforts of unseen mothers. There was a curious, animal distance in Suzanne's face, a measurement of the uncanny place she'd found herself.

She straightened when I approached. "Look at you," she said. "All clean and scrubbed." I saw a new harshness in her face: a blood blister under a fingernail.

I didn't say anything. I couldn't. I kept touching the ends of my hair. It was shorter—Jessamine had cut it in the bathroom, squinting at a how-to article in a magazine.

"You look happy to see me," Suzanne said. Smiling. I smiled back, but it was hollow. That seemed, obliquely, to please Suzanne. My fear.

I knew I should do something—we kept standing under the awning, increasing the chance someone would stop to ask me a question or introduce herself to my sister. But I couldn't make myself move. Russell and the others couldn't be very far away—were they watching me? The windows of the buildings seemed alive, my mind flashing to snipers and Russell's long stare.

"Show me your room," Suzanne announced. "I want to see."

...

The room was empty, Jessamine still at the Tuck Shop, and Suzanne pushed past me and through the doorway before I could stop her.

"Just lovely," she trilled in a fake English accent. She sat down on Jessamine's bed. Bouncing up and down. Looking at the taped-up poster of a Hawaiian landscape, the unreal ocean and sky sandwiching a sugary rib of beach. A set of the **World Book** Jessamine had never opened, a gift from her father. Jessamine kept a stack of letters in a carved wooden box and Suzanne immediately lifted the lid, sifting through. "Jessamine Singer," she read off an envelope. "Jessamine," she repeated. She let the lid bang shut and got to her feet. "So this one's your bed." She stirred my blanket with a mocking hand. My stomach tilted, a picture of us in Mitch's sheets. Hair sticking to her forehead and neck.

"You like it here?"

"It's okay." I was still in the doorway.

"Okay," Suzanne said, smiling. "Evie says the school is just okay."

I kept watching her hands. Wondering what they'd done exactly, as if the percentage mattered. She tracked my glance: she must have known what I was thinking. She got abruptly to her feet.

"Now I get to show you something," Suzanne said.

The bus was parked on a side street, just outside the school's gate. I could see the jostle of figures inside the bus. Russell and whoever was still around—I assumed everyone. They'd painted over the hood. But everything else was the same. The bus beastly and indestructible. My sudden certainty: they would surround me. Back me into a corner.

If anyone had seen us standing there on the slope, we would have looked like friends. Chatting in the Saturday air, my hands in my pockets, Suzanne shading her eyes.

"We're going to the desert for a while," Suzanne announced, watching the flurry that must have been visible on my face. I felt the meager borders of my own life: a meeting that night for the French Club—Madame Guevel had promised butter tarts. The musty weed Jessamine wanted to smoke after curfew. Even knowing what I knew, did a part of me want to leave? Suzanne's dank breath and her cool hands. Sleeping on the ground, chewing nettle leaves to moisten our throats.

"He's not mad at you," she said. Keeping a steady simmer of eye contact. "He knows you wouldn't say anything."

And it was true: I hadn't said anything. My silence keeping me in the realm of the invisible. I had been frightened, yes. Maybe you could pin some of the silence on that fear, a fear I could call up even later, after Russell and Suzanne and the others were in jail. But it was something else, too. The helpless thoughts of Suzanne. Who had sometimes colored her nipples with cheap lipstick. Suzanne, who walked around so brutish, like she knew you were trying to take something from her. I didn't tell anyone because I wanted to keep her safe. Because who else had loved her? Who had ever held Suzanne in their arms and told her that her heart, beating away in her chest, was there on purpose?

My hands were sweating, but I couldn't wipe them on my jeans. I tried to make sense of this moment, to hold an image of Suzanne in my mind. Suzanne Parker. The atoms reorganizing themselves the first time I'd seen her in the park. How her mouth had smiled into mine.

No one had ever looked at me before Suzanne, not really, so she had become my definition. Her gaze softening my center so easily that even photographs of her seemed aimed at me, ignited with private meaning. It was different from Russell, the way she looked at me, because it contained him, too: it made him and everyone else smaller. We had been with the men, we had let them do what they wanted. But they would never know the parts of ourselves that we hid from them—they would never sense the lack or even know there was something more they should be looking for.

Suzanne was not a good person. I understood this. But I held the actual knowledge away from myself. How the coroner said the ring and pinky fingers of Linda's left hand had been severed because she had tried to protect her face.

Suzanne seemed to look at me as if there could be some explanation, but then a slight movement behind the shrouded windshield of the bus caught her attention—even then, she was alert to Russell's every shift—and a businesslike air came over her.

"Okay," she said, urged by the tick of an unseen clock. "I'm taking off." I had almost wanted a threat. Some indication that she might return, that I should fear her or could draw her back with the right combination of words.

I only ever saw her again in photographs and news reports. Still. I could never imagine her absence as permanent. Suzanne and the others would always exist for me; I believed that they would never die. That they would hover forever in the background of ordinary life, circling the highways and edging the parks. Moved by a force that would never cease or slow.

Suzanne had shrugged a little, that day, before walking down the grassy slope and disappearing into the bus. The queer reminder in her smile. Like we had a meeting, she and I, at some appointed time and place, and she knew I would forget.

I wanted to believe Suzanne kicked me out of the car because she'd seen a difference between us. That it was obvious to her that I could not kill anyone, Suzanne still lucid enough to understand that she was the reason I was in the car. She wanted to protect me from what was going to happen. That was the easy explanation.

But there was a complicating fact.

The hatred she must have felt to do what she'd done, to slam the knife over and over again like she was trying to rid herself of a frenzied sickness: hatred like that was not unfamiliar to me.

Hatred was easy. The permutations constant over the years: a stranger at a fair who palmed my crotch through my shorts. A man on the sidewalk who lunged at me, then laughed when I flinched. The night an older man took me to a fancy restaurant when I wasn't even old enough to like oysters. Not yet twenty. The owner joined our table, and so did a famous filmmaker. The men fell into a heated discussion with no entry point for me: I fidgeted with my heavy cloth napkin, drank water. Staring at the wall.

"Eat your vegetables," the filmmaker suddenly snapped at me. "You're a growing girl."

The filmmaker wanted me to know what I already knew: I had no power. He saw my need and used it against me.

My hatred for him was immediate. Like the first swallow of milk that's already gone off—rot strafing the nostrils, flooding the entire skull. The filmmaker laughed at me, and so did the others, the older man who would later place my hand on his dick while he drove me home.

None of this was rare. Things like this happened

hundreds of times. Maybe more. The hatred that vibrated beneath the surface of my girl's face—I think Suzanne recognized it. Of course my hand would anticipate the weight of a knife. The particular give of a human body. There was so much to destroy.

Suzanne stopped me from doing what I might be capable of. And so she set me loose into the world like an avatar for the girl she would not be. She would never go to boarding school, but I still could, and she sent me spinning from her like a messenger for her alternate self. Suzanne gave me that: the poster of Hawaii on the wall, the beach and blue sky like the lowest common denominator of fantasy. The chance to attend poetry class, to leave bags of laundry outside my door and eat steaks on parents' visiting days, sopping with salt and blood.

It was a gift. What did I do with it? Life didn't accumulate as I'd once imagined. I graduated from boarding school, two years of college. Persisted through the blank decade in Los Angeles. I buried first my mother, then my father. His hair gone wispy as a child's. I paid bills and bought groceries and got my eyes checked while the days crumbled away like debris from a cliff face. Life a continuous backing away from the edge.

There were moments of forgetting. The summer I had visited Jessamine in Seattle after she had her first child—when I saw her waiting at the curb with her hair tucked into her coat, the years unknit themselves and I felt, for a moment, the sweet and blameless girl

I had once been. The year with the man from Oregon, our shared kitchen hung with houseplants and Indian blankets on the seats of our car, covering the rips. We ate cold pita with peanut butter and walked in the wet green. Camping in the hills around Hot Springs Canyon, far down the coast, near a group who knew all the words to **The People's Song Book.** A sun-hot rock where we lay, drying from the lake, our bodies leaving behind a conjoined blur.

But the absence opened up again. I was almost a wife but lost the man. I was almost recognizable as a friend. And then I wasn't. The nights when I flicked off the bedside lamp and found myself in the heedless, lonely dark. The times I thought, with a horrified twist, that none of this was a gift. Suzanne got the redemption that followed a conviction, the prison Bible groups and prime-time interviews and a mail-in college degree. I got the snuffed-out story of the bystander, a fugitive without a crime, half hoping and half terrified that no one was ever coming for me.

It was Helen, in the end, who ended up talking. She was only eighteen, still desirous of attention—I'm surprised they stayed out of jail as long as they did. Helen had been picked up in Bakersfield for using a stolen credit card. Just a week in a county jail and they would have let her go, but she couldn't help bragging to her cellmate. The coin-operated television in the common room showing a bulletin of the ongoing murder investigation.

"The house is way bigger than it looks in those pictures," Helen said, according to her cellmate. I can see Helen: nonchalant, thrusting her chin forward. Her cellmate must have ignored her at first. Rolling her eyes at the girlish bluster. But then Helen kept going, and suddenly the woman was listening closely, calculating reward money, a reduced sentence. Urging the girl to tell her more, to keep talking. Helen was probably flattered by the attention, unspooling the whole mess. Maybe even exaggerating, drawing out the haunted spaces between words, as in the incantation of a ghost story at a sleepover. We all want to be seen.

All of them would be arrested by the end of December. Russell, Suzanne, Donna, Guy, the others. The police descending on their tent encampment in Panamint Springs: torn flannel sleeping bags and blue nylon tarps, the dead ash of the campfire. Russell bolted when they came, as if he could outrun a whole squad of officers. The headlights of the police cruisers glowing in the bleached pink of morning. How pitiful, the immediacy of Russell's capture, forced to kneel in the scrub grass with his hands on his head. Guy handcuffed, stunned to discover there were limitations to the bravado that had carried him that far. The little kids were herded onto the Social

Services van, wrapped in blankets, and handed cold cheese sandwiches. Their bellies distended and scalps boiling with lice. The authorities didn't know who had done what, not yet, so Suzanne was just one of the skinny jumble of girls. Girls who spit in the dirt like rabid dogs and went limp when the police tried to handcuff them. There was a demented dignity to their resistance—none of them had run. Even at the end, the girls had been stronger than Russell.

It would snow in Carmel that same week, the barest slip of white. Class was canceled, frost crunching thinly under our shoes as we tromped across the quad in our jean jackets. It seemed like the last morning on earth, and we peered into the gray sky as if more of the miracle were coming, though it all melted into a mess in less than an hour.

I was halfway back to the beach parking lot when I saw the man. Walking toward me. Maybe a hundred yards away. His head was shaved, revealing the aggressive outline of his skull. He was wearing a T-shirt, which was strange—his skin flushed in the wind. I didn't want to feel as uneasy as I did. A helpless accounting of the facts: I was alone on the sand. Still far from the parking lot. There was no one else around but me and this man. The cliff, starkly outlined, each striation and pulse of lichen. The wind lashing my hair across my face, dislocating and vulnerable. Rearranging the sand into furrows. I kept walking toward him. Forcing myself to keep my gait.

The distance between us fifty yards, now. His arms were honeycombed with muscle. The brute fact of his naked skull. I slowed my pace, but it didn't matter—the man was still heading briskly in my direction. His head was bouncing as he walked, an insane rhythmic twitch.

A rock, I thought crazily. He'll pick up a rock. He'll break open my skull, my brain leaking onto the sand. He'll tighten his hands around my throat until my windpipe collapses.

The stupid things I thought of:

Sasha and her briny, childish mouth. How the sun had looked in the tops of the trees lining my childhood driveway. Whether Suzanne knew I thought of her. How the mother must have begged, at the end.

The man was bearing down on me. My hands were limp and wet. Please, I thought. Please. Who was I addressing? The man? God? Whoever handled these things.

And then he was in front of me.

Oh, I thought. Oh. Because he was just a normal man, harmless, nodding along to the white headphones nested in his ears. Just a man walking on the beach, enjoying the music, the weak sun through the fog. He smiled at me as he passed, and I smiled back, like you would smile at any stranger, any person you didn't know.

terrible. [illegible] the [illegible] into [illegible]. I kept walking [illegible] myself to keep my pace.

The distance between us [illegible] now. [illegible] [illegible] with [illegible] [illegible] [illegible] [illegible] [illegible] [illegible] [illegible] [illegible] head [illegible] walked [illegible] [illegible].

[illegible] [illegible] [illegible] [illegible] [illegible] my [illegible] into the [illegible] [illegible] [illegible]

The [illegible] [illegible]

[illegible] [illegible] had looked [illegible] [illegible] [illegible] the [illegible] [illegible] how the [illegible] [illegible] and [illegible] [illegible] were [illegible] [illegible] [illegible] [illegible] [illegible] [illegible].

And [illegible] was [illegible]

[illegible] I thought [illegible]. Because [illegible] was [illegible] [illegible] [illegible] nothing [illegible] the white [illegible] [illegible] [illegible] [illegible] [illegible] [illegible] [illegible] [illegible] [illegible] [illegible] [illegible] and [illegible] [illegible] [illegible] [illegible] [illegible].

ACKNOWLEDGMENTS

I would like to thank Kate Medina and Bill Clegg for invaluable guidance. Thank you also to Anna Pitoniak, Derrill Hagood, Peter Mendelsund, Fred and Nancy Cline, and my brothers and sisters: Ramsey, Hilary, Megan, Elsie, Mayme, and Henry.

ABOUT THE AUTHOR

EMMA CLINE was the winner of **The Paris Review**'s Plimpton Prize in 2014. She is from California.

emmacline.com
Facebook.com/EmmaClineWriter